A CHERISHED BETROTHAL

SCOUTS OF THE GEORGIA FRONTIER
BOOK THREE

DENISE WEIMER

WILD HEART
BOOKS

ISBN-13: 978-1-943365-84-9

CHAPTER 1

JULY 12, 1775
FORT CHARLOTTE, SOUTH CAROLINA

"*D*inna touch me, sir!"

The sharp command from the captain's residence stopped Lieutenant Alexander Morris in the process of striking the British colors in the fort's yard. The act itself had already given him pause, for there could be no going back from this. The taking of a crown fort—even one in the backcountry—was no less an act of aggression for the lack of bloodshed.

But what was a Scottish woman—unmistakable, from her lilting brogue—doing here?

Alex's men had been instructed to supervise Captain George Whitefield's family as they packed and prepared to be escorted from Fort Charlotte. A wagon awaited them with horses already hitched in the yard. They would travel northeast to the town of Ninety Six, along with whatever munitions Major James Mayson chose to transfer to the fortified town.

Where the Whitefields went from there mattered not, so long as—having refused to join the Patriot cause—they left the area.

The undeniable rumble of an argument proceeded through the open door of the captain's quarters. Alex folded the flag over his arm, smoothing the King's Colours with his scarred hand. He'd fought with the Georgia Rangers under this banner, but never again. The line had been crossed now. Swallowing past the unexpected tightness in his throat, he pivoted and went to see what might be out of kilter with the Whitefields.

He was about to enter the captain's cabin when a petite form in a blue bodice and linen petticoat swept through the door, nearly colliding with him. The young woman stopped, one hand flying up to secure her tilting straw hat.

Alex made a small bow. "What seems to be the problem, lass?"

"Miss Lawrence," Sergeant Sean McTavish supplied. He stood behind her, his ginger-bearded face a thundercloud above his blue coat with red facings. "We found her visiting with Mrs. Whitefield and more than a bit contrary about takin' her leave."

Lawrence. Now, why was that name familiar, like a moth tickling about the edges of his recollection?

"I'm not contrary. I only wanted to say a prayer." Miss Lawrence lifted moist blue eyes to Alex's, blinked, and sucked in a breath. She peered at him, no doubt catching sight of the edge of the scar that ran from beneath his cocked hat to the tip of his left eyebrow.

Alex was well-accustomed to people staring, but somehow, this woman's perusal shortened his patience—not his best quality even on a good day. "Prayer?"

"For safety for the Whitefields' journey. I was only askin' for one last, peaceful moment alone in their home, to cover them with the Lord's protection."

"And I told her, we don't need no Loyalist prayers. We'd

thankee to mount yer horse." Sergeant McTavish leaned the tip of his rifle toward the extra mounts at the hitching post. "We willna keep the major waiting."

"Let her have her prayer, Sergeant," Alex said.

When Miss Lawrence's full pink lips parted, he gestured toward the doorway.

"Thankee, sir," she whispered. "Lieutenant...?"

No call to further this acquaintance. Even had he been assigned here at Fort Charlotte rather than the town of Ninety Six, he possessed no skill with ladies. Nor the desire to develop it. Alex stuck his head into the cabin and ordered the remaining privates away. "The Whitefield family wishes a moment of reflection before they depart."

After the men scrambled out, squinting against the bright sunshine, Miss Lawrence entered and crossed to Mrs. Whitefield, who clasped her bairn to her bosom while a toddler clung to the leg of the English captain. The three joined hands, and Alex waited only long enough for Miss Lawrence to begin in a quavering voice, "Most merciful God..." before himself stepping outside.

Sergeant McTavish scowled at him. "A cryin' shame, a sawny lass hand in glove with Loyalists."

"Why is she here on her own, anyway? Where does she come from?" Alex wiped his forehead with his sleeve and surveyed the fifty-by-forty, four-bastioned enclosure, which swarmed with blue-coated men. Barrels of gunpowder and ammunition were being hefted onto wagons and two small brass field pieces secured on carriages. The full-sized guns would remain, though a want of platforms and working caissons made them somewhat redundant. The stone fort had cost a thousand pounds sterling to construct a decade before but now greatly needed repair.

"She said her father is the minister at the Presbyterian mission just north of here on Russell's Creek."

It was Alex's turn to frown. "Aren't most parsons in these parts itinerant?"

"Not this one. Apparently, Reverend Lawrence has been holdin' services for the British soldiers at the fort as well as for our countrymen in these parts. And they say they have Cherokee children at the mission."

Alex's face went slack, and McTavish gave a grim nod. Fort Charlotte might be the colony's westernmost outpost on the Savannah River, but he hadn't expected a reason for an enemy more dangerous than the Loyalists to regularly come and go.

"Lieutenant Morris." Alex's captain, Moses Kirkland, strode toward them, his brow set in a harsh line. "Where are the Whitefields? Our company has assembled, and Major Mayson is waiting to mount up." Captain Kirkland jerked his chin toward the parade ground, where their commanding officer inspected the cannons.

"I will fetch them, sir." Indeed, they would need every bit of light for their lumbering party to reach Ninety Six—named for its distance from the important Cherokee town of Keowee—before dark, even on this mid-summer day.

Sergeant McTavish pulled a face. "They needed to say their prayers first, sir."

Captain Kirkland scoffed. "They will need them. Round them up, Lieutenant Morris, with no further mollycoddling."

Kirkland's tone—brusque as ever—rankled Alex. How much of the man's current distemper stemmed from losing the appointment of major to Mayson? Alex might regret heeding his cousin Finn's invitation to sign up under this particular former Regulator, but he'd let nothing interfere with his chance to prove himself in a worthy cause. He belonged here, in uniform. Not behind a plow in Georgia's recently ceded lands. He saluted, then handed the flag to the captain. "As requested —the King's Colours."

Though the Patriots had no banner as yet to fly in its place,

Major Mayson would present the British flag to Captain White-field to carry with him to his own commander.

Kirkland snatched the folded bundle and pivoted for the parade ground.

In the dim interior of the captain's quarters, Alex found Captain Whitefield latching a traveling trunk while the women embraced. Frances Whitefield wept softly. "You have been a kindly friend for me in this lonely place, Elspeth."

Elspeth...so that was the name of this lass with flaxen-blond hair such as he hadn't seen since...

"And you to me." Dropping Frances's hands, Miss Lawrence glanced at him.

Alex cleared his throat and addressed Captain Whitefield. "Sir, Major Mayson awaits yer presence on the parade ground. Some of my privates will fetch yer luggage."

Alex's refusal to remove his hat might be marked as a lack of respect, but he couldn't bring himself to do so under the watchful gaze of Miss Lawrence. To track the disintegration of her poorly concealed interest from shock, to horror, and finally, pity—a reaction he'd witnessed too many times. And that made him as irritable as Captain Kirkland. What cared he what this prim miss thought?

If he was offended, Captain Whitefield gave no indication. He straightened with a sigh, almost seeming resigned. Did he share their Patriot leanings, as some suspected? Was that why he hadn't fought back when Major Mayson had demanded the surrender of the fort?

Whitefield set his cocked hat atop his gray wig, as immacu-late in his red coat, white breeches, and black boots as if he were conducting a review of His Majesty's troops rather than surrendering barely more than a dozen men to a foe His Majesty did not even recognize. "Thank you, Lieutenant. Come, ladies." He gestured for the women to proceed him from the cabin.

Outside, the formal surrender took place in the fort's yard while Alex and his men assisted the civilians. After loading the Whitefields' luggage onto a supply wagon, Alex helped the captain's wife and toddler girl into the back. Miss Lawrence handed Mrs. Whitefield her baby boy, then turned to look at him.

"Do one of the mounts here belong to you, miss?" he asked.

"No, sir. My father has our horse. He left me here to visit Mrs. Whitefield while he went to call on a friend in New Bordeaux."

At least that satisfied his concern that this beautiful young woman's father would allow her to traipse across the country-side on her own. "Very good. New Bordeaux is along our route to Ninety Six. We will drop you off there."

She hesitated. Surely, she was not thinking of awaiting the reverend's return at a fort occupied by strangers, without another woman or chaperone. "Are you going? To Ninety Six?"

Her question brought him up short. "Aye, miss. That is where I've been posted. Now, please, allow me..." He held out his hand.

She took it, but rather than climbing into the wagon, she stepped closer to him. "Lieutenant, what is yer name?" The question was barely above a whisper. Her blue eyes bore into his, tugging at something long furled up in his memory. Something he wanted to keep that way.

"Why would ye need me name?"

"Because I think I ken you. I think we...grew up together." The heat from her small fingers just might burn holes through Alex's white gloves.

Despite the momentous surrender of the fort taking place only yards away—the result of the first act of aggression by rebel armies on South Carolina soil—Mrs. Whitefield and Alex's men all stared at him and this strange Scottish lass. He sought to dispel their interest with a soft, scoffing breath and a tight smile.

"That canna be the case, for I have no memory of ye." And he certainly would, did he ken her.

Confusion, followed by what appeared to be deep disappointment, swam in her eyes. Then, before he could register her intent, she swiped his hat off his head. A dark, sweaty lock of hair fell loose from his queue, though it wasn't enough to cover his scars, judging by the flash of emotion on Miss Lawrence's face. But it wasn't the pity he expected. It was the most intense joy he'd ever seen, twisting his gut into a paroxysm of longing and alarm.

"It *is* ye." A small sob bubbled from her lips, and she released his hand to cover it at the same moment she dropped his hat—and slumped toward the ground.

~

lex. Alex. Alex.

Elspeth's mind repeated the name she'd once awakened from her nightmares calling out but which her faint heart lacked the strength to give voice, even now, as she jostled along in the wagon with her head pillowed on Frances's shoulder. Could it be? From the moment she'd noted the proud grace with which the man carried his lanky body, the set of his jaw, those eyes almost like coals, her heart had thundered. Her palms had grown sweaty, and her knees had shaken. And then, his Scottish brogue, so much deeper but still so musical—

"Elspeth, are you well?" Frances jostled her arm. No doubt the woman wanted back the one patch of herself not taken up with a slobbering babe or clinging toddler.

Elspeth sat upright, running her hand over her eyes. But the gesture did not clear the sight of the man riding his bay stallion behind the wagon, frowning in her direction. *Great*

God in heaven, could Ye have heard my prayer after all this time? And was she about to be parted from the boy she'd sought for years, before he would even acknowledge her? Tell her his story?

The possibility seized her with such panic, she clutched her middle.

"Are you about to cast up your accounts?" Frances looked around, presumably for a vessel. "'Twould not be unusual, after a faint."

Elspeth stopped the woman's search with a hand on her elbow. "I dinna faint. I only went a wee bit dizzy." Although she possessed only the fuzziest memory of the lieutenant scooping her up and lifting her into the wagon, a spectacle for all to see.

Frances gave a light shudder. "No wonder, given the sight of that man's scars. Such fearsome damage could only have been done at the hands of the Indians."

"They were not so bad, the scars." Indeed, his hair had covered most, and they were healed to silver-white and old— fifteen years old, to be exact. But the tightening of her fingers on the edge of the wagon gave the lie to her words. The scars might not be bad now, but that day...

She pressed back a groan and shut the lid on the memory as solidly as she had on the chest of her dead mother's belongings that still sat at the foot of her father's bed.

Frances eased forward, into Elspeth's view. "And do you know him, as you thought?"

"I do." The confirmation of his name would punctuate her statement, though. She still hadn't heard it. And still couldn't speak it.

"From Long Canes Creek?" Frances knew Elspeth's story, the rare-spoken name of the place where she'd lost all family save Da, and she said it even now in the softest tone, almost looking apologetic. But intensely curious, just the same.

Elspeth drew breath to reply, but instead, a demand rang

out from the head of the column. "Halt! What is the meaning of this? Where are you taking munitions that belong to the king?"

Major Mayson's reply reached them with equal clarity. "These munitions now belong to the provincial government of South Carolina, as does Fort Charlotte, from whence they came."

As their wagon rumbled to a stop, she raised herself in its bed for a view of whomever confronted Major Mayson, his adjutant, and Kirkland—the unpleasant, corpulent fellow whose troop now escorted them while the other captain of the South Carolina Regiment of Horse, Caldwell, remained with his company at Fort Charlotte. Captain Whitefield rode his stallion beside the Patriot officers. And now, a knot of mounted men in civilian clothing blocked the road leading into New Bordeaux—and not the French Huguenots who lived there.

Frances had swiveled around in the wagon. "Who is it?"

"Friends of yer husband's, I believe." She recognized the Cunningham brothers, Robert and Patrick, as well as Jacob Bowman, all of whom were outspoken proponents of King George.

Frances squeezed her hand. "Pray God there is not trouble."

Indeed, the lieutenant Elspeth believed was Alex had circled his men around their wagon even as they spoke. He leaned closer from the back of his horse, saying in a hiss, "Get down."

For a moment, she met his eyes, searching for some sign of recognition, some connection, but his were blank...though they narrowed.

"Sit...down...*miss*."

She was just about to do so when an agitated voice called her name. "Elspeth?"

She whirled around. "Da?" What was he doing here?

Mounted on his gelding, her father edged up the side of the road past the Cunningham brothers. "Oh, thank God, 'tis me daughter! Ye must let me reach her. She has no business in all this."

He sounded all affright. When Elspeth raised the hem of her petticoat in preparation to step onto the wagon wheel and jump down, Alex's hand landed firmly on her shoulder.

He jerked his chin at her. "'Twould be foolish to get in the middle of this confrontation. We ken not where it will lead."

"He is right, Elspeth." Frances patted the rough board next to her. "Sit here while they talk."

Elspeth sank between little Betsy and her mother. The toddler sucked her thumb. The drawn lines of her friend's face and the arm she wrapped around them both emphasized the danger only a few feet away. Would the Loyalists attempt to take the guns and powder by force? Had a battle been avoided at the fort only to break out on the road?

As her father said, she had no part in this. For years, they had successfully straddled the worlds of those who found fault with the king's governance, those who thought he'd done no wrong, and the Indians, both Creek and Cherokee. They'd focused on proclaiming the truth of God's love for all.

Would that fragile peace end here, today?

How foolish of her. It had already ended, the moment these newly recruited Patriot rangers had seized Fort Charlotte on orders of the provincial government's Council of Safety.

The firm, proud voices of the men carried to them for a few minutes, but Elspeth couldn't make out their words. At last, her father and an officer bearing more trim and fringe than Alex approached, faces tight.

Da reached out and grabbed her hand. "Elspeth, are ye well?"

"I'm fine, Da." But would her father recognize Alex? She nodded toward him, but he was saluting his superior.

"Adjutant," Alex greeted the man. "What's happening?"

"Given the presence of civilians, the Loyalists have agreed to avoid bloodshed, though a portion of the powder will be returned to Fort Charlotte. They think it less likely to create contention there, out of the way as it is."

Alex pressed his lips together. "I suppose they think we canna blow anything up without it." He turned to her. "And I suppose that means ye can hie home with yer father, Miss Lawrence."

"Actually, Lieutenant Morris..." The adjutant frowned and swiped his glistening brow. "Major Mayson wishes you to accompany the Lawrences to their mission and overnight with them."

"What?"

"Morris?" Elspeth's father broke in. "Alexander Morris?" He was looking at Alex much the way Elspeth imagined she had, leaning sideways to catch a glimpse under the cocked hat. "Why, is that really you, me boy?"

Alex's tanned cheeks had gone white. "That is me name, sir, but I fear ye share the same mistaken idea as yer daughter. I dinna ken ye."

Had Elspeth remained standing, her legs would have failed her. She grabbed Frances's hand, though the woman had no idea what this meant to her. Poor Frances allowed her to squeeze hard, though, not uttering a word.

"Yer father, he was Malcolm Morris, no?"

A brief nod was all the answer Alex gave, making Elspeth wish she could leap from the wagon and get her arms around him.

Thankfully, the adjutant gave a grunt and picked up the dangling thread of conversation. "Major Mayson heard the young lady recognized you. Reverend Lawrence told him he is expecting a small party of Cherokees."

"Aye, by tomorrow," Da confirmed.

Elspeth stiffened.

The young officer nodded, his steely gray eyes still on Alex, who kept his head down. "Reverend Lawrence will introduce you as his friend, Lieutenant Morris, and you will then issue an invitation for the Cherokees to visit Fort Charlotte on behalf of the provincial army. It is of the utmost importance to the major that the Cherokees know we are their friends."

If Elspeth had wanted to leap from the wagon before, it was all she could do to stifle her moan of dismay now. Alex appeared far too stricken to utter any such protest himself—even if he had such a right while under orders. Could anything more difficult be asked of him? Had he even had dealings with the Indians these past years, as she had? Not likely—unless he'd met some of the Creeks in battle when they had last risen in Georgia, early the year prior.

"And if they willna come?" The words seemed to slide out through the lieutenant's stiff jaw.

The adjutant straightened. "Then you will join us in Ninety Six."

"And the reverend has agreed to this?"

Why did Alex ask the other officer, as though Da was not sitting right there?

Da, bless his heart, answered, anyway. "I have, Alex...er, Lieutenant Morris. My daughter and I will feel safer with ye at the mission while things are all arsy varsy. Besides, 'twill be good to catch up with ye."

"Verra well." Alex did not return his tentative smile. Instead, he saluted the adjutant. "Will that be all, sir?"

The man's mouth pursed, then he jerked his head toward a stand of pines nearby. Both men wheeled their horses in that direction and conferred in low tones. What was this about? Something they did not want her and Da to hear? And wasn't inserting their man at the mission—a supposedly neutral place —a way for the Patriots to nudge them into their camp?

"Come, Elspeth." Da drew his gelding next to the wagon and held his arm out.

Elspeth hugged Frances tightly. "Goodbye, my friend." She would dearly miss having a companion nearby. Indeed, having a female friend at all. In her experience, those were hard to come by.

"Goodbye, dear Elspeth. Keep safe. Write to me in Charlestown." Frances helped Elspeth cross the wagon wheel and get a leg over her father's mount while the men's backs were turned.

As she settled on the front of the saddle, she angled her body and whispered, "Da, can ye believe it? Is it really him?"

"Aye, lass, I think so, though for some reason, he doesna want us to ken that."

"Then why are ye allowin' him to come to the mission?"

"His major was verra suspicious of my appearance with the Loyalists." He spoke quickly, his tone low. "I crossed paths with them in Bordeaux and learned what was afoot. All I could think of was to get to you, my child. I would do anything to accomplish that."

She nodded. "I am glad ye're here."

"Besides, do ye not want to talk with him?"

Oh, more than anything. But would he talk?

The main column lumbered forward, the Loyalists having dispersed. Elspeth blew a kiss to Frances and little Betsy in the back of the wagon. The adjutant galloped off, and Alex Morris turned his horse their direction, his square, bristled jaw set, his eyes unreadable under the ever-tilted hat.

He was going home with them—the boy she'd longed to see for fifteen years. Yet he wasn't a boy any longer. He was a man, hardened and guarded. And either he was playing a part she had yet to grasp or he truly did not remember them. She couldn't decide which would be worse.

CHAPTER 2

*H*ow had he ended up here, trotting his stallion up the Fort Charlotte and Cherokee Old Path? And with these people who stared at him with awareness beyond what Alex himself possessed—or wanted to? People who harbored his sworn enemies? If they truly had shared the traumatic losses of his childhood, how could they do that?

The natural riches of Piedmont South Carolina had drawn settlers into these parts even before the Cherokees had agreed to cede the land. Some of Alex's earliest memories were of the trip down the Great Wagon Road from Virginia, following the Calhoun family, who had settled near here. Hunters had reported to them in Waxhaws, on the border between the Carolinas, about the forests of massive trees spaced so far apart that deer and buffalo could be seen from afar. They heard of more than a hundred buffalo grazing on a single plot. Herds of deer numbering upwards of sixty. Rich clay hills with fertile, sandy loam along the streams.

Indeed, it was still so. Under the shade of spreading oaks and along blackberry and green brier thickets, deer paused their grazing, flicking their white tails while watching them pass. Black walnut and chestnut trees formed their green husks, promising an autumn harvest. Wild pea vines yielded their bounty even now. From low-growing clusters of leaves along the road, spiky white flowers of Culver's physic and stems of baneberry shot upward, the white eyes with black spots appearing to observe their progress. The almost deafening chorus of birdsong, the chatter of squirrels, and the screech of crickets warned of their presence.

But Alex could hardly enjoy the scenery, so tight was the tension in his body, his dread of this visit ahead. Perhaps he should have waited to sign up. Georgia lagged behind the other colonies in patriotic fervor, often drawing the censure of South Carolina—partly because Georgia's governor was a respected man, fair overall as royal politicians went, and partly because trouble with the Creek Indians had demanded the colony's attention. But some parishes, including St. Andrew's on the coast, where Alex's mother's kin lived, had eagerly adopted the resolutions of the First Continental Congress, which had met in Philadelphia the September past. Surely, Georgia would get around to forming their own Patriot militia and ranger companies.

Alex had been beholden to Finn, though, and especially to his uncle, Gilroy. They had taken him in back when the Georgia Rangers were disbanded back in 1767, shortly after Alex had received his training as a raw lad of sixteen. He'd been set against returning to Darien. His uncle and cousin had given him a home and the Morrises' land to farm. They'd also given him a local militia to join. And when Finn's wife had turned up with child, Alex signing up in Gilroy's place had allowed the grandsire of their little clan to stay home and look after the family. Far be it from Alex to leave a debt outstanding.

What would the cost of this one be, though? Higher than he'd thought, something told him, and not a battle in sight. At least, not a battle with powder and shot.

He followed the gelding carrying the Lawrences, father and daughter, into a dirt clearing that supported a cabin—in dogtrot style with a breezeway connecting the two squares of living space—plus a small barn and a corncrib. Chickens clucked and scratched about the yard. A lush grapevine draped an arbor lined with rough benches in the shade of the trees, while tall green corn plants marched down toward what must be Russell's Creek.

He hastened to dismount and loop Charlie's reins around the hitching post so that he could offer assistance to Miss Lawrence. She took his hand, swinging her leg over the horse. No proper sidesaddles here on the frontier, but he ken enough to look away. Then to reach up for her as she braced herself on his shoulders. Her waist—'twas tiny but firm in his hands. She landed inches from him but had to look up to speak.

"Welcome to our mission, Lieutenant."

How was it she smelled of lavender while sweat ran in rivulets down his back?

Was he still holding onto her? Eejit!

He snatched his hands back just as he could've sworn the good reverend stifled a chuckle. Thankfully, a movement at the door drew everyone's attention.

Alex froze as three slim figures in buckskin and trade cloth filed onto the porch.

"Tea-cher." The first girl came forward, black braids framing her bronze face, which had lit upon sight of Miss Lawrence. But her gaze stumbled over Alex. In fact, his bright uniform drew all three pairs of eyes. And he couldn't stop staring either. Frowning? Yes, he was frowning. The girls, all seeming between the ages of nine and twelve, shuffled back into the arms of an old Indian woman who appeared in the doorway behind them.

Miss Lawrence smiled and gestured them forward. They came, hesitantly, halting at the top of the steps. Then, as her father dismounted, she took Alex's arm. "Lieutenant, I would like to present Galilani, Kamama, and Ayita." She pointed to each in turn. To his surprise, they all curtsied. Miss Lawrence had been imparting European manners. "And Ulisi. Her name is Udelida, but we call her Ulisi, which means *grandmother*, for she truly is grandmother to Galilani and Kamama. She helps look after our charges and run our household."

Miss Lawrence not only taught these children, but she employed an Indian as her housekeeper?

She squeezed his arm. "It is part of our agreement with the chiefs. And it is best for all." She turned back to her little flock and began speaking in a foreign tongue, *their* foreign, heathen tongue.

Alex pulled his arm away.

She concluded her statement by slowly stating his name, "Morris. *U-na-li-i.* Friend." And she patted his shoulder firmly.

"I will take care of the horses." Alex reached for Charlie's reins, turning away from Miss Lawrence's dismayed perusal. Before he could escape to the stable with both mounts, Reverend Lawrence clamped his other shoulder.

The man spoke low in his ear. "I ken 'tis a lot to take in, lad, but we shall talk after supper."

A lad, was he? Could these people not see he wasn't the boy they remembered? He was a soldier, an officer, and right now, he had an assignment to complete. He would complete it and report back to Mayson, and after that, he'd never need to see the Lawrences again.

He unsaddled and brushed down the stallion and the gelding under the watchful eyes of a milk cow and two goats. He took his time feeding and watering the mounts, but finally, it was time to seek out his hosts.

Voices came from the left side of the dogtrot. In the main room, a small fire had been stirred up despite the day's heat, presumably to warm a pot of something. Reverend Lawrence sat at the head of a long board, the three Cherokee girls along one side. One of them held a small vase of wildflowers, but her lilting voice speaking in her own language ceased with Alex's steps.

Miss Lawrence and the grandmother, as they called her, served up supper on wooden trenchers—salted ham, thick slices of bread with butter, and snap beans. When his form darkened the doorway, Miss Lawrence whirled, and her face... well, it lit.

Alex's gut bottomed out, for no one had looked at him like that. Ever.

She hurried forward, his plate in her hand. "I hope ye dinna mind a simple supper, Lieutenant. With having been gone all day..."

"'Tis far better fare than I'd have had at either of the posts, miss." He ducked his head. Thankfully, they did not seem to notice that he left his hat on.

"Please, take a seat." Reverend Lawrence gestured to the empty side of the table.

Never did he think he'd be breaking bread with his mortal enemies, even children. Alex stared at the bench a moment, then sat.

Miss Lawrence slid onto the other end, while the old woman took her plate to a rush-bottom chair in the corner.

Abruptly, he stood. "She can have my seat." He'd be far more comfortable eating in silence, without the stares of the trio of girls.

"Oh, no." Miss Lawrence tugged on his arm. "Ulisi always sits there to eat. Dinna ask us why."

"She no longer sits on the floor, so 'tis progress." Reverend Lawrence chortled. "Shall we say grace?"

Slowly, Alex sank back onto the bench. The three girls folded their hands and bowed their heads. He did likewise. The reverend spoke each short sentence in English, then, presumably, in Cherokee. "Creator God, we thank Thee for this Thy bounty. We thank Thee for reuniting us with Lieutenant Morris. Be present in our home, in our conversation, and in our land. Amen."

Alex dug into the meal, suddenly aware of his aching stomach. He'd eaten precious little this day, and he was plumb chapt. He washed down bites of bread and meat with the cool, fresh cider in the pewter tankard at his place.

"So...Lieutenant Morris..." The reverend leaned back. "Have ye lived in South Carolina all this time?"

"No, sir. I have split my time between Georgia and Carolina. I was in Darien as a youth, south of Savannah."

A soft gasp escaped Miss Lawrence. "Is that where ye went? We thought...well, we thought..."

Her father picked up where she left off. "We thought ye and yer mother might return to Waxhaws, as we did."

So that was how it was to be? Polite conversation for suppertime. They would not speak directly of the dreadful event that had marked a turning point in their lives—at least, not yet. He would do all he could to keep it that way. Perhaps the presence of the three girls wasn't all bad. How much did they understand? How careful did he need to be?

He cleared his throat. "My mother had kin on the coast. When I was sixteen, I joined the Georgia Rangers. The next year, when they were disbanded for want of conflict and funds, I went to live with my uncle's family south of here." Hopefully, that would satisfy their curiosity.

Miss Lawrence looked up from handing one of the girls half of her slice of bread. "Yer mother didna protest?"

Of course, she would inquire about that. He gave a brusque laugh. "Protest? Nay. She had a new husband, a new family." And was undoubtedly more than glad to be shed of him, seeing as how she'd never once asked for him to come back.

Reverend Lawrence slanted a slightly quelling look at his

daughter but posed another question of his own. "And that is where ye have been since?"

He offered a patient smile. "Not exactly. In 1773, the Georgia Rangers were reorganized. I served a year with them before word of the new land cession. Thought I'd try my hand at farming." He grunted. "'Tis more skilled clutching a rifle."

Miss Lawrence's eyes rounded. "Did ye see action, Lieutenant?"

"Against the Creeks. Aye. Some of them were less than happy about the land given up. William's Creek had a wee something to do with me becoming an officer in the South Carolina Regiment of Horse." That and Uncle Gilroy's influence with William Kirkland. And this was as good a place as any to bring the conversation back around to one of the purposes for his visit. "When I got a chance to serve the provincial government, I jumped at it—as any freedom-lovin' Sawny would. Or perhaps you dinna see things the same way."

The reverend leaned in. "Oh, we were as flustered by the Intolerable Acts as any. Yes, we deserve powers of assembly, representation, and trial here in the colonies rather than having to be transported to England to defend ourselves. And we shouldna be forced to quarter British troops sent to enforce these unfair laws." He sipped his cider, then held up an index finger. "However, can we trust the lowlanders to give us that?"

"Aye." Alex lowered his fist to the table with a soft but emphatic thump. "Already, the provincial council offers far more seats to the backcountry than the royal government ever did. 'Twas the biggest thing we fought for as Regulators, in both Carolinas. And now, to see it become so..."

Reverend Lawrence tilted his head first to one side, then to the other. "Aye, it bodes well. But the way they have treated Alexander Cameron has been a cryin' shame."

"I have heard conflictin' talk of Cameron." Alex sat forward. The Lawrences could be privy to vital information about the superintendent for Indian affairs in the southern district that could prove helpful to his commanders. "A fellow Scot who wields great influence over the Cherokees, they say."

"Aye, they call him Scotchie. He took a wife from the Estatoe village, the daughter of a prominent chief. They have two children."

Many traders and Indian agents did claim native wives. "His plantation lies near here, no?"

Miss Lawrence nodded. "On Penny Creek of the Little River. His estate, Lochaber, is quite grand. Mr. Cameron recently hosted the famed naturalist William Bartram on his trip through these parts."

Reverend Lawrence grunted. "And then to have a visit from Andrew Williamson, another Scot, on behalf of the Council of Safety, accusin' him of being in league with Indian Superintendent John Stuart to stir up the Cherokees on behalf of the British."

Alex tore his final strip of ham in two with his teeth. "I was told that when they searched Stuart's correspondence, they found a letter from Cameron that showed it might be true."

"Of course, it isna true." Reverend Lawrence's pleasant demeanor slipped as he fairly spat the words. "I have spoken with him meself on this verra topic. Cameron wants to keep the Cherokees out of this conflict, as we do. Ye must take my word for this, Lieutenant."

"Verra well, sir," Alex said. "As I dinna ken the man meself, I willna say ye nay."

Miss Lawrence smiled. "We only want peace. We can see the positives and negatives on both sides. Talkin' would accomplish so much more than fightin'."

"I dinna think they want to hear us over there in England, Miss Lawrence, any more than they did when we so politely asked fer our own king in Scotland. Me grandsire died at Culloden. Did yers?" He peered at her.

"Aye, actually." Her fingers tightened on the handle of her spoon. "But things are different here. I shan't pretend the English dinna look down on us—at least, some of them. Call us crackers. But many of our countrymen have been given land by the king. Land we never would've had in England or Scotland. Positions and opportunities abound here. We're treated with respect when we apply ourselves."

"Ye mean when ye show yer loyalty." Disdain seeped into his words.

"I *mean* when we keep our heads down."

"I ken what ye're sayin'. That is how my uncle feels." Alex offered the olive branch. He could speak his mind without needling the lass. "His biggest fear is losin' his land." Uncle Gilroy had bought the acreage from Kirkland and would follow the man to hell to keep it. He was that sure Kirkland sensed the direction the wind was blowing.

"Aye." Miss Lawrence brushed bread crumbs from her hands. "Another thing the royal government has done right is to enforce boundary lines that will protect both us and the Indians. Where there have been issues, the settlers have been at fault."

"Have they, now?" Alex couldn't help the sarcastic tone. Hadn't Miss Lawrence's father explained to her how the Cherokees had reneged on their agreement with the settlers in Long Canes?

She wilted a bit under his glare, sliding off her bench to circle 'round and wipe the face of the smallest girl. She whispered something in Cherokee in her ear, and the girl scrambled outside. The other two quickly followed. Miss Lawrence began clearing the board.

The reverend lowered his tankard to the table. "What my daughter means to say, Lieutenant, is that we have worked hard to establish peace here on Russell's Creek, and whatever we may think about His Majesty's policies, we will do all we can to maintain it."

"That may not be possible for long, sir. Ye may be forced to take sides."

A gentle smile tugged the corners of the man's thin lips. "Ye'd be surprised how far the love of Christ goes, my son."

Somehow, the statement he'd doubtless intended to mollify only increased the tension in the room. Alex forced his shoulders to relax. Mayson needed to ken who his allies and enemies were in this area. And he wanted any friends of the Cherokees to be his friends. Alex wouldn't accomplish that by offending the Lawrences.

He blew out a soft breath and thanked Miss Lawrence as she took his plate. "So how long have *ye* been here, Reverend?"

"Ah, let's see..." He formed a steeple of his fingers, drumming them together. "We came back here in sixty-six. Ye were—what?—thirteen, Elspeth?"

"Almost." She swept around behind Alex, refilling his cider, her scent of lavender wrapping around him like a silken cocoon, no less binding for its invisibility.

"I was trained in Waxhaws by William Richardson." Reverend Lawrence produced his pipe and a pouch of tobacco. "There was a traveling preacher here before me who also went into Cherokee lands. He started this cabin, though he began his mission work and teaching in their towns. When he passed on of a fever, I became his replacement. Waxhaws ken I had a daughter of me own, so the students would have to come here."

"English—is that all ye teach them?"

A smile crinkled the wrinkles about Reverend Lawrence's light-blue eyes. "I suspect ye expect my answer to be mathematics, too, and aye, we do teach them that, but primarily, Lieutenant Morris, we teach them about God." He filled the bowl of his pipe and tucked his pouch away in his waistcoat.

"And their parents, their chiefs, allow this?" He couldn't fathom it.

"We do it in ways they can picture. We speak of the Great Creator and His son. We tell them stories from the Bible. Often, these stories have parallels in their own traditions. We cannot push them, ye see, but we can spark their curiosity. And we can certainly answer questions." That benign smile returned to his face as he lit his pipe. "Those who are called will hear the truth."

"But there will be those who disagree. And when they find out, you could become the recipients of their anger." Alex shouldn't care what became of them any more than he would any other settlers. Yet an unnaturally strong sense of panic rose in him the longer he listened to this foolhardiness. He turned to find Miss Lawrence staring at him from the sideboard. "*Why* would ye persist in putting yerself in danger?"

"Oh, Alex." She strode across the floor to him, kneeling and taking his hand, of all things, as though speaking his given name hadn't been enough to totally shake him. "Ye mustn't fash yerself for us. The Cherokees ken us as friends. Would that ye ken us that way also."

How could he answer the pleading in her voice, in her words? In her eyes? He pulled his hand back. "I dinna understand. If ye are who ye say ye are…"

"'Tis true, Alex." Reverend Lawrence rose, his fair countenance darkening as he clutched his pipe before his barrel chest. "We ken yer family well. We were yer neighbors. We were there the day ye lost yer father and brother…as we lost my wife and two bairns." He drew an unsteady breath. "Not only that, but ye and Elspeth were rescued together, three days after the massacre."

Alex's swallow snagged on a ragged obstruction in his throat. That must be why their last name had sounded familiar. He would've heard his mother mention it, if only long ago.

The minister drew his lower lip up. "I dinna ken what yer game is, or what yer dandy commander whispered in yer ear, but ye can trust us."

"Game? I play no game, sir."

"Then talk to her." Lawrence jerked his chin toward his daughter. "I would say 'tis long overdue."

CHAPTER 3

*a*lex had the look of a man who'd sighted a kelpie—those mythical water creatures of Scottish lore—as Elspeth led him from the cabin toting her brace of buckets on his broad shoulders, presumably to clean the dishes and fetch water for washing up tonight. But truly she just wanted to get him out of the house and into the honesty of nature, where she might see if any trace of the boy she'd known remained. Where she might speak words that had a chance to break through his shell.

And oh, she longed to do more than look and speak. She'd been but six and he but ten when last she'd seen him, but being torn from him after what they had endured together had been almost more than she could bear. She'd wanted to throw her arms around him since the moment she'd seen him. But she would not do that. No, she would not.

He spoke as they brushed past the cornfield, the sibilant whisper of a breeze in the green leaves. "I dinna ken what I'm supposed to say to ye."

"Say what ye want. I will listen. And answer yer questions."

"'Tis a fine piece of land ye have here."

Not that, not more polite talk. "Thankee." Elspeth gave a soft sigh. The muggy heat of the evening dissipated beneath the canopy of trees leading to the creek.

"But a good bit to manage for yer father, given his religious responsibilities, what with no sons." Alex's statement cut off abruptly, as though he had just remembered there *had* been a son.

Elspeth chose to turn the conversation in another direction. "Aye. Ye may have noticed we have only girls here now. 'Tis why tomorrow's visit is so important."

"What do ye mean?" They had reached the creek, startling an otter, which slunk into the current and swam away. Alex set down the buckets, and she went about unpacking one, the dirty trenchers and spoons along with her corncob and lye soap.

"Tomorrow, the party of Cherokees will arrive from the north with a boy. At least, that is the agreement. We have been askin' for a long time for the chiefs to send us a boy. Ye see, the founding church in Waxhaws would view that as a success, even though the Cherokees give just as much status to their women as to the men."

Alex stood stiffly on the creek bed while she scrubbed the trenchers in a quiet pool. "How many do ye think will come?" His fingers rested on the ivory handle of the dragoon pistol he wore on his hip.

"When the girls were dropped off, two or three braves accompanied them. I'd expect the same." She stood. "Alex, 'tis important we say nothing to provoke them. Will ye be canny?"

"I've a message to deliver from my commander, and deliver it I shall." His dark brows drew so close they almost formed a single line over his eyes.

Unexpectedly, a small bubble of a laugh slipped past Elspeth's lips.

One of his straight brows quirked up. "What are ye laughing at?"

She bit her bottom lip. "At ye, ye noddy. Deliver it with that countenance, and no fightin' words will be needed."

As a child, he would've met such a challenge with like teasing. Given the lack of a pigtail, he might've pulled on her ear. But this Alex grasped her forearms and leaned forward. "How can ye make light of this?" The words were hissed with an intensity that doused her with shame. Almost immediately, he seemed to realize his error—familiarity. His face slackened, and he released her and stepped back. "My apologies, miss. That was out of line."

"Ye dinna need to call me *miss* any more than I intend to call ye *Lieutenant Morris* any longer. Do ye not ken me, Alex? Even a little? Why are ye actin' this way?"

He turned his face away. "Because I dinna remember ye, Miss Lawrence. Ye say ye were there...at Long Canes Creek..." His throat bobbed. The name had cost him something. "But I dinna recall any of it."

She gasped, her heart bottoming out. "Nothing?"

"Nay."

"Not before...or after?"

He rubbed his jaw, dark with bristles. "I remember our house there. Huntin', playin' with me brother. Sittin' through some everlastin' preachin' services. And after...I have memories of Darien, growin' up with me mother's kin. Bein' taught to ride and handle weapons by the men there. Leavin'." Another swallow.

Why would he have left Darien? But more importantly... "So the first memory ye have of me..."

He met her eyes. "Is when ye nearly ran me over this mornin'."

"I dinna run ye over. Ye nearly whammed into me, ye big lout."

The corner of his mouth twitched. The tiniest gesture, but it spiraled unreasonable hope all the way through her. She stepped closer. "Ye saved me, ye ken. I'm alive because of ye."

"I truly doubt that." His lips pulled downward. "A lad of me age shoulda given a better account of himself."

"Nay. Ye hid me in the canes. I was afeared to go in there because of the panther tracks in the mud. I'd just spotted them and dragged ye over to show ye. 'Tis why we were away from our families. I wanted to impress ye, to let ye ken what ye had taught me about trackin' had stuck. Ye always were keen on the outdoors, weren't ye? So I'm not surprised ye're a ranger...a scout."

His eyes brightened, just a flicker. "I did always like to track. Da taught me...and Ethan."

"Yes, Ethan. Yer brother. Ye both protected me. He was so brave." Suddenly, Elspeth's throat thickened and burned. A memory flashed before her eyes, and his face hardened as he watched her.

He held up his hand. "I dinna need to remember. I ken what happened. Mother told me, when she finally believed I couldna recall. And that is all I need."

"But when ye block out the bad memories, ye also block out the good. Friendship. Courage. Sacrifice. Do ye ken how long I've wanted to thank ye, Alex Morris?" She took his hands, wrapping her fingers around his. His were callused but warm. She drew one to her face and rubbed her cheek against it, closing her eyes. He was real, right here in front of her. No longer a figment of her imagination.

He sucked in a breath, then pulled his hands away. "Ye have no need to thank me, but if ye must, consider yer duty discharged. Now, Miss Lawrence, I willna leave ye alone by the creek, so I suggest you get to cleanin' the dishes."

The golden July light seemed to leave the bank as she stared at him. All the words she wanted to say floated away like thistledown on the current. Was this, then, the best she could ever hope for from Alex Morris?

~

*H*e'd hurt her—Elspeth. No. Miss Lawrence. He couldn't think of her as Elspeth, even though her knowledge of him confirmed her father's statements. As he followed her back to the cabin, her shoulders hunched, and she clutched one arm about her middle as though she might be holding herself together. The fact that he'd pained her gave him no pleasure. In truth, it made him feel like the lout she'd called him. But she did not understand.

By all accounts, she'd lost more than he had. But what remained—her father, her faith—had lent her a bulwark Alex had never had. His survival had depended on never looking back. On focusing his pain into purpose. He couldn't allow her to strip away his defenses. Not to mention, when she looked at him as she had... How was a man to respond to that type of deep emotion? The pleading she surely intended to reach his younger self and reestablish a connection threatened to stir more than either of them could safely explore.

But neither could he allow the distance to continue to build between them, not if he was to accomplish his mission.

The silence lasted until they approached the cabin. The shutters hung open on the right side now, and giggles and chatter in Cherokee spilled forth.

Alex tilted his head in that direction. "Is that where they live?"

"That is where they sleep, with Ulisi. You will be relieved, I'm sure, that you willna have to share quarters with them tonight." She dropped her arm and raised her chin as she mounted the steps.

He ignored that bit of baiting. Though he did wonder

where they would stow him. In the barn with the animals? That would suit him best. "And where do ye hold yer lessons?" Alex lowered the buckets to the porch.

She shrugged. "Everywhere. Anywhere. The fields, the forest. They teach me as much as I teach them. We use the room they sleep in for spinning and weaving, the common room where we ate for English and arithmetic."

"How did ye do it?" The question popped out of him, stopping her as she turned toward the door. When she faced him, he swallowed. This much he had to know.

"Do what?"

"Forgive them." He forced the two raspy words past the tightness in his throat.

Her face softened—if ever it had truly been hard. With a countenance like a china doll's, 'twas difficult for her to look fierce. "Alex, those girls were not even born when the attack came on Long Canes."

"Ye ken what I mean. Why have *anything* to do with them?" He balled his fists at his sides.

Elspeth released a soft breath and moved closer, though she did not meet his gaze. "For years, I had nightmares. Nothing Da did could stop them. When he felt the call to minister here, he ken it to be part of his healin', to turn what the enemy meant for evil to good, as the Scriptures promise. But he was afeared to tell me. Finally, the Reverend Richardson worked it outta him. Turns out, it was part of my healin' too. When the first girl came to us, she was only a little younger than me. She became...my friend." Her voice broke. "I saw that she was much like me. I saw that with peace sown, friendship could grow."

Alex's head started to shake slowly, as if of its own accord. "Perhaps we canna lay the fault at the feet of little girls, but ye canna place yer trust in the boys. They grow up to be merciless warriors who will do again what was done at Long Canes Creek. Ye saw it with yer own eyes. Ye remember it, even if I dinna. Did yer father not tell ye, the Cherokees broke their agreement with the settlers? They had given over the Flat-woods, legally surveyed by Patrick Calhoun."

Her lips firmed. "Nay. Da told me that he later learned that by the treaty of 1747, the land was not open, no matter what the Calhouns thought or did."

"And that gave the Indians the right to massacre twenty-three settlers and leave dozens others maimed for life?" His voice rose with a twist at the end that gave away more than he'd intended. Many more would have perished, had one of the Cherokees, a young woman, not ridden ahead to warn the settlers, allowing the first group to get off to safety though the second was ambushed crossing Long Canes Creek.

Her hand encircled his wrist. "Nay. Nay, of course not. But please..."

She wanted him to quiet for the sake of the Cherokee girls. He blew out a hot breath. This was why he shouldn't speak of these things. The fire he could usually keep banked, like hot coals under a curfew, threatened to blaze up. And this was not the time or place. "I'm warnin' ye...yer fine words, Elspeth, will hold no weight with them."

Her lower lip quivered. "Ye called me Elspeth."

Alex shook free of her. Was that all she had heard? His lapse? "Listen to me, woman. They didna parley then, and they willna now. Nothing has changed."

He expected the look of hurt to return, but something glistened in her eyes. Not tears. "Everything has changed. Because God changed it in here." She clasped her fist to her chest. "Ye asked how we could forgive them. By the grace of God. By the strength of His Spirit. Ye can have that, too, Alex."

He stared at her. Perhaps she had more gumption than he'd thought. Good for her. She would need it. But he wanted nothing that would make him weak and foolish, as her misplaced trust did. He would not argue with her again, however. He let out a sigh. "Where will ye have me sleep, lass?"

Elspeth dropped her hand to her side. "Ye will find a cot in the loft. Da moved mine to the nook downstairs for the summer. I'm afraid ye might be rather warm."

Not nearly as warm as she made him. He looked forward to the escape.

~

*T*he loft offered him no respite. The piece of fatwood Elspeth had nipped into the tin candleholder showed him that even though she'd abdicated to cooler environs below, she must still use the space for reflection. For Scripture reading and prayer, if the open Bible on the table beneath the small window was any indication. A vase of dried wildflowers sat beside it, and from a shelf above, a doll of stuffed and stained linen looked down on him with a painted-on face. He picked it up and turned it over in his hand, fingering the linsey-woolsey cloth of its simple dress.

Had it belonged to Elspeth? Surely, for the young woman's presence permeated the area. He could no longer *Miss Lawrence* her in his head. Even when he opened the shutters and let in the light of the silver moon, the hoot of the owl from a nearby branch, and the cry of a wolf from a faraway hill, the place smelled like lavender. Indeed, the herb hung above his head, drying.

With a sigh, he divested of his accoutrements and finally allowed himself to remove his hat. Necessary for a wash in the basin Elspeth had sent up with him. If only the cool water could cleanse the ache inside. He preferred the fire to the ache. His life held no room for longing.

Alex eased onto the cot—covered with a lavender-scented quilt, of course. Tomorrow, he would draw on every ounce of strength he possessed to issue the invitation to the party of Cherokees that his commander required. If fortune was with him, they would decline. Because he had no more come here to make friends with his enemies than he had to fall prey to a set of pleading blue eyes. Nay. He had come here to fight a war. One long overdue.

~

Someone screaming his name shot him from bed like a cannon ball.

"Alex!" The two syllables held all the fear and desperation he'd felt in a lifetime. And she needed him. Elspeth.

He grabbed his pistol and scrambled for the ladder, clumsy in the moonlight. His heart thundered. Had the Cherokee party arrived early? Invaded the house?

"Stop!" The command came in English before he could lower his foot to the floor. Reverend Lawrence stood behind him, his hand raised, his face like a prophet's of old.

"But sir..."

From the back of the cabin, Elspeth still called for him, though her voice had become plaintive, child-like.

"Turn around and go back up the ladder. I will handle this."

It took everything in him not to push past the man and sprint across the floor. "Is she in danger?"

"No more danger than her nightmares put her in."

"She is calling..." *For me.* He couldn't fathom it.

"It is hardly the first time." Even in the semi-dark, the somber lines of Reverend Lawrence's face were notable. "Though God knows, I thought we'd banished these demons. I fear yer presence has stirred them again. I will go to her. Pray with her. All will be well."

But all was far from well. Alex's limbs shook like a newborn lamb's as he climbed the ladder. His breath came in short puffs.

Visions of himself bending over Elspeth's bedside rather than her father assaulted him. She had needed him for years while he'd been unaware she was alive. And now, his mere presence had plunged her back into a fear her faith had since overcome.

All the more reason to high tail it to Ninety Six tomorrow and never look back.

CHAPTER 4

*W*hen Alex descended the ladder the next morning in full uniform, bristling with weapons and his expression reflecting the gravity the day's task would require of him, Elspeth faced the hearth. Her fingers shook as she unwrapped yesterday's cornmeal mush. Rather than handing it to Ulisi, who waited over the iron spider with butter already sizzling, she dropped the slices onto the posnet herself.

Ulisi plunked her hands on her hips and harrumphed.

"Fetch us some fig preserves," Elspeth directed in Cherokee. "Oh, and serve the men their cider, please, Ulisi."

Slightly mollified, if the relaxing of her mouth was any indication, the woman shuffled away with no idea she was providing Elspeth some small salvation. She couldn't look at Alex, even as he greeted her father and took a seat at the table. Not after she'd awakened not just calling but *screaming* his name last night. And him with no memory of *why* she might do such a thing. 'Twas too shameful to bear.

Why had the nightmare returned? She ken why. The one person her soul had been searching for the last fifteen years had returned, but she had no more access to him than she ever had. *God, give me strength.*

The mush fried up far too quickly. Ulisi topped it with fig preserves and a bit of cream, and Elspeth turned to serve it with a smile.

This time, it was Alex's gaze that sought something in hers. "Mornin', miss." His furrowed brow inquired if she was well.

"Mornin'." She choked it out, but her knees wobbled. Before she knew it, she was heading for the door, flinging an explanation back over her shoulder. "I shall just go see what is holdin' up the girls." They should have been back in with the milk by now.

As she crossed the porch, her mind remained back at the table beside Alex. Then her vision focused, for not three figures but six approached the cabin. Beside her students stood a boy slightly shorter than they...and two braves. Their bare chests gleamed. Feathers fluttered from roached locks. Bows and quivers of arrows poked up behind their backs. Above breech-clouts and leggings, tomahawks hung from woven belts.

'Twas the sight of those blades that made her brace herself on the post. Made her mouth dry up. Made her libel to disprove all her notions of forgiveness and goodwill by running, scream-ing, back inside.

By the grace of God, she would not do that. She repeated her earlier prayer with far more earnestness, and a calming warmth flowed through her, seeming to congeal in her legs. Lifting her chin.

"*Tsi-lu-gi.*" Welcome. For that they were.

The older man stepped forward. "*Si-yu.*"

Elspeth turned her face just a couple of inches and raised her voice a notch. "Da? Our guests are here." Pray God that Alex remained inside for now. These first few moments would be crucial.

She gestured to the girls. Two lugged the milk bucket. The other held a basket of eggs. "*Ha-wi-ni,*" Elspeth said. *Inside.* They trudged up the steps and indoors, obeying her, giving no indication of how they felt about their new schoolmate.

Her father exited as they entered—thankfully, without Alex. Da gave her a nod, as if reading her mind. He must've told Alex to wait until he was called. He gave a solemn smile and bowed his head to the braves, resting his hand on his chest, and spoke the Cherokee word for *preacher*. "*A-la-tsi-do-ho-s-gi.* Lawrence."

Elspeth barely registered the Cherokee names of the men as she stepped back, slightly behind her father.

The older man tugged the boy up next to him, keeping an arm around him. "Inoli. Black Fox."

English from the lips of braves always startled her, though she usually found some reason to make herself scarce when they visited. She might have lathered herself in God's grace and still found this one spot impossible to reach.

Yet the bright, intelligent eyes of the boy drew her. His skin was lighter than that of the others. Was he of mixed blood? He stared at them with open curiosity. Judging by the conversation, mostly in Cherokee, between her father and the brave, this was his nephew, not his son. But it was a start. Eventually, they might send a son of a chief, which would guarantee the continuation of the mission. Waxhaws Presbyterian might even appoint someone to help her father, should she marry. The clock was ticking on that.

She stopped that thought right there.

Her father was telling the braves all the things they would teach Inoli and how grateful they were to have him. The braves stated this was only a temporary visit, which would end at the start of the fall hunting season.

A movement at the door drew their attention.

Alex stood behind the partially open threshold, but the flash of blue and white was enough to send bronzed hands to tomahawk handles.

Elspeth gasped and stumbled backward. Alex seized her and drew her inside. "Wheesht, lass." He whispered the Scottish term for *hush* in her ear. Though he wrapped his arm around her, trembles had taken over. Thankfully, he had the sense to remain there with her while her father explained.

"We have a guest." Speaking in Cherokee, Da held up both hands. To his great credit, he took a slow step down from the porch. Then another. "A messenger from the soldiers who have taken over Fort Charlotte who want to be free of the Great White Father. He comes in peace. Will ye hear him?" He waited until the braves looked at each other, then by unspoken, mutual consent, uncurled their fingers from their tomahawks. Da made a gesture behind him.

Alex took a step forward, but Elspeth snagged his arm. "Ye should leave off yer weapons."

Incredulity flashed in his eyes. "Meet them unarmed whilst they remain armed to the teeth? Not a chance." But he held out his hands, palms down, as he stepped onto the porch. He glanced at her father. "Will ye translate for me?"

Da nodded. Everything Alex said in English, he echoed in Cherokee.

Two slender arms wrapped around Elspeth's petticoat as Galilani peered past her. The other girls crowded 'round. Warmth and reassurance flooded Elspeth, and she rested her hands on the girls' shoulders. These sweet children had sensed her distress and come to comfort her every bit as much as they were driven by curiosity. This was why she was here, whatever might happen with the Loyalists and Patriots, and even with Alex.

Alex spoke firmly, almost flatly. "The commander of Fort

Charlotte asks that ye accompany me to meet him, to receive his gifts and assurances of friendship. To make promises. The colonists will govern themselves without the king. They will govern these lands. They would be yer allies. They will live beside ye in peace. Will ye come?"

Silence but for the cawing of a crow fell over the clearing. The men stared at each other. Alex scarcely seemed to breathe. What would he do if they agreed?

Finally, the younger warrior muttered something Elspeth's father did not translate. And thank God he did not. *The scarred one speaks with hate in his eyes.* Elspeth's heart set to thumping, but the man jerked his chin at Alex. Da translated his response.

"Our people will make no promises with yours. You may kill each other, but we have no part in white man's war."

Abruptly, the older brave knelt next to Inoli. He untied the eagle feather that dangled beside his own face and secured it in the boy's long, shiny locks. He murmured instructions in their language, then straightened and faced the cabin with a grim nod.

Alex stiffened as if he'd been slapped. He sucked in air, and his fist balled up, inches from his pistol handle. He was trembling violently.

Elspeth's heart raced with alarm. "Alex?" she whispered. As her father took charge of Inoli, she shook free of the girls and went to the frozen figure in blue. "What is it?"

He recoiled at her touch. His face had gone white as bread dough, his pupils dilated. "Nothing. It is nothing." His sudden steps down the porch drew a small cry from her, but he only headed for the stable.

Everything in her ken it was not nothing. In that moment, before the two braves had turned and strode away, something had changed. Something that could bring danger on them all.

∾

*H*ow mistaken he'd been when he'd thought yesterday held more revelations than a man could countenance. Today just might prove his undoing.

First, the dream—his, not Elspeth's. The sliver of a memory had jerked him awake at dawn. It had started with that funny-faced doll, clutched by a little girl. Not Elspeth. Someone even younger, with almond-shaped eyes and dark hair like that of the woman on whose lap she sat. The doll had dropped, almost falling beneath the squeaking, rolling wagon wheel. He had snatched it up in time and returned it.

The woman's musical voice had said, "Tell Alex thankee."

"Thankee," the child had called.

And that had been it. His first memory of the time he'd blocked. He'd yet been sorting it when the Indians showed up early.

His hands were still shaky as he entered the town of New Bordeaux southeast of Fort Charlotte, with its log homes on half-acre lots along narrow streets. The predominance of French spoken there excused him from exchanging civilities with the citizens he passed. He breathed easier when vineyards stretched along gentle slopes toward the Little River, evidence of the Huguenots' main industry. And easier still when trees resumed on either side of the road.

He felt better with every mile he put between himself and those Indians. Yet wasn't this what he'd come here for— revenge? Nay. Restitution.

The winter prior, he'd feared battle with the Creeks might undo him, paralyzing him with memories, but he'd made a discovery. The fire he kept locked deep inside, once unleashed, gave him courage. Combined with the training from the High-landers of Darien, it made him a formidable fighter, commanding the respect of far more seasoned soldiers.

Today he'd feared again...that he would not be equal to the encounter with his real enemies...the Cherokees. But he'd done his duty as a soldier. That his invitation had been scorned only meant he'd need bide a while longer before he could meet his enemy on the field of battle—for make no mistake, those tawny warriors were more his enemies than the lobster backs.

Then the older brave had given the boy the feather that covered his ragged ear. And the words of Alex's mother flooded into his memory, turning him cold from head to toe.

Before Alex had locked all memories of the massacre from his mind, he'd told her, in those first gut-wrenching moments of reunion, that Ethan had died defending him...but not before parting their attacker's ear with his knife. Alex had ken in the moment the Cherokee had said his farewell to the boy that he'd found his brother's killer. It was the same man who'd left the imprint of his tomahawk forever on Alex's head, shoulders, and hands, evidence of what escaped his memory—that he'd curled into a ball when he could not defend himself.

Reverend Lawrence had further confirmed the brave's identity when he'd told Alex he was called Split Ear from the mark he'd received in the Cherokee War.

It had taken all Alex's restraint not to ride after those two braves and ambush them on the trail home. A rifle shot followed by a pistol shot would make quick work of them. But he couldn't risk his service as a ranger or retribution on the Lawrences. And he couldn't tell Elspeth the reason he'd taken his leave so abruptly. She'd been far too shaken by the mere appearance of the braves. He could still feel her trembling under his arm. Somehow, the revelation of her weakness made her more relatable.

He had, however, warned her father. Reverend Lawrence's countenance had gone slack when Alex shared his discovery. Obviously, Elspeth had told him far more of what she and Alex had faced during and after the attack, separated from their parents, than he himself had guessed. The minister had requested a promise that Alex wouldn't do anything rash. Out of respect and in return for a guarantee that Lawrence would keep his daughter away from Split Ear, Alex had given it.

And now, upon a rolling ridge, he rode past a fort of poplar logs in a meadow sprinkled with wildflowers, the blockhouse with portholes and a stone chimney so wide it took up most of one end. Though this palisade was not military, swivel guns and blunderbusses studded the openings. They gave testament to the determination of the fort's builders...the very people who had been driven off by Long Canes massacre.

Uncle Gilroy had told Alex about how the Calhouns and some others had returned to the Ninety Six District, settling near their previous location and constructing Fort Boone under the watchful gazes of hired Chickasaw guards. What bravery. What determination, he'd said. And that was why the English wanted the Scottish all along their borders.

The English, the Scottish, the Indians, the Patriots and Loyalists...all had fought their battles different ways and at different times. Now was the season for him to fight his.

Sweat rolled down Alex's face as Charlie trotted past the rolling hills to their right that proceeded along a southerly turn to the town of Ninety Six. Natural growth of oaks, black walnut, and hickories gave way to fields of corn, hemp, and oats. Harvests of other crops were in full swing. Threshers with scythes finished cutting the wheat, workers pulled up the yellowed stalks of flax, and wagons rumbled past full of indigo to be soaked in the first of three graduated vats for extracting the precious dye England demanded.

Located at the crossroads of a dozen paths and three notable roads connecting the Indians, Charlestown, and numerous small villages, Ninety Six made an impressive sight in the backcountry. A dozen residences surrounded taverns, shops, and a newly constructed courthouse and jail.

A two-story frame residence, painted a soft gold, drew Alex's eye. 'Twas hard not to notice, with its double porches and double brick chimneys. Back in June, when the Second South Carolina had enlisted here, Roger Bailey had sent his African housekeeper out with cider and cakes to refresh the recruits waiting in long lines on the courthouse lawn. Alex had heard the men of the area speak of the man with respect. Not only was he a justice of the peace, but he also owned a sizeable plantation in the district. So it hadn't surprised Alex when Reverend Lawrence had given Bailey's name as that of a man he could call on in a crisis. A moderate and a level head, as Lawrence had described him.

Those were certainly much in demand these days.

Major Mayson had established his headquarters at the massive frame courthouse and brick two-story jail at the south-west corner of the town. Alex had no sooner dismounted to walk Charlie through the encampment's hubbub than someone called his name.

His cousin Finn strode up, red hair ablaze in the bright July sun. "Alex! Whatever happened to ye, man? I saw ye ride off with that reverend and his daughter. Ye sly boots." He took a swig of strong-smelling rye whiskey from his pewter tankard.

"Supposin' that is what ye get for promisin' me my own commission." Alex thumped his cousin's shoulder. Knowing Finn had his back while serving together as Regulators had provided a sense of kinship he needed—until his cousin and uncle started taking their sense of justice too far. A number of men who'd volunteered to help keep the peace until law could be established on the frontier had ended by dispensing discipline in far too harsh a manner. No, it was better that as lieutenants, they both had their own men to oversee now.

"How is it ye get to sally off into the sunset with a braw lass while I'm stuck in these tight quarters with a bunch o'boggin' soldiers?" Despite the teasing words, Finn's ruddy face lacked its usual cheer. "A lot has happened in yer absence, Alex."

Alex stopped and faced him, holding Charlie's reins. "What did I miss in a day?"

Finn shrugged, not meeting his eyes. "The men have mixed feelings about occupying the town. Holding the river crossing at the fort was one thing, but being here in Ninety Six shows an intention to command the entire region."

Alex nodded. "True, but as much as I signed up to fight the Indians, not the Loyalists, this is what we signed up for." His muscles tensed, and he leaned forward, dropping the volume of his voice. "I was sent to the Presbyterian mission because they received a party of Cherokees this morn. One of them turned out to be the brave who killed Ethan."

Finn's jaw dropped. "How do ye ken?"

Alex ran his finger over the top of his ear. "He was missin' a chunk here. The reverend said he lost it in the Cherokee War."

Finn's Adam's apple bobbed. "What did ye do?"

"I delivered the message Major Mayson told me to, invitin' him and the other one to Fort Charlotte for tea."

"Blessed virgin! Did they accept?"

Alex let out a huff. "Well, I'm here, aren't I? Not there? But now I ken he is still alive. The reverend swears the Cherokees willna get involved in the disagreements between Patriots and Loyalists, but if Split Ear's reaction was any sign, I have a chance of finishin' what Ethan started soon enough." A grin tugged at a corner of his mouth as he led Charlie to a water trough on the side of the courthouse. The stallion drank deeply, and Alex took the opportunity to seek his own refreshment.

Finn shifted his weight. "What would ye do if the Cherokees joined on the side ye're pledged to?"

"The Patriots?" Lowering his canteen, Alex shot his cousin a sharp glance. "Ye were there, maybe in the first group that got to Tobler's Fort, but ye saw what they did."

"Aye. I imagine ye'd do all in your power to avoid allyin' with them, wouldn't ye?"

"As should you."

Angling closer, Finn narrowed his eyes. "What we should do is whatever guarantees our land and livelihood after all this is over."

Alex met his stare. "There are lines we dinna cross and alliances we should never make, or did yer pardon from yer Regulator days wipe clean yer memory?" Although he'd heard his Uncle Gilroy in recent months speak the same sentiment Finn had.

"Family is the only alliance I never compromise. As it should be for you." Finn shoved Alex's arm. "What's stuck in yer craw, anyway? Did the lass naysay ye?"

Alex tethered his stallion on the nearby hitching post before answering, allowing a bit of space from Finn's looming presence. "The reverend and his daughter ken me. 'Tis why I was selected to go with them. They were there, too...at Long Canes. Elspeth Lawrence was the one...the one..."

Finn's hazel eyes went wide. "The one ye were found with?"

After three days. "Aye." It was barely a breath.

"Lawrence. Right. My mother had a letter once that mentioned them movin' back here."

"She—Elspeth—wanted me to remember. And I did. At least, I remembered something. A doll. I believe it was her sister's, the one who died."

Foolishly, he'd told her as much when he'd said goodbye. She'd looked so forlorn, and he hadn't been able to answer her questions about when they would see him next. Never, if he could help it. Because, as always, he only brought the darkness. But after her scare, he'd had to offer her something. So he'd told her about the memory. The resulting flash of hope in her eyes made him feel even worse.

And something niggled him. Why keep a token of her

younger sister on display, but none of her baby brother? Her mother?

"Nay..." Finn slowly shook his head. "Not died. Was abducted. The Lawrences' younger daughter was taken by the Cherokees."

CHAPTER 5

*A*lex should've paid attention to Finn's disposition when he'd arrived in Ninety Six. Should have taken heed to the hushed voices and sideways looks whenever he entered a room or approached a circle of soldiers unannounced, rather than submersing himself in thoughts of the past, of Elspeth Lawrence and her lost sister. Even Alex's meeting with Mayson had flustered him. It had been clear his answers about the loyalties of the Lawrences and the mood of the Cherokees had failed to satisfy the major. Mayson asked him to further renew his acquaintance with the reverend and his daughter. Their contacts made them important.

How would Reverend Lawrence and his Elspeth take his overtures of friendship? They would either suspect his motives or worse, believe him to be sincere and seek more than he could give.

Alex had forgotten to lay all that aside and focus on the present. Had he retained his normal vigilance, he surely wouldn't be in this position now, five days after the taking of Fort Charlotte—standing behind a rough shed while his cousin held a secret meeting with his men on the other side.

He'd sought fresh water upstream in the Spring Branch that ran at the bottom of the hill west of town. Churned mud and horse droppings marred the banks nearest the jail. Here, a copse of trees and an abandoned settler's outbuilding offered a rare patch of shade—and privacy. Somehow, he'd approached unseen and unheard, and now he couldn't unhear the words Finn had just whispered.

"Our scout has spotted Fletchall's men a few miles out. They should be here within the hour to challenge the Patriots. Kirkland has resigned, as he told us he would. Now is the time for us to flee."

Flee? Alex's heart pounded. What Finn suggested sounded like desertion. Treason. But wasn't Thomas Fletchall colonel of the Upper Saluda District Militia—for the cause of freedom, like them? And yet if he was coming to challenge the Patriots, could Finn be changing sides?

Alex couldn't let this pass, but he was unarmed save for his *sgian-dubh,* the small knife that most men of Highland origin wore in their boot or garter. He would confront his cousin, though it needed to be later, just the two of them.

Could he sneak away without being spotted, or would it be wiser to remain in place and wait for the men to finish their conference? As he swiveled to survey the landscape, a small rock rolled out from beneath his boot.

"What was that?" one of the privates asked.

Another answered, "Someone's back there."

Nothing for it now. Dropping his bucket with a thud, Alex stepped around the shed, drawing the startled gazes of the half dozen men standing there. And the barrels of one or two pistols. Still, he spoke without wavering. "What is the meaning of this?"

"Alex!" Finn's complexion turned several shades ruddier than normal. He gave an out-of-control-sounding laugh and waved down his sergeant's weapon. "What are ye doin', followin' me?"

"Fetchin' water from the brook." Alex jerked his head to the left. "What are *ye* doin', skulkin' around sheds and speakin' of fleein'? Fleein' what? If there's danger, ye should be aimin' those pistols at the enemy, not me."

"The problem is, I'm not sure ye ken who the enemy is."

"Has Fletchall joined the King's Men, then?"

"Aye." Finn gave a slow blink, as if waiting for Alex to catch onto something. "And so have we."

No one moved, then everyone did—Alex for his knife, Finn's soldiers for Alex. Three of them tackled him, twisted his arm behind his back, and wrested away his sgian-dubh before he could roll away. The swarthy sergeant held him down, Alex's face inches from the mud.

Alex let out a growl. "Have ye lost yer minds?" Was this what Finn had meant when he'd said a lot had been going on? They had been planning a...defection? "Is this about Kirkland's jealousy of the major?"

The man holding him scoffed. "Ye're thinkin' too small, Lieutenant."

"I'm sorry, Alex." Finn's voice came from closer. He was bending down. "I would have left ye alone, had ye not showed up at the wrong time. I ken ye wouldna join us, with yer undying loyalty to a cause. Hopeless as our grandsire, ye are."

"At least he ken what he believed in. Do ye, Finn?" Alex twisted to get a sideways view of his cousin's thin face, the lower half speckled with uneven ginger scruff.

"Aye." Finn straightened. "This *is* about Kirkland. About the land we bought from him. The people he kens. And they all think it would be most unwise to rebel against His Majesty."

"Land is no' worth yer honor."

"As though *ye* would understand. We tried to give ye a

home, a plot of yer own ground. But ye have the soul of a gypsy. Ye dinna ken what home is. Ye have no loyalty where it truly matters...to family."

Alex's eyes closed briefly, the words shooting a pain to his heart. How could Finn say that, knowing how he'd lost his own parents and brother? "I'm here for ye, aren't I? For yer da?"

"Nay. Ye're here for yerself. To fight the war which has been goin' on inside ye since Long Canes Creek."

The unexpected insight silenced Alex.

"Well, the rest of us would like to stay here." Finn went on, as smug in his predictions as he was boastful in his cups. "What do ye think will happen when this little drama plays out, hm? The might of the English army and navy, the fierce anger of the Cherokee...all will be unleashed against the colonists. I dinna ken about you, but I dinna want to be on the receivin' end of that."

"This is treason." Alex heaved against the sergeant, and a burly private added his knee to Alex's back.

"Nay...ye *Patriots* are treasonous. Tie him up."

Alex drew in a deep breath, but before he could let out any further sound, Finn stuffed a dirty kerchief in his mouth. He spat it out, bucked, and kicked backward, making contact with the sergeant's knee.

The man yelled and relaxed his hold just long enough for Alex to break free. His cry of triumph ended in a grunt of pain as something hard made contact with the back of his head, and he slumped into the dark pit that opened up beneath him.

~

Shouts roused Alex. His head throbbed, sharp pain shooting to his temple with every beat of his heart. Evening light filtered through the gaps between rough-hewn logs. He sat slumped inside the shed where he'd confronted his cousin, gagged and bound.

Had he really just been betrayed by his own flesh and blood?

He tried to spit out that notion along with the kerchief, to no avail. Why should Finn's treachery surprise him? Like Kirkland, whose reputation included selling rum to the Indians and dealing in fraudulent land warrants, his primary concern had always been himself.

Knowing that did not make the betrayal hurt any less.

Shouting and the drumming of horse hooves continued from near the jail. When Alex found the rope around his wrists to be secure, he tried bellowing past the material in his mouth, but the noise from nearby drowned out any hope of his being heard.

What was going on?

He shifted and placed an eye to the crack. Men in the rough clothing of the frontier swarmed the area, some mounted and some not, all carrying rifles. A group marched from the direction of the courthouse toward the jail, dragging a figure in blue. Mayson! Some of the faces of his captors were familiar. Alex had seen them on the road from Fort Charlotte. They shoved the major up the steps and into the brick building.

Alex sat back, his speeding pulse creating starbursts before his eyes. Where were the rangers? Surely, they hadn't all deserted, even his own men. He had to get out of here. Now.

The shed was empty save a couple of old barrels. Alex scooted over to one and positioned himself. He pulled on the lower metal band until the wood gave way enough to loosen the tip. Then he leaned forward and rubbed the rope binding his hands against the sharp band, back and forth, back and forth, until the fibers began to slacken.

With a cry, he broke his hands free, snatched the kerchief from around his jaw, and made quick work of the knots binding his ankles. He scrambled back to the crack facing the jail and crouched there to observe.

Guards had been posted in all directions he could see. Dozens more Loyalists surrounded the buildings, carrying crates and barrels from the courthouse and the jail to waiting wagons. If any Patriot rangers remained, they had most likely been taken captive like Mayson. And Alex had left his weapons inside the courthouse where he and the officers had slept.

Not to mention, he found the door to the shed bolted from the outside. The wood was old enough he might be able to kick his way out, but that would attract notice.

He sat back down and rubbed a hand over his face. How was he to effect a rescue with no weapons and no soldiers?

Duncan Lawrence's parting words came back to him. Roger Bailey was a fair man, a moderate man. But was he trustworthy? Or, if Alex went to him, would the justice of the peace only turn him over to the Loyalists?

Did Alex have a choice? Even if Charlie was still safely picketed in the meadow, fleeing town without even trying to do something to help Mayson stank of cowardice. Perhaps Bailey could at least give him information about where the other rangers might be.

Making up his mind, Alex checked the view from all points around the shed. Finding no one near and the Loyalists still at work emptying the village of Fort Charlotte's munitions, he found a spot where the hewn log was already cracked, laid on his back, and kicked at it over and over with all his might.

Finally, large enough pieces splintered away for him to be able to crawl through. Keeping to the trees as much as possible, he circled north of town. Even without his blue-and-red coat—which was in the courthouse with his accoutrements—and even with his waistcoat and breeks covered with dirt, their white material stood out like a surrender flag. A small field of cornstalks offered a likely approach to the residences along

Island Ford Road. He passed through an orchard and let himself through the fence to the back door of the golden-painted house.

The woman with the glowing golden-brown complexion who had served him cider in June stepped onto the back stoop and flung out a pot of cooking water, stopping in mid-swing when she caught sight of him. "Have mercy!" Her hand flew to her bosom, and her eyes went wide.

Alex approached with his hand held out. "I mean ye no harm, ma'am. I just need to speak to Roger Bailey...if he will speak with me." He searched her eyes for the answer to his unspoken question. He was placing his trust in this servant he'd only seen once before. "Please."

Finally, she gave a slow dip of her head. "Come up onto de porch, sir."

"Thankee." He did as requested. "Tell him...tell him I come at the suggestion of Reverend Lawrence."

At that, the slave's shoulders relaxed a measure. "Wait here." She let herself back into the house.

Alex scanned the yard until the door opened again. He found himself looking into the piercing green eyes of a man every bit his height and sturdy build. He wore his wheat-gold hair tied back with a black ribbon and his stock loosened above his finely woven waistcoat. Alex hadn't expected the man to be so young—thirty, at most.

"I'm Roger Bailey. How can I be of service?" His gaze lowered to take in Alex's attire and state of dress, and awareness of the dangerous situation Alex found himself in flooded his aristocratic features.

"I am a friend of Reverend Lawrence." Alex did something he normally did not do. He removed his hat. That snapped Bailey's notice up right quick. His eyes widened at the network of scars that ran under Alex's hair, and his throat bobbed. "I ken his family as a child, and he says I can trust ye."

"Of course," Bailey said. "Come in, come in." But rather than lead him through the door he'd just come out, Bailey opened up a room built onto the back porch, the type many who were flush in the pocket kept for travelers. He followed Alex into a space where a small rope bed, a washstand, a chest, and a chair sat atop a braided rug. "I take it you are one of the Patriot rangers."

Alex nodded, his hat now firmly back in place. "Lieutenant Alexander Morris, sir, of the South Carolina Regiment of Horse. Reverend Lawrence said ye were a fair and moderate man. Can I trust ye?"

Bailey lifted his head. "I would never betray the confidence the reverend places in me. And 'tis true, like him, I have assumed something of the role of an ambassador in these parts. He sees it as his religious duty, and I see it as my civil duty."

"Verra well, then. I came from Fort Charlotte with Captain Kirkland and Major Mayson, but I stumbled upon the plot to defect by some of Kirkland's men and was attacked and bound. When I came to, the town was swarming with King's Men. I saw Mayson thrown in the jail."

"Mm-hm." Bailey gave a murmur that indicated his awareness of these events, if not his opinion on them, and fingered his clean-shaven chin. "And where are your own men, Lieutenant?"

"I dinna ken, sir." If his fears proved correct, Finn had gotten to them during Alex's absence, and they were long gone. "I had hoped ye might have word if any Patriot troops remain in the area."

"It is my understanding that all of Kirkland's rangers departed before Colonel Fletchall arrived with his militia. I suspect they will have gone for now to one of the plantations of the Loyalist leaders."

The confirmation pierced Alex in the gut. So Kirkland's men *had* not only deserted...but defected. He took a step forward. "Do ye ken any who would join me to free Mayson? He has done nothing but bring supplies from Fort Charlotte to Ninety Six under orders."

Bailey pressed his lips tight and shook his head. "Not enough to challenge that troop at the jail and courthouse. No, Lieutenant, your wisest course of action would be to return to Fort Charlotte, or at least to lie low and see what the morrow brings. My body servant tells me the Loyalists are packing the munitions."

Alex cast an eye toward the window, curtained in muslin, through which dimming golden light slanted. "I dinna fancy stumblin' upon Loyalist patrols in the dark, nor desertin' me commander...even if I am his only loyal man remainin' in Ninety Six."

"Then you will stay here. I will send my manservant at first light for information."

Alex cut his gaze back to the man before him. "Are ye certain, Mr. Bailey?"

Bailey placed a large hand on his shoulder. "Roger. Any friend of Duncan's is a friend of mine. And yes, I am certain."

"Until first light, then." His skin prickled at the delay, the inactivity, the unfamiliar surroundings. Alex walked to the window and peered through the crack in the material, but all it afforded him was a view of the garden.

"Pray, do not attempt anything rash, Lieutenant Morris. I can see that you are a man of action, but there are moments when it behooves us to be still."

Alex turned and took Roger Bailey's measure. "I can see why the reverend speaks well of ye."

A hint of a smile tickled laugh lines bracketing Bailey's mouth. No doubt, the ladies found him irresistible. "I will send Rosa with water and food. Should any unwanted company appear, she will warn you in time."

Alex nodded, but a check in his spirit left him pacing the

short length of exposed flooring after Bailey took his leave. What about the company that might be wanted? Would Bailey send word to Colonel Fletchall the moment Alex laid his head down?

He wouldn't sleep a wink.

CHAPTER 6

*E*lspeth blew a sticky strand of hair from her face and stirred the crushed-up cone of sugar Galilani had just added to the simmering peaches in the pot. 'Twas always miserable, laboring over the fire so long at the tail end of August, but they would be right glad of the preserves during the winter. The rain drumming on the wooden shakes off and on made the humidity even harder to bear.

She had the girls take turns stirring, but only Galilani was truly helpful. The others preferred to play with the colored glass jars lined up on the table or steal pinches of the sugar. By now, they were quite giggly, living up to the meaning of their names, Kamama—*butterfly*—and Ayita—*first to dance.*

A shadow crossed the threshold. Elspeth snuck a peek as Inoli strode in and back out and called over her shoulder in Cherokee, "What are you doing?"

As usual, he failed to answer. After the last break in the rain, he was supposed to be sweeping the dirt yard and then feeding the chickens...although last time she had looked, he was chasing them up into the trees with the broom. Sweeping the yard made no sense to one unaccustomed to yards. Or chickens.

With her father off to visit an ailing friend and Ulisi on one of her wild herb forays, which always seemed to take half the day, 'twas all Elspeth could do to keep the boy occupied. He'd proved a quick learner, but his limited English and boundless curiosity made a tricky combination. He set about to master everything they taught him with grave determination, but he did not like to speak in English until he was certain of what he could say. That might have something to do with the girls' giggles.

Truly, he needed a man's hand, and even Da was not always equal to the challenge. A man like Lieutenant Alexander Morris was needed.

Where was he?

On the Sunday service Da preached monthly at the fort— and had continued to do, lest they be branded Loyalist traitors —she had strained to catch sight of that tall, aloof figure. Had fretted for his welfare ever since they heard of how the Loyalists had stormed Ninety Six. Both truth and rumors streaked through the backcountry faster than a black racer snake after a rat. Captain Caldwell had told them that the King's Men had left almost as quickly as they had arrived, releasing Major Mayson on bail to later answer charges of robbing Fort Charlotte. But of Lieutenant Morris he had no word.

Had he turned coat with the rest of Kirkland's men? Or had he been captured or wounded in the fray? Elspeth gnawed her lower lip. He'd given her no reason to hope they might further their friendship, if one could call it that, but when he'd told her of the memory with the doll—

Boom!

Elspeth jumped and dropped the long-handled spoon into the pot. Not thunder, but musket fire, and just outside! Instructing the girls not to move, she whirled for Da's Brown

Bess...and found its usual spot by the open door empty. Inoli! Her heart hammering, she ran to the porch.

The boy stood just across the clearing, the smoking musket now lowered to his side, the eagle feather twirling at his ear. And through the trees, up the drive, a flash of brown and white —not a deer, either—made her suck in her breath.

"Oh, Inoli, who have ye shot?"

Her first course of action should be to protect the boy. After all, though he'd taken the musket without permission—in fact, Da had strictly warned all the students to never touch the gun —he was but a child. Maybe he had thought he was protecting *them*. Maybe he had been. Some settlers were none too fond of the notion of Cherokee children at a mission school near Long Canes.

She whisked out the door and across the yard. Catching Inoli unawares, she snatched the musket up in one hand and the boy in the other. Elspeth hauled both toward the cabin.

He struggled, pointing behind them. "Look, Miss El." The children found her name difficult to pronounce. "*I di-s-da-yo-s-di.*"

"You shoot—I ken. Why did ye take the musket, Inoli?"

"Elspeth!" Her father's cry halted her halfway up the steps.

Her hand flew to her heart, and she spun. Had Inoli shot at her father by mistake?

The boy broke free and ran down the driveway to meet him, slipping once and skidding into a mud puddle, then springing to his feet as though nothing had happened. He shouted and waved his arms.

Elspeth's pulse only slowed a fraction when Da came into the clearing, no red stains on his person. "Are ye all right?" she called.

"Aye." He slowed and dismounted, leading his gelding toward the bushes. A moment later, he popped back up, holding a dead red fox by its long, fluffy tail. "But he isna."

She covered her face, and the air rushed out of her. Then she glowered at Inoli and shook a fist at him. "I have half a mind to take the broom to ye, ye eejit!"

Good thing Inoli's English was not up to par, for rather than taking offense as a Cherokee young man of his self-respect would be sure to do, he grinned broadly. "*Go-hu-s-di a-da-s-da-yv-di.*"

Da hooted from the yard. "Something to cook, he says!"

Behind her, a trio of soft giggles sounded. The girls, peeking out the door, no doubt.

Elspeth planted her hands on her hips. "I dinna find it a bit funny, especially after he took the musket without permission. Ye must deal with him, Da, else next time, he might be shootin' the neighbors."

Her father led his mount up to the porch, where he handed her the limp fox.

Pressing her mouth tight, she held it out lest it drip a pool of blood onto the floorboards.

He winked at her. "A bit betwattled today, are ye, love? Dinna fash yerself. I shall have a chat with the boy. Remind him that boys his age shoot blowguns, not muskets. And for you, I have a surprise."

"Besides this poor dead creature, ye mean?"

"Aye. Tomorrow, we shall go to Boonesborough. Ye will like that, won't ye? Gettin' a wee break from yer labors?"

Tomorrow was Wednesday, not Sunday, so Da could hardly be needed to preach. Before Elspeth could ask him what was to be at Boonesborough, he settled his free hand on Inoli's shoulder and led him toward the stable with a stern command.

∾

*E*lspeth had hoped that Alex might be among the rangers escorting Reverend William Tennent to Long Canes, but she was disappointed, for while there were rangers present, the one she longed to see was not in the company. Her father's anticipation of hearing the minister of the Independent Presbyterian Church of Charlestown, a man educated at both the College of New Jersey and Harvard, though he was only thirty-five, overrode his normal reticence to involve them in political affairs. For while Tennent did preach, this gathering beneath Farmer Harris's shed was more rally than service.

It would seem the Council of Safety found the backcountry in need of a good upbraiding. In light of the Loyalist troubles, they had sent a committee of three, headed by the fiery politician and orator William Henry Drayton and including Tennent, to set the region straight regarding the reasons for the rebellion against the king. The day before, Drayton and Tennent had combined their powers of persuasion to sway an enthusiastic crowd at Ninety Six, then split up to cover more ground.

Tennent had concluded his sermon and turned to the real topic of his visit, the need to raise more militia for the Patriot cause. His cautions about the looming threat of the Cherokees made Elspeth's skin prickle. More than one speculative and inquisitive glance turned their way as they sat beneath the shed.

Da covered her hand with his. Her father assured her their Indian neighbors would stay out of the fight, but his talks with the superintendent had taken place some time ago, and the braves who occasionally visited the mission for the children's sake were almost always stoic. With how much truth would they truly trust a white minister?

The young lady seated beside Rebecca Calhoun was said to be the new bride of Philip Guthrie, from Augusta. Though rather plain, she looked sweet and friendly—until she answered Elspeth's hopeful, curious glance with a sour look.

A fat drop of water from last night's rain plopped onto Elspeth's gray linen petticoat. She brushed it away and smoothed the sleeves of her cotton bodice, embroidered in a vining flower pattern—her second-best dress. Perhaps she should have worn her work petticoat and apron. Maybe then the other women would take some pity on her, see she only wanted a friend. Was it simply their mission work that created distrust?

Andrew Pickens, whom they had known back in Waxhaws, straightened from where he leaned against a post and launched a question into Tennent's first pause. "All that may be true, Reverend, but how are we to answer yer call for volunteers, how are we defend ourselves against the Cherokees, if we have no ammunition?"

Murmurs of agreement sounded around him. If Pickens, the owner of a fine plantation along the Keowee, felt such a lack, what of the farmer who barely cleared enough corn and wheat to put bread on his family's table?

"A fair question, Mr. Pickens." Tennent extended his hands, palms down. "What I propose is that we raise three companies of militia from these parts. Drayton and the Council of Safety have authorized me to take this measure. We will supply your powder and shot. You will elect your own captains and officers. In the face of this double threat, men of Long Canes, are you willing to rally to the cause of freedom?"

"Aye!" Pickens was the first to respond, his craggy brows drawn low over his long, hooked nose. A dozen others quickly followed his lead, standing and adding their voices.

"You have made your new government proud this day." Tennent smiled with not a little relief, though the dark circles beneath his eyes belied his enthusiasm. No wonder, for he had traveled thirty-six miles the day prior and likely passed a damp and uncomfortable night. "Let us seek some refreshment while you talk amongst yourselves, then we will reconvene and cast the ballots."

After two hours of oratory, no one argued with that suggestion. People stood, stretched, and chatted while they sought hampers to spread their food on the rough-hewn logs laid over stumps for tables. Elspeth rose, suddenly shy. When her father stepped over to speak to one of the elder Calhouns, her mouth went dry.

Rebecca Calhoun smiled at her. "'Tis good to see ye, Elspeth."

"And ye, Rebecca. How are yer children?"

"Very well, thankee. 'Tis a lovely dress."

"Oh, thankee." She smoothed her hand down her bodice. "I dinna get much chance to wear it, I'm afraid. And I daresay less comin', what with fall on the horizon." Autumn was undoubtedly the busiest time for a woman, setting by stores of food and candles for winter.

Young Mrs. Guthrie edged into view at Rebecca's elbow. "Did I hear it spoken aboot that ye have a boy stayin' at the mission school now too? Not just girls?"

"That is correct. Inoli. He is...quite a handful."

"For sure and certain." The girl's lips turned down. "How will ye ever find a husband if all yer time is taken up with heathen children?"

Elspeth's mouth opened and shut as she sought an answer. "I...well, I suppose I reckon that if I am called to do the Lord's work, He will provide the husband when the time is right."

Rebecca nodded. "Well said, Miss Lawrence."

"Miss Lawrence? Miss *Elspeth* Lawrence?"

The deep voice of an African man at her elbow couldn't have been more welcome.

"Aye?" She turned. "I am she."

"I has a message for you, which I's carried here from Ninety Six."

As Elspeth accepted a small, stained envelope from the servant, who must be traveling with Tennent's party, Mrs. Guthrie tugged Rebecca aside. Her whispered entreaty carried to Elspeth's ears. "Givin' herself airs that she be some sort of teacher. Imagine. Come, Rebecca. I have apply tansey in me basket."

Rebecca offered an apologetic smile as she allowed herself to be led away.

Elspeth fought down the prickly lump in her throat. So that was it? Other women spurned her friendship because she was learned and sought to apply that learning? And with the Cherokees, of all people.

Love your enemies, bless them that curse you, do good to them that hate you...

So be it. She lifted her chin. If that was the cost of doing what God had asked her to do alongside her father, the very model of forgiveness and grace if she'd ever seen one, it was a small enough price to pay.

Elspeth turned over the envelope. The letter *B* imprinted the red wax seal. She pressed her finger over it with a soft laugh. Apparently, her commitment to her work had not discouraged everyone. She unsealed the short letter and read it, then stood there blinking and thinking, almost oblivious to the chatter of the women and impassioned words of the men around her.

Da slid a hand through her elbow and whispered in her ear. "Methinks 'tis time for us to depart, daughter, before they break out the Association and strong arm us into signing."

She looked at him. "What?"

"I said..." He eyed the paper she held. "What is that? A missive?"

"From Roger. He and his mother have invited us to town for me birthday celebration. He will send his buggy and driver."

"Oh...daughter." Da breathed out the soft exclamation. "What think ye?"

"I dinna ken, Da. I do enjoy the company of Miss Charlotte. Verra much." She was the only woman in these parts to be consistently kind to Elspeth, in fact, even if the reason might have to do more with her own ill health—or her son's affections. "But if I go..."

"He will take it that he may resume his suit."

"Aye, an' he does still hold slaves." Reaching through the slit in her petticoat, Elspeth tucked the letter into the pocket she wore beneath.

"He does, inherited from his father before him." Da shifted his head first to one side, then the other. "But he an' I have had conversations about that, an' I believe him to be comin' around. Not to mention the influence a fiancée—or a wife—might exert."

"I wouldna marry him under the circumstances."

"Then see what this visit brings. I shouldna go, not with Inoli needin' the firm hand he does. But you may, if ye wish. I leave that up to you. But remember, Roger Bailey be an oak of a man. Not one to trifle with. Best make up yer mind soon enough."

No doubt, Roger was the handsomest, most charming, and wealthiest man she'd ever met. But someone else might be found in Ninety Six...or at least, news of him. Elspeth drew in a little breath as she gazed past her father.

"I ken that look, lassie. And I can guess well enough the reason for it." Da squeezed her arm. "Be careful. Not every man would guard yer heart as I would have him to."

CHAPTER 7

"*J*s it too much, Miss Charlotte?"

Elspeth hardly recognized herself in the mirror of the walnut dressing table, her hair drawn up into an elaborate pouf with two ringlets dangling over the shoulder of the gown Roger's mother had lent her. Truly, *gifted* her...for she'd had Rosa cinch her old dress in to fit Elspeth like a glove. She ran her hand over the fine rose brocade material with three flat bows on the bodice.

"Never too much. One of your beauty should be shown to the best advantage, my dear." Miss Charlotte stood behind her, admiring her handiwork, her own thin form quite regal in butternut silk that complemented her golden-and-silver hair.

Heart squeezing with gratitude, Elspeth turned on the padded stool and extended her hand. "Why are ye so kind to me, ma'am?"

Miss Charlotte took her hand and squeezed it gently. "Why would I not be kind to the young lady my Roger favors?"

"Because I'm not English. Nor from a fine family such as yers."

"With the proper loyalties, the first might be overlooked." A smile danced about the older woman's lips. "As to the second, Roger thinks highly of your father, an educated man who is doing important work among the Cherokees. Allies we wish to keep."

"Aye." So the very thing that made them scorned by the Patriots was valued by the Loyalists. "But only with the children —the work, that is."

"Where better to sow the seeds of tomorrow?" With a feather-light touch, Miss Charlotte smoothed Elspeth's curls. "You poor girl. I suspect the lack of mother and sister has left quite a hole in your life."

Elspeth blinked back the moisture that rushed to her eyes. "'Tis just that I dinna find other ladies to be so kind either. The work ye mentioned may be to blame."

Miss Charlotte gave a soft laugh and dropped her hand. "Not just that, I would wager. You're like a rare flower in this rough wilderness, Elspeth. Whether you see it or not, my son certainly does."

Elspeth broke eye contact, for the woman spoke truth. Not only Roger Bailey, but many other men, high born or low, married or bachelor, looked on her with a certain hunger. But not Alex Morris. The one man she wished would covet her attention seemed determined to avoid it. In the two days she'd been in town, she'd not sighted him, and she hadn't been able to figure a way to gracefully inquire about him.

"Now, come along." Miss Charlotte clapped her hands. "We must not keep Roger waiting. I believe he has a little surprise he wants to present to you before company arrives."

Elspeth rose but gave a murmur of dismay. "Oh, no...this supper, this dress...is more than enough." Prize that Roger might be, she was not ready to be beholden to him, not even if local gossips labeled her nearly a spinster upon turning twenty-two. But was she already beholden, just by being here?

"Roger loves any excuse to give a supper, and the dress is from me."

"Of course. Thankee, Miss Charlotte." Elspeth followed her to the door of the fine guest room she enjoyed while staying the week in Roger's home. The blue floral pattern on the curtains and counterpane put her in mind of Charlestown, even though she'd never visited there.

Her hostess paused a moment with her hand on the stair rail.

Elspeth hastened to support her. "Are ye feelin' quite well, Miss Charlotte?"

"Oh, yes. Just a lot of excitement for an invalid like me."

Elspeth cocked her head. "Ye're not dizzy?" Though hardly an invalid, Roger's mother suffered with yearly malarial fevers. Elspeth had tended her during past illnesses more than once.

"Indeed, no, though I thank you for your concern. Let us go down."

Golden evening light illuminated the landing as they started downstairs. Elspeth kept a watchful eye on the older lady. The savory scent of turkey roasting and the sweet of candied potatoes promised a feast.

"Who else will be joining us for supper tonight?" Elspeth inquired as she trailed her hand along the curving balustrade.

"Two local men and two officers, I believe. I'm afraid we will be the only ladies."

Elspeth refrained from saying that was something of a relief. She wouldn't have had the chance.

Roger stepped from his library into the downstairs foyer. His freshly washed hair gleamed in its queue, as did his embroidered silk waistcoat and the buckles on his shoes. But none so much as his eyes when they found her.

Miss Charlotte kissed his cheek and sailed past him to investigate the state of the dining room...and leave them alone in the entryway.

Roger held his hands out to her. "Elspeth, you look...marvelous."

She lowered her lashes, unable to return his fervent gaze. "Thanks to yer mother's kindness."

"Only in small part. Would you allow me a kindness too? Seeing as how it's your birthday?"

Would Miss Charlotte have it otherwise? Elspeth dipped her head in a faint nod. "Although I'm no' deserving, Roger." They had long ago reached the point in their friendship where Christian names became appropriate, but she did not use his often.

"There is none more deserving." He reached into the pocket of his coat with its many brass buttons and produced a small velvet pouch, which he held out to her. "From Mother and me."

And that precluded any argument, did it not? Elspeth loosened the opening and drew out an ivory-carved cameo. "Oh, Roger, 'tis..."

He made a chiding sound and raised his finger, almost touching her lips. Indeed, his gaze rested there for a moment that made tingles shoot down Elspeth's neck. But then he dropped his hand and stepped back. "I would give you much more, should you allow it."

Elspeth swallowed. Up until now, she had put off any official attachment between them with talk of how her father needed her. But the reverend made no secret of his approval of Roger. "Da is still hopeful this next year will prove a turning point in our work. If the congregation at Waxhaws learns of our success, perhaps they will send him an assistant."

"Your dedication does you credit, Elspeth." Roger bowed his golden head and placed a hand behind his back. "I will bide my time, for now."

"Thankee, Roger."

She flushed that this man would demonstrate humility before her. She had just bought herself a year, but what woman would need more than a week to see what a catch he was? His attentions did flatter, his touch did stir. And yet, even if Roger did not own slaves, something held her back. What was missing? Why did he not fill the void in her heart?

"Will you wear the brooch?" His question broke into her musings.

"With gratitude." She pinned it onto the front of her bodice. She'd never owned jewelry so fine.

"Beautiful," Roger said, but he was looking at her face.

She flushed, but before she could respond, boots and voices sounded from the front porch.

"Ah, that will be our company."

Poe, the butler who also acted as Roger's manservant, hurried past them to answer the call of the brass knocker. He opened the door to two rangers in blue and white, doffing their hats.

Elspeth drew in a quick breath, for the figure in the back was the one she'd been longing to see.

The look on Alex's face as he caught sight of her stole the smile that had started to bloom on her lips.

～

*W*hat was she doing here? And dressed like the china doll he so often thought she resembled? Indeed, it had taken him a moment to even recognize her. Why was she welcoming guests with Roger Bailey as though she were his hostess? His wife?

The questions crashed through Alex's mind as Bailey greeted them. "Lieutenant Morris, I'm so glad you could come...and bring Lieutenant Wilson. Not only will you complete our supper party, but you will allow me to right the wrong I did you upon your last visit, when I kept you in my back room." He stopped talking as Alex continued to stare at

Elspeth. "But, of course, you are already acquainted with our guest of honor."

"Aye," Alex said, "though 'tis something of a surprise to find her here."

"A pleasant one, I should expect." Bailey drew Elspeth forward by the hand, keeping hold of it and bestowing a warm smile on her. "I thought Miss Lawrence would enjoy seeing her childhood friend for her birthday."

"Indeed." Elspeth took another step toward him, disengaging from their host as she folded her hands before her. "I have been greatly concerned since I had no word of ye followin' the events that took place here last month." Her gaze entreated information.

Alex shifted his focus to Bailey. "I owe my safety to our mutual friend, for he sheltered me durin' that hubbub and then vouched for me before Major Mayson, that it had been my desire and intent to free him when he was imprisoned. That I had no prior knowledge of the defection of Kirkland's troops."

Elspeth turned to Bailey with widened eyes and parted lips.

He nodded. "And since then, Lieutenant Morris has become something of Major Mayson's right-hand man."

"He does intend to keep me here until Ninety Six be secure." He also expected Alex to be his eyes and ears. The man was understandably paranoid, suspecting plots and enemies all around. In fact, Alex had been ferreting out any potential schemes when Bailey had come upon him at the tavern with his current companion and issued his invitation. And now, Alex turned to the brown-haired man who stood quietly behind him, holding his hat. "This is Lieutenant Connor Wilson, who serves under Captain Ezekiel Polk. Lieutenant Wilson, Miss Elspeth Lawrence."

Wilson stepped forward to offer his greetings. Bailey shook his hand warmly. A spark of Mayson's suspicion flared in Alex's mind. Had Bailey known when he'd insisted both of them come to this "birthday supper of a dear friend" that Kirkland's defection had created a ripple effect of doubt in Polk's company? Was he eager to further that?

A woman of regal bearing and some years appeared from a side door, was introduced as Bailey's mother, Charlotte, and ushered them all into a parlor. Alex declined her offer of a drink while they waited for the two local gentlemen yet expected, but Wilson accepted and settled onto a settee looking like a fish out of water. A gulping, happy fish as he surveyed the fine furnishings, porcelain vases, and puddling lengths of curtains.

Indeed, what were they doing here? Had Bailey truly thought only of Elspeth with this invitation? The man stood behind her chair with solicitous attention, though Elspeth's gaze sought Alex's.

He avoided it. His scalp might as well be on fire, so conscious was he of his scars in the evening light coming through the wavy glass. He'd had no choice but to surrender his hat to the butler. One hardly sat at a supper party wearing one's hat.

When the final two members of their party arrived, Alex's discomfort fled. For the guest introduced as Thomas Brown bore scars much fresher and more alarming than his. The man's wig couldn't fully cover the front of a raw patch of skin that had undoubtedly been made by a scalping knife. He walked with a pronounced limp despite the soft material of the shoes he wore and his youth—mid-twenties, Alex would guess. Brown took a full glass of rum and a seat beside the planter, Edward Nash, whose land adjoined Bailey's.

While Bailey attended to his newly arrived guests, Elspeth sat alone. Her lashes fluttered, and her skin had drained of its normal pinkness.

Alex found himself going to her. He leaned over and whispered, "Are ye well, lass?"

"Aye. Thankee." But her fingers fluttered up to grasp his on her shoulder. And her eyes told a different tale. Memories, usually hollow but now brought to vivid life, flashed behind them.

A chill went down Alex's spine. No words were needed. He squeezed her hand. But he dropped it when Charlotte Bailey's gaze clamped onto the gesture. And narrowed.

So that was how it was.

The manservant spoke low in Mrs. Bailey's ear, and she rose and extended her hands with a little bow. "Gentlemen, supper is served."

Bailey returned to claim Elspeth, escorting her across the hall and into the dining room, followed by Mr. Brown with Mrs. Bailey. Nash, Alex, and Wilson trailed them. At the doorway, Wilson tucked a discreetly placed elbow into Alex's rib and raised his eyebrows. While they hadn't broken out the fine china—for a man of Bailey's standing undoubtedly possessed some—the light of fragrant bayberry tapers flickered over white creamware, silver, and crystal. Alex stared at the assortment of utensils with more unease than he had the Loyalists who had invaded Ninety Six. In the backcountry, most ate with knife and spoon—or just one's hands.

They took the seats their hostess indicated. As the slave who had served Alex during his prior visit, Rosa, offered onion soup from a tureen, Thomas Brown leaned over to Elspeth. "Miss Lawrence, you have recently arrived from near the Savannah River, is that correct?"

"Yes, sir." She darted the briefest glance at him. "My father and I have a mission on Russell's Creek."

Alex cut her a glance. She had said *yes* rather than *aye* and *father* rather than *Da*. Trying to play down her Scotch-Irish roots?

"I have heard of Reverend Lawrence. We are grateful for the goodwill he shows the Cherokees."

No doubt of it, if by *we* the man referred to the Loyalists. Alex kept his face impassive as he sipped his soup.

"Thankee, sir." Elspeth offered Brown a fleeting smile. "'Tis the calling God has put on our hearts, to forgive, to offer service where we may."

Brown's nose wrinkled as if he might snort, but instead, he smiled. A gesture that struck Alex as contrived. "Tell us, is that area still being assaulted by the fiery rhetoric of Drayton and Tennent?"

Elspeth blotted her lips with her napkin. "We did hear Tennent speak at Fort Boone, but we didna stay long, as they turned to signin' the Association and raisin' several militia companies. Besides, Tennent himself was called away."

"Called away?" The middle-aged planter, Nash, cocked his head. "By whom?"

Alex was more concerned with Elspeth's comment that she and her father had left before signing the Association.

"By a message from Drayton, 'twould seem. They had news of Lieutenant Morris's former commander, Captain Kirkland, raisin' troops to march on Fort Charlotte."

Alex sat up straight. "Was it true?" He waved away Rosa's offer of oysters on the half shell. He had no stomach for the slippery things, especially now.

Elspeth met his gaze. "I dinna ken." He almost smiled as her usual accent rolled off her tongue. "When I left, Tennent was at Fort Charlotte, advisin' Captain Caldwell to mount some of his big guns and send out patrols. He had them cut the tops of the corn outside the fort and strip the blades so as to offer no shelter for attackers."

"He will make the fort secure." Caldwell was an honorable man, the type of captain Alex should have served under. He had studied surveying under Patrick Calhoun and mapped most of Ninety Six. But now, Mayson commanded Alex's loyalty. Alex cringed just thinking of the cousin he'd once laughed and ridden with possibly attacking the fort he'd sworn to defend. Would he one day face Finn in battle? "What uneasy times we live in."

"I take it you were assigned to Fort Charlotte." Disdain fairly oozed from Thomas Brown's observation. He stared at Alex as Rosa set a platter of roast turkey filled with chestnut stuffing before him.

Alex met his gaze. "Originally. I will remain in Ninety Six for the foreseeable future."

"That might not be too long, Lieutenant." Unmistakable challenge hardened the man's expression.

Alex forked several lima beans, then paused, tilting his head. "Brown...be ye the Brown of Brownsborough? In Georgia?"

If possible, Brown's jaw tightened even more. But he managed to bolt back another swallow of rum. "Was. I now reside here, in Ninety Six."

"I, too, hail from Georgia. I recall hearin' about yer hamlet bein' founded south of my plot in the Ceded Lands. Ye brought colonists with ye from England, no? And the governor appointed ye magistrate of that region?"

"He did, though all that is in the past. I will never return to Georgia, except as an instrument to wipe the Patriot scourge from her soil."

Elspeth stiffened.

Wilson lifted his brows.

Alex made not a move or sound.

Bailey looked slightly grieved, though not surprised, at this outburst.

Lieutenant Wilson broke the silence as he rubbed his chin. "Forgive my ignorance, but I thought Georgia was loyal to her royal governor."

"Governor Wright is a good man, a fair man, but the Sons of Liberty are running rampant over him. As they assaulted me, in body, not just in principle." Brown's hand clenched. "All I asked was to hold my own opinions. If they are such advocates of freedom, why not let a man counter their Association? Hypocrites!" He banged the table, making its occupants jump along with the crystal.

"My dear friend..." Bailey patted his mouth with his napkin, then lowered it to his lap. His green eyes glowed with compassion. "'Tis pain you speak from, and rightfully so. In respect for the differing opinions of my guests, I ask that you refrain from personal insults. But I do think it only fair that those in our company be summarily apprised of what you suffered, and at whose hands."

"Ha! At the hands of the Sons of Liberty." Brown fairly spat the name. He raised the edge of his wig and pointed to his temple. "You think this the work of a Cherokee knife? Not by a mile. I would sooner trust my life to a red man than those who call themselves Patriots. For they are the ones who dragged me from my own home, tied me to a tree, roasted my feet over the flame, and tarred and feathered me."

"Thomas—" Bailey sought to interrupt, but Brown was on a tirade.

"A blow from the butt of one of their muskets fractured my skull and has left me with debilitating headaches. I have lost two toes. But the worst of it all—the worst, I say—was being carted through their settlements, forced to pledge my allegiance to their cause. As if I will not bring down God's vengeance upon every one of them the moment I have the chance!"

Alex shot to his feet. How could he sit in the face of such hatred? Brown rose too. They stared at each other, their breathing the only sound in the room.

Then Elspeth gave a little sob, muffled in her napkin.

Alex grasped the edge of the table and leaned toward the man. "Apologize at once."

"I will never apologize for speaking the truth."

"Not to me. Not for the truth." Although he couldn't say Brown's story had not rattled him to his bones. Would Bailey countenance such a tale, were it not true? "To the ladies, for the manner in which ye spoke it. Ye have upset them."

Brown's gaze shifted toward Elspeth as a tear slid down her cheek.

Mrs. Bailey reached over to take her hand.

He stood stiffly a moment, then affected an equally stiff bow. "Miss. Ma'am. I do apologize for my bluntness. It was not my intention to ruin your birthday supper."

Bailey laid his hands on the table. "Lieutenant Morris was correct...we should have saved the details for the men's parlor. However, I am a firm believer in hearing out those of differing opinions. Only by listening to each other's stories can we begin to understand, and then, hopefully, reach an accord. Now, gentlemen, would you please both resume your seats?"

Alex weighed Bailey's apparent sincerity and Brown's apology, however forced, against his anger that their host would have placed them in such a position. Had he been brought here in an attempt to sway him? He wanted nothing more than to march out of the room and never see Roger Bailey or Thomas Brown again.

Then his notice fell on Elspeth, and his chest constricted. Her pleading look drew him down into his chair. Whatever this had been about, she hadn't deserved this outcome. He gave her the smallest nod, and her mouth wobbled, then drew taut.

"Thank you, sirs." Mrs. Bailey dipped her head. "Let us not allow any discord to spoil the rest of Rosa's feast." She waved her hand to indicate the dishes on the sideboard—acorn squash, baked celery, hominy pudding, and sweet potatoes. More bounty than Alex had seen in a lifetime, although the rich foods would taste like sandy river soil in light of what he'd just heard. "Now...let us speak of more pleasant topics."

"I have one—a corn shucking!" Mr. Nash raised his index finger. "You're all invited to my place later this month. Lieutenants, bring your men, your friends. You can meet the local ladies and drink your fill of rye whiskey and peach brandy."

"Oh, but my harvest will come in ahead of yours," Bailey protested. "And I've engaged the best fiddler in the district."

Alex paid little heed as they discussed the dates. Wilson filled his silence, obviously eager to further his acquaintance with these wealthy men. Did he not care where their loyalties lay? They would be wise to keep their own council and keep to their own kind...the Patriot troops. To do their duty and nothing else. Lines were too easily blurred. They were living in a cauldron about to boil over.

As soon as they had finished the plum pudding and adjourned from the dining room, Alex made his excuses.

"But you can't go yet." Bailey laid a hand on his shoulder. "We shall enjoy port and madeira while my mother plays the harp. And Miss Lawrence has agreed to sing. You don't want to miss that, do you?"

For the first time, Alex glimpsed something behind Bailey's benign pleasantry. Some sort of satisfaction? He guessed exactly how much Elspeth's presence in his house had rattled Alex—not to mention the revelations of his outspoken guest.

"Thank ye, sir. I believe I've witnessed quite enough for one night." Accepting his hat from the butler, Alex pressed it onto his head.

"Well, do you mind if I stay?" Wilson asked from the other side of Thomas Nash.

"Suit yerself." Wilson was not his man. Any more than Elspeth was his woman...or ever could be. She'd have to make up her own mind about Bailey and his convictions. But he did bow over her hand and wish her happy birthday.

For one brief moment, the longing in her gaze made her

appear libel to follow him into the night. But she went to Bailey's side before the door closed behind Alex.

He strode across the yard, breathing deeply of the early September air tinged with the smallest hint of fall. Partway down the street, when another sound mingled with the chorus of the cicadas—the faint notes of a harp and Elspeth singing— Alex stopped, his heart thudding.

"'Drink to me only with thine eyes, and I will pledge with mine...'"

A voice so sweet could only come from a pure heart. Did her eyes not pledge him...so many things? And did that not make her worth fighting for? Did he want such a fight, with all the risks it would demand?

CHAPTER 8

"*A*lex, come see..."

The echo of the voice that had awakened him beckoned him even now, lilting, brimming with child-like wonder. The flash of memory that had come, as before, on the edge between sleep and waking, lingered before him. A twirl of blond hair over wide blue eyes, cheeks reddened by cold, a small outstretched hand.

He'd taken to horseback just after dawn in hopes of clearing his head, never expecting to glimpse a familiar figure in a blue riding habit trotting out of town. And now he followed again.

Where was Elspeth going? Was she meeting someone? His business all the more, if so.

He passed a patch where dew-drenched pumpkins yellowed in muddy rows beneath damp leaves. Corn in tall green lines. An indigo field where workers prepared to get in the second harvest before the next shower, which indeed the heavy sky promised.

Finally, she turned off on a bridle path leading away from the Island Ford Road. Did she ken he was behind her? She never turned around, and Alex kept his distance.

Moisture dripped from the trees as he came into a clearing that surrounded a dilapidated cabin, obviously abandoned, and there stood Elspeth by her horse, holding the mare's reins and watching for him with a tiny smirk at the corners of her mouth. "Some scout ye are."

"I wasna tryin' to be chary."

"So ye trust me, then? Ye ken I wouldna lead ye into an ambush?"

He swung his leg over Charlie's back and drew the stallion closer to her mare. "I was more concerned with ensurin' yer safety. What is this place? What are ye doin' here?"

She shrugged, and they both looped their mounts' reins around an old hitching post. "Just a spot I found on a visit some time ago. I come here when I need to think."

"Ye canna think in that grand mansion?"

"Not at the moment." One corner of her mouth quirked up. Did that mean she resented being waylaid by Bailey's guests, or that Brown's story had stirred her sympathy?

"Last night 'twas not the celebration ye deserved. Still, ye shouldna be ridin' aboot by yerself. This is a lonesome place. Not a safe one."

"I ken this land." She crossed to the front steps, him following, and seated herself on the edge of the porch. "I'm not afeared of it."

He lowered himself beside her, drawing one booted knee up on the top step. "Ye should be afeared of its men, though." He fingered the edge of the fabric of her dress, a light woolen, woven fine. Was Bailey clothing her now? And what did that mean? "Seein' as how ye're..."

When he stopped himself, she turned her head his way. "I'm what?"

Alex cleared his throat. "Ye're a bonny lass." From the corner of his eye, he caught the slow smile that spread over her face, but he hurried on. "A young, unmarried lass such as yerself shouldna be gallivantin' around the countryside alone. Why is Bailey not with ye?"

She lifted her chin a fraction. "He had a meetin' with his overseer. Something to do with the harvest."

"Hm." Alex couldn't resist the opportunity to point out that the man was not a saint. "I s'pose he'd have to keep close accounts of his slaves."

She shot him a sharp glance. "I didna wish for his company, anyway."

Alex's heart stuttered. So she had been upset with him? And Alex's company...had she wished it instead? Not that either mattered. "Ye are courtin', are ye no'?"

A sigh escaped her. "I suppose that depends on who ye ask. Mr. Bailey and his mother have laid plans, but I havena made up me mind. For now, Da needs me at the mission."

He gave a brief nod. So there was no betrothal—yet. "Will ye be goin' back there soon, then?"

"Sunday, after the prayer meetin' at Roger's."

Roger, was it? And the man held prayer meetings? Ach. "I take it ye're in agreement with Bailey's views?"

"What a lot of questions ye have, Lieutenant." She pressed her hands onto the floorboards on either side of her and sat straight.

"I only ask out of concern for ye, lass. After last night, I canna say other than that Bailey has Loyalist leanings, no matter how he tries to play them off as diplomacy." And Mayson would ask. He would expect a full report from Alex this very morning. "Anyone who would have that man, Brown, in his house..."

Elspeth's fingers tightened. "I ken." A slight shudder passed through her.

"Ye should wear a cloak, lass. The damp, it settles into yer bones." Alex shrugged out of his coat and draped it around her shoulders. When she drew it close about her neck, he smiled. "There, ye look a right Patriot now."

Her brow crumpled, and her nose wrinkled. "'Tis not that I am a Loyalist, Alex. Brown affrighted me to death. I thought *ye* were angry..."

Alex frowned. She compared him with that hateful rum-swiller?

"I believe he will do great damage in the backcountry," she continued, "and I wish Roger would have nothing to do with him. And of course, I dinna agree with slavery. How could I? I want every man to have his freedom. But ye canna say what was done to Brown was freedom. What type of men are these Sons of Liberty? Who are they to say a man canna feel loyalty to a king who gave him land and kept him safe from Indian attack? And are the land-hungry Patriots not themselves at fault when they settle farther and farther west on land that doesna belong to them?"

Alex drew a slow breath and studied his hands. "These are yer reasons for no' signing the Association, then." He had to admit, they were not bad ones. He might feel the same, were he more attached to land.

"I suppose. Although, on the other hand, I do believe we colonists deserve better say in our own government. Because I'm torn, I canna in good conscience pledge meself to either side."

"There may be abuses, aye, but in the end, isna our God-given freedom the most important thing?" He searched her face for agreement.

"Aye." She let out a soft sigh.

A hopeful sign, that. In the end, she would come out right. But the dark clouds looming over the backcountry threatened to dump their contents sooner rather than later. "If ye dinna pledge to the Association, Elspeth, ye could be in danger."

"An' I could be in danger if I do. This town one day belongs to the Patriots, the next, to the Loyalists."

"We willna lose the backcountry."

"Then I'm goin' to need a friend. A friend who can cover me...like this coat." She buried her nose—pink at the tip—in the red collar. Was she sniffing it?

Something in Alex's stomach fluttered, but her appeal for his protection went far deeper, touching something innate in his core. He did not need to agree to an understanding that was already in place. That just was. But how could he watch over her when she persisted in putting herself in harm's way? He rose from the porch and stood before her, his fingers tightening on the handle of his pistol.

"Ye should go home, Elspeth. Not be seen here in town with Bailey. Mayson will have his eye on him."

She raised her head—and her eyebrow. "*Yer* eye, ye mean?"

He gave a breath of a laugh. "I shall do as ordered, but I shall also do all I can for yer father and yerself. In the name of...our past friendship."

"But why?" She breathed out the question as she joined him in the yard. "Ye dinna even remember that friendship."

He hesitated a moment, his fingers twitching, his gaze skittering away from hers. "I saw ye this morning, as I woke..." He met her eyes as they widened, and his throat tightened. "Not ye now. Yer face, then. Just a glimpse, but I think it was right before..."

She drew closer, reaching for the hand that hung by his side and squeezing it. "Whatever ye do or dinna remember, Alex, I believe ye ken my heart. And that we aren't traitors."

"Tell me something." If he was to vouch for her, he needed to fully understand her.

"Anything."

"Yer sister..."

"Leana." Elspeth blinked and nodded. "What of her?"

"Me cousin, Finn, he said she didna die in the attack. That she was taken. Is that true?"

"Aye." She whispered the word softly, her fingers loosely woven through his in a grip that felt unsettlingly right, her focus now on the ground.

"Yer work at the mission, then... Did ye come here partly in hopes of gettin' wind of her?"

She caught her lower lip between her teeth. "I believe Da thought so at first, and he made his inquiries, but as the years went by with no word of her..." Her slender throat worked between the edges of his coat collar. "We had to assume she was either taken far into the Nation...or perhaps she didna make it."

He released her hand and braced her arm, something firming in him. "Dinna give up hope, lass. These times, they may change things. And if they do, I will help ye look for her." If there was any chance, any chance at all, that he could get his father or brother back, he would ride to the ends of the earth. Someone should do the same for Leana Lawrence.

Elspeth met his eyes. "Aye. We should do all we can to get back what was stolen." She raised her hand to touch the side of his face. "But sometimes, that isna something physical."

Alex's brows lowered, and he stepped back. "I remembered ye, lass. Is that not enough?"

"That meant everything, but I wasna speaking of yer memory."

He stared at her a moment. Then he shook his head. He did not want to know what she meant. He turned toward Charlie. "We should go. Ye should ride out ahead of me." They had already been here too long. Being seen alone with him would ruin her reputation. "I will wait a few minutes, then follow and keep an eye on ye."

She trailed him to the hitching post but made no move to untether her mount as he did his. She merely stood there, watching him. "I prayed for many years to see ye again, but as always, God had just the right timing. He ken when I would again be in need of yer protection."

Alex paused just long enough to add a stone or two to the wall around his heart. He couldn't allow her to draw him backward, and he must keep focused on his mission going forward. "I can only help ye if ye use caution yerself. Tell Bailey ye need to head home today...tomorrow at the latest. Make whatever excuses ye need to. If he willna send ye, I will ask permission to escort ye."

"The braves are due back Sunday, to take Inoli with them on the fall hunts." Elspeth's calmly spoken words drew Alex's head up. "I could use that as an excuse. I told Da he needed me there to help persuade the braves to let him stay longer, but he said I shouldna return until Sunday."

The journey from Ninety Six would take most of the day. If she waited until Sunday, she would arrive after the Cherokee party had gone. Reverend Lawrence had heeded his warning about Split Ear. Much as the need to encounter his brother's killer might eat at him, he could be drawn up on charges for an unprovoked attack. Nay, it was best they both stayed away from the mission until the Cherokees had departed. For now. Where Elspeth's safety was concerned, Bailey presented the lesser threat.

Alex flicked his fingers toward her, indicating she should mount up. "In that case, ye should do as yer father bids." He held Charlie's reins in one hand while extending the other to her.

She took it, frowning. "But why?" She studied his face. "What aren't ye telling me?"

"If Bailey is connected to the Loyalists, it may be best not to arouse his suspicion. Just leave things as they are. But stay away from Ninety Six in the future."

"Does that include Roger's farm?"

His eyes locked on hers. "Why would ye be goin' to his farm?"

"For the corn shuckin'. Weren't ye listenin'?" The corners of her lips twitched.

"I have no interest in merry-makin'." Would the woman just put her foot in the stirrup?

Elspeth tilted her head. "'Tis a shame, for the boy I ken was keen on laughin' and havin' a good time. Perhaps if ye took me to the shuckin', folks wouldna call me a Loyalist."

"I willna attend any future functions hosted by Roger Bailey...or his friends. And ye shouldna either."

"Verra well." Elspeth raised her chin, shoved her boot into the stirrup, and pushed against his hand as she thrust herself onto the saddle. He unlooped the reins and handed them up to her. "Thankee," she said, but her tone had chilled. Drawing her mare back from the hitching post, she looked down at him with color in her cheeks. "Protectin' me doesna include tellin' me what to do, Alex Morris. I dinna intend to hide meself at the mission forever. So if ye willna come with me to the corn shuckin', I will have to go alone." She tapped her heels into her mare's sides and trotted from the clearing.

Oh, but he'd gotten her dander up. And that had him wanting to call her back, for what sight was sweeter than a Scottish lass in a temper? Good thing he had a reason. "Elspeth!"

She turned her mare's head and her own, her pink lips in a pout.

"My coat?"

Understanding dawned, and she went red, then walked her mount back to him and dropped the heavy garment upon his head. Completely unexpectedly, a laugh stole out of him. At the sound, her eyes went wide—as he spied when he removed the coat.

Perhaps she was right. He couldn't recall the last time he'd truly found humor in anything. Somehow, she shone a ray of sunshine into his dark clouds. When he smiled at her, she drew back as if he'd struck her. Might as well surprise her a wee bit more. "I canna say aye yet, but if circumstances permit, maybe I shall see ye at the corn shuckin'."

CHAPTER 9

*E*lspeth sat at the long dining room table, still dressed in the riding habit she'd worn on her early-morning outing. As a light rain splattered the long-paned window, she sipped her aromatic tea and stared at the golden center of her egg.

Each time her hope for a future that included Alex Morris faltered, he did something to draw her back. Opened up a crack in his armor. Showed her something she longed to see. 'Twas as if he ken in his soul, even if not in his mind, what she needed from him. For instance, the way he'd come to her when Brown's appearance had stirred dark memories. And then to challenge the man on her behalf. He'd left abruptly last night, but could she blame him? Speak of an ambush. Roger had certainly laid one for him.

Then this morning, Alex had followed her. Of course, she'd spied him the minute he set off from the courthouse. If the Regiment of Horse wanted to employ rangers as scouts, why in heaven's name did they dress them like peacocks?

She stifled a giggle behind her hand, drawing Miss Charlotte's gaze. Oh...she'd quite forgotten she was not alone.

Elspeth smiled and sipped her tea, and Roger's mother went back to spreading jam on her toast. Elspeth went back to her memories.

As they had spoken in the clearing in the wood, Alex might have been gruff—'twas the way he'd hardened himself, was it not?—but he'd not only shown her once again the loyalty and protection that were so much a part of his nature. He'd also vowed to find her sister if ever given the chance. He hadn't fallen prey to her machinations where the corn shucking was concerned, but she rather admired him for that. He was not a man to be led by the nose. Yet he'd softened in the end, and when she had dropped his coat right over his startled expression, he'd laughed. Truly laughed. Those enchanting creases by his mouth! And oh, she'd hated to give up that coat, for it had smelt of him, of spice and sweat and pine.

"Are you quite well, my dear?" Miss Charlotte cocked her head, observing her intently.

"Aye, why do ye ask?"

"Why, you are quite pink, and your breathing is rather rapid."

"Oh." She flushed even more in that hot way that always betrayed her heritage. "Verra well. Just the effects of a good ride, I suppose." *Lord, dinna strike me dead.*

Elspeth took a swallow of tea and willed her heart to be still. To halt its mad gallop after a man who might not prove himself worthy of her yearning. What was she doing, sitting at Roger's table in his mother's riding habit, eating this bounteous breakfast with a smirk on her face put there by another man? She who had never paid heed to anything in breeks was now the worst of vixens.

She held great affection for Roger. Great esteem. Maybe even a dram of desire. And if he proved willing to reconsider his position on slavery, she had intended to consider his suit... until Alexander Morris had risen like a specter from her past.

Had intended?

She would clear her head, and clear it now.

Miss Charlotte pursed her lips. "I cannot imagine what is keeping Roger. Or what was so pressing that it could not wait until after breakfast."

As if summoned, he came through the front door, laying off his cloak and shaking water from his hat. He entered the dining room with a weighted brow. "My apologies, ladies. Things did not go as planned this morning."

"Trouble at the plantation?" Elspeth tracked his movements as he kissed his mother's forehead, then took a seat at the end of the table.

"No." He waited while Rosa filled his coffee cup. After she stepped away, he sighed heavily, and his shoulders sagged. "I cannot lie to you. I did not meet my overseer. I rode out to Peach Hill to warn Robert Cunningham."

"What?" Miss Charlotte gasped. "Why?"

"Drayton is in town. At least, he shall be here within the hour with over two hundred men, militia he mustered and rangers from Fort Charlotte."

Rosa returned with bacon and eggs steaming on a creamware plate, which she set in front of Roger.

Elspeth sat up straighter as he tucked into his food. "But why did ye need to warn Mr. Cunningham?"

"Drayton is on the warpath against any he sees as a threat to his precious Association. He will want to round up the Loyalist leaders. Trouble will follow if he gets ahold of them."

"Nay...I mean, why did *ye* need to warn him?" She made sure to place unmistakable emphasis on the key word.

He met her gaze. "Could you, in good conscience, consign those who have been your friends to the same fate as Thomas Brown?"

Her tongue grew mysteriously thick, but she found a way to use it. "That wouldna happen again. Not here."

"Would it not? How can you be certain? No." He cut into his eggs. "It is in the best interest of all concerned that never the twain shall meet."

In the interest of all? Or in the Loyalists' interest?

Miss Charlotte responded to Elspeth's silent staring at Roger by extending her hand upon the table. "We must trust Roger's wisdom in this, my dear. He has long been a stabilizing influence in Ninety Six."

She dropped her gaze, asking Roger a question rather than answering Miss Charlotte. "What will Drayton do?"

"He is likely to further fortify the town and use it as a base of operations. Reports say he has four swivel guns in tow."

"Saints preserve us." Miss Charlotte raised her hand to her temple. "Will war descend upon Ninety Six? Lexington and Concord right here?"

"Not if Drayton finds out where the Loyalists are assembling. I would imagine he would march out to attack. Regardless, Elspeth, it would be best if you extended your stay with us. I will send a message to your father." He did not even look at her as he spoke, then knifed a sliver of bacon to his mouth.

Elspeth's stomach fled to her toes. "I would prefer to leave as planned, on Sunday."

Roger met her gaze, chewed, swallowed, and then laid down his utensil. "I am not prepared to risk your safety traveling in this area with all the troops about. I promise, I will send you home with Poe the moment the situation is resolved."

"And how long might that be? Weeks? Months?" Panic lanced through her at being thus bound, and she slid her chair back from the table. "Nay. I will leave Sunday. Alex will take me."

"*Alex*?" Roger's fair brows drew together. He pushed his plate away, then rose as well, shooting a glance at Miss Charlotte. "Mother, will you give us a moment?"

"Of course." Mouth in a tight line, the older lady hastened from the room.

Roger approached, taking Elspeth's hands in his. Unlike Alex's, they were smooth. Cool. "Dearest, I know how eager you are to return to your father and students, and that is laudable. But would it be so bad if we had a bit more time together? Although..." He hung his head. "I cannot blame you. I have been a terrible host, subjecting you to words no lady's ear should have to hear, especially on her most special day. And then, I disappeared again this morning before I had even had a chance to offer my apologies. Of course, you want to leave. I can't blame you one whit."

"That is not it...at least, not all of it." She couldn't lead Roger on when Alex kept intruding into her thoughts. When their lives seemed destined to merge in some cataclysmic way, though she hardly could see the end of it yet.

Roger snapped his chin up, his green eyes seeking hers. "I vow, I did not know Brown would show so little discretion. I am only recently acquainted with him myself, and I hoped...well, I hoped his tale might be a cautionary one."

"It was, Roger, and I dinna hold ye responsible for his words. Neither am I a wiltin' lily. Ye *ken* what I've been through."

"Then is it so reprehensible that I would spare you anything further?" His fingers squeezed hers until she tugged them back.

"Nay." She dropped her hands to her sides. "But tell me true, did ye even intend to meet yer overseer this morn?" If he had lied to her earlier, he could easily lie again.

"I did. I wanted to return and tell you I had spoken with him about a plan to gradually emancipate the slaves. To show you I have taken your viewpoint not only into consideration, but acted upon it."

Elspeth drew in a quick breath. "Ye would do that...for me?"

"What would I not do for you? To have the hope of calling

you my own? Rest assured, the business with Cunningham might have superseded today, but that is a conversation that *will* take place." He reached for her hand again, raised it to his lips, and placed a kiss on the back.

The warm, soft touch sent tingles racing down Elspeth's spine. This man seemed willing to rearrange his life for her.

Would Alex do the same? Would Alex come even one step in her direction?

"Will you stay?" His eyes pleaded with her. Like two jewels, they were. Somewhat mesmerizing.

"Aye." She released a soft breath. "For a while, I will stay." She owed him that much, at least.

And what of Alex? He would be nearby as well. Doubtless, she would see him again.

She shut out the tantalizing voice in her head.

A knock at the door and Poe going to answer it caused Roger to release her hand. When the butler brought a folded, sealed paper on his silver tray into the dining room, Roger went toward him, hand extended.

With a quick blink, Poe averted the tray. "Er, sir, it's not for you." If he could have blushed, he probably would have.

"Oh." Roger tucked his hand behind his back. "Who is it for?"

"For Miss Lawrence."

Elspeth startled when the servant spoke her name. Reluctantly, she stepped forward and received the missive. Poe departed, but Roger remained a few feet away, watching her. She broke the seal, unfolded the note, and read a short message in an unfamiliar hand.

Miss Lawrence,

Major Mayson has asked me to escort you to Russell's Creek on Sunday morning and to make a delivery upon our arrival. He has ordered that we set out as early as possible, so I regret that you will

be unable to attend prayer service. Please confirm that you will be
ready to depart shortly after dawn.
With regards, Lieutenant Alexander Morris

Elspeth frowned. Alex had indicated that Roger could arrange to send her home. Now Alex wanted to take her? And what did it mean that he had a delivery? Her mouth tightened. The Cherokee delegation. He must have mentioned it to Major Mayson. What else had he told his commander?

Roger moved closer. "Is something amiss?"

"Nothing I canna handle." She gave Roger a quick smile, though she couldn't meet his eyes. "Pray, excuse me."

With a slight bow, he moved aside to let her pass.

She had just told him she would stay, and she would not be used as a messenger between a Patriot major and his coveted allies. She simply must write back and tell Alex she couldn't go. He should be happy not to have to deal with the Cherokees again. Although he would not be happy to learn she was staying on at Roger's.

As she mounted the steps to her room, she felt her host's eyes on her from the foyer. Surely, she was a pawn in an elaborate chess game played by powerful men with conflicting motives. Which side would prove the cannier? Which side was worthy of her loyalty?

And more importantly...which man?

～

Sunday morning at the picket line outside the courthouse, Alex wrapped the three muskets Mayson had entrusted to him in a length of linen, then bound them behind his saddle. His saddlebags held powder, shot, fine Virginia tobacco, and whiskey—none of which were presents he approved of. But Major Mayson was determined to issue another invitation for the Cherokees to parley at Fort Charlotte.

How would Reverend Lawrence react when Alex showed up without Elspeth? What explanation could he give when he had none himself? Would Lawrence even allow him to speak with the Indians?

He still couldn't believe the message he'd received back yesterday from Elspeth. Why would she decide to stay on at Roger's when she'd just told him she would be leaving Sunday? Had the man coerced her?

Alex had almost called on her last night, but the last thing he needed was to get into an altercation with Roger Bailey. Nay, Elspeth had shown herself to be more than capable of exerting her own will. If she wanted to stay with the man, who was Alex to say her nay? She could make her own bed.

So he told himself. And told himself again as he filled his canteen.

Horse hooves pounded the dirt—the pre-dawn patrol returning from the Island Ford Road. One of the riders broke off and headed his way. "Morris!" Lieutenant Wilson raised his voice. "If you're off for Russell's Creek, I'd advise you to hurry. And go to Roger Bailey's on the way."

"Why?" Alex's pulse kicked up a notch. Last night, he'd aired his grievances to Wilson. The man ken how he felt about his assignment. And probably how he felt about Elspeth... although he couldn't grasp that himself just yet.

"The Loyalists are amassing east of here. Colonel Fletchall and his Upper Saluda Regiment are with them. We expect an attack before tomorrow."

It took only a moment for the words to register. Then Alex leapt into action, untying Charlie from the picket line and shoving his boot into the stirrup. "I have to get Elspeth." Surely, under the threat of immediate attack, she would flee with him.

"Quickly," Wilson said, "before Drayton can detain her. His men are at Roger's house now."

What had Mayson done? No, what had *Alex* done? He'd been careful to avoid discussing Elspeth, but his report to Mayson yesterday had revealed his suspicions about Roger Bailey's loyalties. How stupid not to consider the possibility that Mayson might take his concerns straight to Drayton. By mere association, Elspeth could get caught in the Council of Safety's net.

Alex spurred his stallion and cut across to the street that ran through town.

CHAPTER 10

The front door of Bailey's house stood open, so Alex stepped inside.

Multiple trails of muddy boot prints led into the entrance hall. The slamming of cabinet doors and the thudding of books came from the rear study, but soft weeping drew Alex to the front parlor. Clinging to each other on the settee were Mrs. Bailey and Elspeth—with the muzzle of a Patriot ranger sergeant's rifle tilted their direction.

"Alex!" Elspeth jumped up.

Alex lunged across the space and angled the soldier's weapon upright. "What is the meaning of this? Ye fool! Ye have no call to hold ladies at gunpoint."

The ruddy-cheeked lad—probably no more than twenty—snapped off a salute. "I was ordered to keep an eye on the women, sir, while the house is searched."

"An eye on them, not the end of yer rifle."

"Mrs. Bailey kept trying to interfere with the search, sir." The lad's widened gaze fixed on Alex with more than a hint of alarm. Doubtless, prior, he'd glimpsed Alex at Major Mayson's side.

Alex moved toward the settee, taking Elspeth's cold hand and nodding to Mrs. Bailey. "Are ye well, ladies?"

The older woman blotted her face with a lacy handkerchief. "As well as one can be whose home is being destroyed."

Elspeth murmured, "I am now," squeezing his hand.

Resisting the urge to pull her out of the house and onto his horse that very moment, Alex released her and glanced back at the sergeant. "Who is in charge here?"

"I am." A lieutenant with brownish-red hair, a massive chest, and legs like young oaks nudged Roger Bailey ahead of him through the doorway. "And you are...?"

"Lieutenant Alex Morris."

Bailey's perfectly molded face twisted. "This is the man responsible for your orders today."

"I ken nothing of this."

"Oh, but you are responsible, just the same." The man's green eyes fixed on him with a threatening, unwavering intensity.

Alex had made another enemy.

The lieutenant—who seemed as disinterested in giving his name as Alex was in receiving it—jingled a ring of keys around his index finger. "My orders came directly from William Drayton. Anything of concern we find today or as we peruse the correspondence will be sent to the Council of Safety. You can answer to them for your Loyalist connections, Mr. Bailey. Now, Lieutenant Morris, what is *your* business here?"

"My business is a pressin' assignment from Major Mayson, which involves this young lady." Alex tilted his head toward Elspeth. "She must depart with me immediately."

Bailey cried, "Absolutely not—"

"No one is leaving," the lieutenant said at the same time. When Bailey fell silent, the officer continued. "Nobody is to leave this house until I am satisfied with the results of the search."

"Miss Lawrence has aught to do with Roger Bailey's business." Alex took a perverse delight in proclaiming that when the man had no power to naysay him. "She is but a guest here. And I havena time to argue. We are to meet a delegation of Cherokees at her father's mission this afternoon. Should we miss that meeting, I will be sure to let the major ken 'twas yer doing."

The lieutenant glared at him, then called his sergeant aside for a low-spoken consultation.

Bailey took the opportunity to step closer to Alex and practically hiss, "She is not going anywhere with you, you traitor."

Alex kept his voice low as well. "Dinna be a fool, man. An attack is expected on this town before daybreak. If ye care for her at all, ye will do all ye can to see her away."

Bailey's eyes went wide, and he swallowed. Either he was a superb actor or he truly ken nothing about the assault.

Behind Alex, Elspeth drew in a trembling breath. She stood and came forward, taking Bailey's hand. "'Tis all right, Roger. Alex will keep me safe."

Though he clearly took no comfort in those words, Bailey nodded. "Anything for you, remember?"

Alex firmed his lips. Had Elspeth downplayed the level of understanding she'd reached with her suitor?

The officer broke off his conference and jerked his chin at Elspeth. "The sergeant will accompany you to fetch your things. You must allow him to examine all that you pack. Is that clear?"

She bobbed her head. The glance she darted at Alex confirmed that she did not need to be told to hurry.

"Take only what ye can carry on me horse." Alex turned from giving Elspeth the instruction to find Bailey glaring at him with unmistakable disgust. Despite the man's questionable loyalties, losing his regard did not come easily. "Whatever ye think, Bailey, this was not me wish."

"Of course, it wasn't." A sneer commandeered his handsome face. "I won't forget this, Morris."

~

*R*iding in the saddle in front of Alex on Whitehall Road, Elspeth saw rangers and militia mobilizing around the courthouse, the jail, and in the surrounding fields. The muzzles of the swivel guns brought from Fort Charlotte poked from each ground-floor window of the jail, sending a shudder down her spine.

Once they passed the farms outside Ninety Six, however, one would never know trouble was brewing nearby. The wind sighed through the pines and whistled through the hardwoods, sending sprays of water down on them as they rode beneath the spreading branches. Faint touches of yellow painted the underbrush, while the sentinels of the forest labored over their fall bounty—the shagbark hickory's green husks, reddening spicebush berries, and the oblong fruit of the pawpaw.

Still, Elspeth couldn't relax—partly because of the anxiety of the past twenty-four hours, and partly because of the proximity of the man behind her. She clutched the saddle with one hand and her woven bag in front of her with the other. She hadn't been able to ride behind Alex because of the muskets strapped there...another thing that disturbed her. But he kept a firm hold on her with one hand. Neither had spoken since they'd left Ninety Six. Yet his presence and the warmth of his body created a palpable force.

Finally, turning her head slightly, she asked a question that had been nagging at her. "What did ye tell yer commander about us?"

"*Us*?" The emphatic syllable stirred the hair on her neck. "I thought ye understood the importance of leavin' Bailey's house, yet I received a message that ye'd be stayin' on for—how did ye put it?—an unforeseen time?"

"Unforseeable." She sniffed. "Lucky for you, then, the King's Men decided to attack the town."

His fingers at her waist curled. "Ye seem to think I have some control over events. I'm just a soldier who obeys orders, Elspeth."

"Such as reportin' to yer major."

"Aye. Just that."

"Did ye need to throw Roger under the wagon? He was kind to ye. He gave ye shelter when ye were in danger. Had ye into his home. And how did ye repay him?"

"I didna offer me own opinions to Mayson, lass. But I wasna going to lie about who was at that dinner. Bailey brought Drayton's notice on himself the minute he played host to Thomas Brown. So dinna be blamin' me."

Elspeth clutched her bag closer. "I suppose ye told Mayson I was a guest as well."

Alex's silence answered before he did. "Aye. I couldna—"

"Ye couldna lie. I ken." She let a sigh escape. "I certainly canna fault ye for that. It was me own choice to stay at Roger's. Although I did try to go home." For some reason, she needed Alex to realize that. "But he had heard of the King's Men mustering and begged me to stay until it be safe. He didna think they would attack the town."

"Let us pray he is right about that. I hate to think of civilians in harm's way."

"He truly doesna want a war, Alex. He has done all he can to avoid it." She swiveled a wee bit to bestow a sincere glance upon him, catching a glimpse of dark eyes and firm mouth.

"I can believe that. War would threaten everythin' he has worked for. Or...his slaves have worked for. Wealth like that isna built...or sustained...without the sweat of many."

"He told me he was plannin' to set them free. He kens I dinna approve." She made the admission softly, more to defend her own judgement than Roger's.

"He must truly care for ye, then." Did the tightness in Alex's voice betray that the realization did not set well with him? Or did he merely disapprove of Roger for political reasons? "Although he ought to care more for what the Almighty thinks than his woman. Will ye marry him, then? And ally yerself with his Loyalist ideas?"

Ire flashed through Elspeth at his choice of words. Did these men think she was naught but a prize to be dangled and won? Did they think she had no brain of her own? "First of all, I am not *his woman*. I dinna belong to anyone, save God. And I will decide for meself which cause to ally to, when I'm good and ready, not by happenstance of whom I marry."

Alex's chest rumbled—indeed, the man was chuckling. "Eh, lass, dinna get yer nose out of joint. 'Tis only that a betrothal announcement would put the lie to me assurance to the major that ye in no wise share all Roger's views."

"Ye told him that?"

"Aye. I told him the Lawrences were true moderates, peace-lovers who only wanted to stay out of the fray. Practically Quakers."

He was laughing at her again, but she minded not. For he spoke the truth, and any cause for Alex's mirth lightened her own heart. It also afforded her an opportunity. She peered back at him. "On that note, I ken those muskets and whatever is making yer saddlebags so fat are for the Cherokees. I dinna like the way the major forces me and Da to be party to his dealings. He may court the Cherokees as much as he desires, but this will be the last time he does so through the mission. Will ye tell him that too?"

Alex raised his brows, then blew a little puff of air from his nose. "Aye, lass. He willna like it, but it suits me well enough."

She nodded. "There. Ye're welcome. I've relieved ye of yer responsibility."

"One of them, maybe." The way he looked at her sent tingles to her toes. "Ye seem to keep landin' in danger, and I feel this uncanny duty to watch out for ye."

A little tremble ran through her. Perhaps he sensed the connection between them, after all, despite his limited memory. But it would be unwise to reveal just how strongly she felt it. "I can watch out for meself."

He made a slight scoffing sound. "What happened to needin' a friend?"

She gave an abrupt nod. "Friends are useful in these times."

"Then why don't ye lean back on yer friend?" He released her waist to brush a stray curl from her cheek. "Ye're stiff as a board. Ye're gonna be saddle sick and sore all over if ye don't relax a wee bit."

Elspeth gulped. "Verra well." She did not budge an inch. "But I need to ask ye one more thing." And she was not sure how he would react.

His sigh tickled her cheek. "What is it, then?"

"The muskets. Dinna give them to the Indians, please. If ye do, they will only expect more from yer major. A much larger shipment...and powder."

"I believe that is just what he will offer." His jaw worked.

"Ye canna approve. Ye canna arm them, push them to enter this conflict. We have worked too hard for peace."

His brow lowered. "I have me orders, Elspeth."

Aye, but did his loyalty to her run deeper than his oath to the provincial army?

She had said enough. She leaned back against him, turning her face to one side.

He released a heavy sigh, then tucked his chin over her head and his arm around her waist. A wash of something warm and heavy and wonderful stole her breath, and she squeezed his arm. Let the Indians and the Patriots and the Loyalists rage. Her soul rejoiced. The piece of herself that had been missing had returned.

CHAPTER 11

"Nay! Oh, nay!"

Alex startled at Elspeth's exclamation. She sat up from the relaxed posture she'd assumed for the second half of their ride—a posture he'd enjoyed far more than he should have—when they came within sight of the turnoff to the mission. Foolishly, he'd been looking down at her—at her small hand resting atop his, contemplating what it would feel like to turn that hand over and lace his fingers through hers—rather than at the lane. It took him only a moment to note the source of her dismay.

The Cherokee party traversed the road ahead...bound north. Two braves and a boy. They had already been to the mission and were taking Inoli away with them.

"Oh, Alex, we have to catch them. But ye mustn't startle them. Ride to the turnoff and stop there."

He did as she asked, but only so he could get a better view of the men. He halted Charlie in the shade of a red oak. When Elspeth started to swing her leg over the side, Alex tightened his arm around her waist.

She struggled against him. "Let me go. I must catch them."

"Wheesht, lass. I must make sure ye are safe."

He was not about to allow her to run to his brother's killer without him. Not even with him. She could rail against him for loss of the boy all she wanted. Her security came first.

"I will never feel safe facing Cherokee braves, but ye will have me back."

Their little flap drew the attention of the warriors. As they turned, Alex's heart thundered and his limbs went cold. The boy's slumped posture straightened like a hide pulled taut on a tanning rack. While Alex recognized the younger brave from before, the man with him was older, past middle age. Gray liberally streaked his hair. Alex's hold on Elspeth slackened.

"Split Ear isna there," he said. Disappointment and relief battled for the upper hand.

Elspeth shot a look at him. "Split Ear? Five Kills is the one who makes me quake in me boots."

"Then maybe ye should let me talk with them."

"Nay. They ken me, and yer uniform is like a red rag to a bull. I must do it, for Inoli." Her quavering inhale showed how strong her fear remained, even with the older man accompanying Five Kills rather than Split Ear. "We were just connecting with Inoli. He could be the one who changes the future."

"Or the one who starts a war." But he held out his hand to help her dismount.

Elspeth tossed her bag down, then slid after it. She turned to glance up at him, brushing back that stubborn curl. "Ye should hang back. Come in a moment with the contents of yer saddlebags."

Was he now taking orders from a pert miss? Alex scowled at her, but she only set off after the braves. She spoke a sentence in Cherokee, and they waited on her. When she drew within a few yards of them, she held out her arms, and Inoli ran into them. Obviously, she'd made headway there, at least. She kept a hand on his shoulder as she spoke with the men.

Alex dismounted and led Charlie deeper into the shade, where the horse found a nice thicket to nibble. While he waited, Alex uncorked the bottles of whiskey and poured the contents into the ditch. That felt good. Mayson need never ken. Then he pulled the pouches of tobacco and shot from the saddlebags.

Judging from the amount of gesticulating, the conversation was not going well. When Five Kills tugged Inoli by the arm and Elspeth sent a rather frantic glance back his way, Alex took his cue. He'd picked up one Cherokee word so far. "Si-yu." He said it as he walked slowly forward.

The braves stopped, but seeing as how Alex's hands were full of presents rather than weapons, they refrained from palming theirs. Their eyes remained suspicious, their bodies almost coiled, as though a twitch could set them off. Alex gauged just how fast he could drop the peace offerings and grab his pistols. Fast enough—especially with that wide-eyed lass in between them, her golden hair blowing in the damp breeze.

She spoke when he drew near. "They say a boy must hunt with the men."

"Tell them the chief at Ninety Six sends his greetings and would like to invite them to parlay at Fort Charlotte." As Elspeth complied, Alex bowed his head—enough to show deference but not enough to give an advantage—then knelt to place the bundles in the middle of the road. The skin on the back of his neck rippled as a murmur broke out between the braves. Had they noticed his scars?

When he straightened, a gleam of respect lit Five Kill's eyes.

Alex backed up a few steps, and the older man came forward. He opened the bag of shot, scooping up a handful of dully glistening lead. Five Kills nodded.

The seasoned brave unwrapped the pouch of tobacco and took a deep sniff. The lines by his mouth creased, the expression of pleasure eliciting a quick blink from Alex. That would be the first time he'd seen an Indian look happy.

He spoke quickly to Elspeth. "Tell them to take the gifts and leave the boy."

Her frantic glance portrayed her unease over using Inoli as a bargaining chip. "But—"

"Hurry," he hissed. They were losing their opening.

Even as Elspeth rattled off a string of nonsensible Cherokee syllables, the old man had held the tobacco to Five Kill's nose, but the brave had knocked his hand away. He did not wait for Elspeth to finish speaking before taking the boy by the arm and turning.

"*A-ga-ti-di-s-di!*" Elspeth's plea for them to wait fell on unresponsive ears. Clasping her hands together, she faced him. "Alex, they canna take him away."

"Where do they live? Maybe he can return after the hunts."

"Too far for them to bring him again so soon and before winter." Her reply strained with her hurry, and her gaze darted after her quarry.

"Tugaloo?" Alex named one of the few town names he'd heard of that lay north and west of here.

Elspeth sent him a sharp look with her brows drawn together—almost as though she ken more lay behind his question than concern for her pupil. Or maybe his queries just made her impatient. "A small town near there. What can we do?"

She was right. To complete their missions, they both needed something from the Cherokees. "Tell them the white chief has another present."

Her eyes rounded. "Nay..."

He'd already pivoted and dashed back toward Charlie. He reached his horse and fumbled with the linen-wrapped bundle. Elspeth was not telling them. She stood in the middle of the road clasping her own elbows and gazing after the retreating figures.

Alex raised his voice. "A-ga-ti..." What was the rest of it? He had no idea, but the braves had looked back. He got the parcel free and headed toward them, forcing his pace to remain the same as before. It would not do for the Indians to think them desperate.

Elspeth's wide eyes and open mouth asked what he thought he was doing.

He spoke low as he passed her. "'Tis three muskets, lass, and not likely they will parley with the major, regardless. Do ye want the boy, or no?"

"Alex, wait."

But the interest that had ignited in the eyes of the Cherokee men—and the unabashed delight on Inoli's face—bid otherwise. Alex laid two of the weapons at the braves' feet, took a couple steps back, and held the third out, low, toward the boy. He couldn't articulate his request without Elspeth's help, but hopefully, his meaning was plain enough.

Five Kills took up a musket in one fluid motion. He looked it over, checking the stock and the flint and sighting along its length. Then he handed the other gun to his companion. He spoke a sentence or two in Cherokee with his glittering gaze on Alex and nudged Inoli forward. As Inoli accepted his prize with a slack jaw, the men turned and left without him.

Alex refused to turn his back on the braves until they disappeared from his sight, but the scent of lavender and slightly shortened breathing alerted him that Elspeth had arrived behind him.

"Come, Inoli," she said, taking the child—and his new musket—under her wing.

"What did he say? Five Kills?" Alex sought her gaze, but she denied it.

"He said if we teach Inoli to use the gun, he can stay. And

they will return when the wind blows warm to check on him and speak with your white chief."

~

*W*ould the peace that had been reached by treaty in mid-September extend to Roger Bailey? And Elspeth?

Those two questions pressed to the forefront of Alex's mind late that same month as he rode with a party of rangers toward Bailey's farm. A nearly full moon rose on the horizon as the evening light found kinship among the turning sumacs, sour-woods, and maples. A cool breeze brought the hint of wood smoke and roasting pork—and groans of anticipation from his companions.

Anticipation was rather the opposite of what rolled in Alex's gut. Even though he had learned upon his return to Ninety Six that Bailey had retained his house and position when his correspondence revealed nothing indicting, the man's ire over the affront could scarce have cooled.

Would Bailey drum Alex from his land? Would Elspeth give him more of the cold shoulder that had driven him away at dawn when last he saw her? Though he'd spared her Inoli, to do so, he'd gone against her wishes in opening the door to arm the braves. Not to mention the boy. And why was he worrying over schoolboy problems when this uneasy agreement between Loyalists and Patriots could be shattered like a glass bottle at a target practice? Mingling at a corn husking was surely ill-advised, and yet, that was exactly what the major had bid them do, in the spirit of goodwill.

'Twould be no small feat when they had almost come to shots fired earlier in the month. When the attack hadn't happened as expected on the eleventh, Drayton had tried for peace. Colonel

Fletchall wavered, almost accepting the olive branch, but Brown and the Cunningham brothers stood firm. Only a flash flood and the resultant rise of the Saluda River had prevented the Loyalists from marching on Ninety Six. No doubt, Drayton's continual volley of public declarations did nothing to soothe their angst. He had declared anyone who had not yet signed the Association a public enemy, along with followers of Captain Moses Kirkland. He'd also ordered the captain's plantation ransacked. Where Finn and his men and the others now took shelter, Alex couldn't guess.

When the Loyalist force had come within four miles of town and dispatched an envoy, Major Andrew Williamson of the militia and Major James Mayson of the rangers had ordered the Patriots drawn up in a hollow square in front of the courthouse. The intimidated Loyalist colonel had quickly agreed to peace talks. The King's Men had made clear they wished to remain part of the British Empire but agreed not to support British troops in case of invasion. The Patriots agreed to respect the rights and property of those who chose not to sign the Association. The whole thing was blamed on a misunderstanding.

'Twas hardly the end of it, whatever they might pretend, especially with the governor of South Carolina fleeing to a British warship in Charlestown Harbor. Yet here they were, Patriot rangers in blue, trotting into Bailey's plantation yard on this fine, early-autumn evening.

A pig roasted on a spit, children chased each other around the big pile of corn at the end of a barn, and ladies placed a bounty of pies on a long table in the clearing. Men in fringed linen hunting shirts stood around the cider barrel, while a slave added an apron full of red and green apples to a tub for the taking. Smoke twirled from the stone chimney of a cabin—not nearly so fine as Bailey's townhouse, but twice as substantial as Alex's home back in the Ceded Lands.

He, Wilson, and the soldiers dismounted and tied their horses to a picket line set up along the trees.

"Welcome, men." Bailey's smooth, booming voice made Alex pivot, his chest tightening. But the man stood there with a smile as wide as his spread arms, somehow no less well-equipt in breeks and a hunting shirt than in a fine suit. "Come, we have rum, spruce beer, and cider, and haunches of venison for those who can't wait for supper."

The rangers surged forward with lusty agreement. Alex followed more slowly. If ever he felt like a fish on the riverbank...

Bailey stepped toward him, and he stiffened. Was the man about to call him out? Nay, for he reached out a hand. "I am glad you came, Alex. Elspeth will be pleased too."

She was here? He'd been torn between the hope that his warnings and the battle they had narrowly avoided might be enough to keep the lass at home and the desire to see her again and set things right. Slowly, Alex shook Bailey's smooth hand. Whatever Elspeth said, he doubted the man would be writing up manumission papers anytime soon. Surely, someone who'd accrued such wealth on the backs of slaves would not be willing to part with them so easily.

"She set me straight about you, by the way. Assured me I had been hasty in laying my trouble with the Council of Safety at your door."

Alex nearly choked on his own spit. Elspeth did truly have the gift of persuasion. "I am sorry for any inconvenience Drayton's methods caused ye."

"No need to apologize. A man must do his duty, mustn't he?" Bailey's hand gripped his to the point of discomfort, and his smile tightened into more of a sneer.

He hadn't been forgiven. Not by a long shot.

Bailey released him abruptly, then slapped him on the shoulder. "Go. Have some cider. I see your comrades have settled on the porch with their pipes. We will start the shucking soon."

As the man headed toward the drive to greet a family in a wagon, Alex approached the refreshment table. A lithe form in a flowered bodice and blue petticoat spun around. Elspeth's eyes sparkled beneath her mob cap and fair curls.

"I was afraid to hope ye would come."

He quirked up one side of his mouth. "Does it count if I'm under orders?"

She wobbled her head back and forth and pursed her lips. "Mm, seein' as how I've felt bad about the way I treated ye since I last saw ye, I will take it. And I noticed Roger made haste to make ye welcome."

Alex bit back a sarcastic laugh. "Aye, he did indeed." Let her have her moment of satisfaction.

"Well, then? Are ye not glad ye came?"

"That remains to be seen." Frolics made him antsy all over. He only longed to ride off into the woods and find himself again. But 'twas hard not to respond to Elspeth's cheer.

"Here's somethin' that might put a smile on that dour mug of yours." She flipped back a woven napkin covering a plate of apple fritters.

He raised his eyebrows. "Did ye make them?"

"No, silly, I'm snatchin' someone else's before 'tis time." She took one up and tore a piece off. "Just see if this doesna tickle yer fancy."

She held up the bite, giving him no choice but to open his mouth. She popped the sample in and smiled with anticipation as he chewed. He answered by way of claiming the remainder of the fritter. She giggled and wrapped her fingers around his elbow.

As they turned away from the table, Alex met a pair of green eyes across the yard. Unmistakable challenge was writ on Bailey's face. But Alex had no intention of leaving Elspeth's side until he was assured things were well between them. For some reason, the slight strain had driven him fair mad these past two weeks. Just for good measure, he drew her hand through the crook of his arm. They strolled over to a bonfire.

He leaned down to keep his voice to a murmur. "For the record, lass, there is no reason to feel bad. I ken ye would be angry with me when I gave the Cherokees the guns."

She play-pinched him. "Then why did ye do it?"

"'Twas a simple tally, my decision. On one side, I share yer distaste of armin' or courtin' the Cherokees. On the other, I had me orders. And also *yer* orders."

She drew back a fraction. "*My* orders?"

"To keep the boy."

"I told ye I wanted to, not that I expected ye to." Elspeth blew out a little breath. "In fact, I expressly recall askin' ye not to give them the guns."

"Oh, but ye did tell me. In not so many words."

"And when was that?" She planted her free hand on her hip.

"When ye looked as though ye might cry at the sight of him leavin'. I couldna have that." He allowed a smile to dance around his mouth.

Elspeth came out with a laugh. "Now I ken how to get to ye, Alex Morris. I just look at ye with me big blue eyes a'wellin'." She fluttered her lashes at him.

"Ach, no tears are needed, lass." He meant the declaration to follow in the same joking manner, but the way she stared at him, suddenly growing quite serious...

A call came from the barn, and the youths around the fire scampered off. The adults began to mill that way too.

Elspeth's fingers tightened on his arm. "Are ye joinin' the huskin'?"

Alex stepped back a fraction, shaking his head. "I'm afraid I'm not one for games."

The hurt that shuttered her expression confirmed that she no more considered this a game than he did. For it mattered not how endless or awkward he might find the chit-chat, how silly the songs. If he uncovered one of the rare ears of red corn, he could claim a kiss from the girl of his choosing.

Her hurt meant she wanted to be that girl.

But did she not understand? He'd determined to make things right with her, and he had, but farther he couldn't go. The war he had to fight lay ahead of him, no less real for the reprieve of a corn husking. It would come, and he would go. And what he must do when it did must not be bound by her demands of grace and forgiveness. Nor weakened by desire for her approval and affection.

She stared at him a moment, then something flickered in her eyes. She dropped her hand from his arm. But she leaned up to kiss his cheek before she walked away.

Now why would she do such a thing? He rubbed the spot her tender lips had touched and went soft as cornmeal mush in his midsection as he watched her find a spot beside the pile of corn. Most of Wilson's crew joined in.

Alex sought a cup of cider and stood at the edge of the barn with the old men, who jawed around their smoke circles about how Drayton had written to Cameron to ask him to go to British Florida and Cameron had responded by leaving Lochaber for his plantation on the Reedy River...inside the Cherokee Nation. And how Robert Cunningham thought no more of the treaty of September sixteenth than a hill of beans.

Bailey had taken a spot across from Elspeth and was tearing husks away faster than the twelve-year-old boys. He winked at her, then he slowly peeled back the edge of a husk to reveal the coveted ruby kernels. Hoots broke forth, and Elspeth went as red as the ear. Alex stiffened. He would lay odds on Bailey having planted that ear. But no one would naysay the man on his own property. Unless Alex did.

But he stood straight as a pine while Roger Bailey rose, circled the pile of corn, and held his hand out to Elspeth. Whistles and cheers erupted from the onlookers. Elspeth glanced around, finding his gaze on the fringe of the crowd. Then she lifted her chin and allowed Roger to pull her close and claim her lips with his.

With a splat, Alex tossed the rest of his cider on the ground. He wouldn't be there when that kiss was done.

CHAPTER 12

*a*lex rubbed a hand over his jaw as he approached the Ninety Six trading post. He'd lost his shaving razor along some winding trail or creek-side camp in the last week, the first in November, and his bristles had turned into a beard. He was half a mind to let it grow, but a clear patch of skin on the lower half of his face was often the only thing that kept him looking somewhat civilized. Not that he'd be kissing any lasses any time soon.

He gave a huff that resembled a laugh, though two dozen mental replays of the embrace he'd witnessed between Roger and Elspeth at Bailey's corn shucking hadn't lessened his ill humor.

Not that he hadn't plenty to keep him occupied. Moses Kirkland had been captured in Philadelphia on a ship bound for Boston to meet with British General Gage. His papers had exposed his plotting with the governor to involve the Cherokees in a backcountry war.

On proof of an affidavit sworn by Captain Caldwell that Robert Cunningham had used seditious language, Cunningham had been arrested and shipped to Charlestown.

His brother Patrick had again roused the Loyalist militia. Failing to free his sibling, he'd got wind of a placating shipment of powder the provincial government was sending to the Cherokees and lingered about the byways until his men captured it. Thus, the week of riding and tracking for Mayson's rangers, which had been redesignated the Third South Carolina. Whenever he did not feel the need to retain Alex as a sort of personal bodyguard—Alex's men having indeed defected—Mayson sent him out with Captain Polk.

Drayton had ordered Colonel Richard Richardson of neighboring Camden District to call up his Patriot militia and start for Ninety Six while Major Andrew Williamson also recruited more men in hopes of attacking the Loyalists. Meanwhile, the Loyalists were beside themselves over a report from an Indian trader that Drayton's meeting with some Cherokee headmen on his way home to Charlestown had aimed to stir a massacre.

With all that afoot, he'd likely not be in Ninety Six long. Best keep supplied.

Alex climbed the steps of the trading post, stepped through the door, and froze. There, by the counter, stood Elspeth. Cold realization swamped him, for her presence here could only mean one thing. He would have gone back out the way he came, but she saw him. Her blue eyes lifted and widened. Nothing for it but to go about his business as though aught was amiss.

"Alex." She whispered his name as he walked past her.

"Miss Lawrence." He tipped his hat and proceeded to the section for men's accoutrements. There, for an exceptionally long time, he examined leather strops, razors, mittens, and sewing kits. Finally, he peeked around a display of tin-and-leather trunks.

She was still there—and she saw him peeking.

Why was he lurking about like a guilty schoolboy? He'd

done nothing wrong. She was the one who ought not to be here.

With a folding razor in hand, he approached the desk and stood a few feet behind her. What could possibly be taking her so long?

She pointed to a tin in the row of spices kept behind the counter and said to the elderly man who ran the store, "Just a small scoop of cinnamon, please, then that will be it." As the proprietor turned to oblige, Elspeth angled toward Alex. "I suppose ye're wondering what I'm doin' here." She had the grace to grimace, but Alex kept his face impassive.

"What ye're aboot is yer own business."

"I'm purchasin' spices to take to a German widow in Londonborough for her Christmas baking. She canna always afford what she needs, and in exchange, she makes treats for the children at the mission as well as sellin' some to the neighbors for a bit of coin."

"Ye rode all the way into Ninety Six to buy spices? Where is yer da?" He made a show of looking around. As suspected, no reverend in his somber black suit.

"No, I..." Her throat worked. "I'm here for Miss Charlotte. Every fall, she takes ill with malarial fever. This year was especially bad. I imagine...the strain of recent events..."

"'Tis very kind of ye."

She was back at Bailey's, despite the man being called out by Drayton. Despite how desperate she'd been to keep Inoli at the mission, where presumably, she'd want to be with him. Despite how fervently she spoke of her dedication as a teacher. Well, her being here said volumes, did it not?

Alex kept his gaze on the proprietor, who had packaged the cinnamon and now awaited Elspeth's instructions.

"When Roger wrote to me," she added, "I couldna say no. He feared for her life."

So Bailey had summoned her. The man had staked his

claim at the corn shucking, and now he used his mother to further his designs. Alex tipped his head. "I believe he has yer spices ready."

"Oh. Aye." Flushing, Elspeth dug in her change purse and laid several coins on the counter. "Thankee, sir." She added the last paper-wrapped parcel to the others in her large woven basket along with the purse, nodded at Alex, and exited.

Was that to be it? Alex released the musky, deerskin-scented air he'd been holding captive and stepped up to make his payment.

But nay. When he came through the door, Elspeth stood on the porch, her basket clutched before her petticoat and a miserable expression on her face. "Ye canna hold nursin' an ailin' woman against me."

"Of course not. As I said, 'tis yer own business." Alex tucked his purchase into an inner pocket of his frock coat.

She moved slightly, blocking the steps. "Why are ye bein' this way? I ken ye willna believe it, but Roger has been a perfect gentleman. In fact, he has quite left me alone."

His eyebrow shot up of its own accord. "As he did at the corn shuckin'?" Now, why had he said that? Twenty-six years of keeping his own counsel, blown to the four winds upon sight of a single beguiling lass.

"Nay. As in, he has been gone since shortly after I arrived. He was wanted on the plantation for the harvest. 'Twas one of the reasons he needed me to stay with his mother." Her eyes narrowed, and she peered at Alex's face as though trying to look into his soul. "Is that why ye left without sayin' goodbye— the kiss at the corn shuckin'?"

He met her gaze at last. "Why would I say goodbye when ye were so well occupied?"

She straightened and blew out a little breath. "Well, 'tis not as if ye would do anythin' but stand around drinkin' yer cider, judgin' everyone who might want to have a good time."

"I told ye, I dinna like games. Far more serious things are afoot than corn shuckin's and kisses. Did ye even notice, Elspeth, the supposed peace reached in September lasted as long as a dewdrop in the sunshine? That me comrades have been chasin' the King's Men and their stolen powder all over creation? We could be at war any day. But if ye choose to put yerself in the midst of it, I canna help that now. Ye have made yer alliances clear."

"Fine." She stamped her foot. "Verra well." She wheeled and marched down the porch steps. But she did not head toward Roger's house. She stomped away from town, her basket thumping her side.

Where was she going? Did she take no notice of the multitude of militiamen and rangers fresh from the backwoods who would follow a young lass alone with the basest of intent? Alex groaned. Then he trailed her. Like a pup at her heels.

~

"Where are ye going?" The exasperated voice behind Elspeth betrayed just enough concern to merit an answer, if not an explanation.

She tossed it back over her shoulder, not slackening her pace. "I thought me business was me own."

"And so it is...when I dinna have to watch ye put yerself in harm's way."

"I'm only goin' to the walnut tree at the edge of that field there." She indicated it with a tilt of her head, just past a black man in the middle of a series of furrows prepared for flax who plowed behind a yoke of oxen. "The nuts have dropped, and the husks should be soft enough to shell without having gone to rot yet."

"Do ye need to make a dye?"

"Nay. Cookies. The widow."

Perhaps the sparseness of her reply would clarify how little she wished to speak to him in this moment, even though he continued to huff along behind her. She'd practically asked him to join in that shucking just so he could have a chance of kissing her, and not only had he declined, but he'd had the gall to scorn her for being claimed by another. Perhaps she *should* marry Roger. He showed great forbearance with those who offended him and great patience with her...and that was far more than she could say for Alex Morris.

They reached the black walnut tree, its yellowing, compound leaves hanging limp in the damp air. She set her basket on the ground and surveyed the area. Green husks with golden and black splotches, some just starting to split open on their own, littered the grass and the woods behind.

"If ye're goin' to stay, ye might as well make yerself useful." She went to work, and without a word, he did too. They dropped nuts in the free end of her basket, carefully timing it so they never met there.

And that was so annoying because all she'd wanted to do was meet him. Her first thought when Roger's plea had arrived by Poe's hand had been that she couldn't turn her back on the only woman who had been kind to her. Her second, not that she would see Roger, but that she might see Alex. Since arriving in Ninety Six, she'd looked for him every day among the rangers coming and going from the town.

She needed to face the truth. What she'd seen in Alex's face at the shucking the moment before she kissed his cheek and walked away was that his soldiering left no room for romance, even should he wish it. The walls he'd built long ago closed her out.

His voice tugged her back out of the pit she'd plunged into. "What of the children?"

She straightened. "What?"

"Ye were so set on yer work with them, with Inoli. How

could ye leave them? And when so much needs doin' before the winter?"

"For a time, they manage well enough with Ulisi to care fer them and Da to teach them." She dropped a walnut into her little pile and lifted her chin. "And I came with me da's blessing, thank ye."

"Oh, I'm certain ye did. Reverend Lawrence wears a mule's blinders where Roger Bailey is concerned."

"For someone who has no opinion, ye sure have a lot of opinions." Elspeth folded her arms. "Admit it. Ye're jealous."

He stepped back as if she'd walloped him. "What am I jealous of?"

"Of the kiss. Of me being here at Roger's. It isna all about keepin' a foolish woman ye feel beholden to out of harm's way. Ye wouldna bother if ye didna care."

His brow furrowed and his mouth gaped. "Elspeth...verra well. I do care." His shoulders slumped, though his admission shot a jolt of something hot and hopeful to her heart. "And I do feel responsible for ye somehow. Our shared past makes ye seem...like part of the family I lost."

She breathed hard from the bottom of her abdomen, trying to dislodge the stone that seemed to have settled there. Like family? Was that how he interpreted the bond between them? Tears prickled at the back of her eyes.

And then came a flash of memory—the way he'd looked at her when they had ridden together on his horse. The way he'd held her against him, tender but firm. Above all, the expression on his face the moment before Roger had claimed his kiss... fury. But at Roger or at her?

From her deep well of exasperation, she let out a screech, reached down for a walnut, and launched it at him as hard as she could. "Ye dolt! Ye eejit!"

He flung up a hand to ward off the ammunition, his eyes going wide. "Lass! What is the matter with ye?"

She palmed a second projectile. "Ye dinna even ken yer own mind, do ye? O'course, ye don't." She threw the walnut and grabbed a handful, stalking forward as she raised her arm again. "Ye forget everything inconvenient!" Wild, sarcastic laughter burbled from her throat as she threw them. If only she could grab and pummel him and—get her arms around him...

But the lieutenant had tired of his indefensible position. He plucked the nut she'd just tossed from the dirt at his feet and launched it back at her. "Stop that, ye crazy woman. Have ye lost yer mind?"

"If I have, 'tis yer fault, always sayin' one thing and doin' another." Elspeth threw her last walnut, but with a lightning-quick movement, he caught it.

He spread his hand open and ran his finger along the broken husk. It came away with the tip blackened. "Heh. This one might be too far gone. But not too far to teach ye a lesson..." The wicked grin he raised to her was not the type she'd coveted of late.

Alarm belted through her, and she took off, meaning to snag her basket and dart ahead of him to town. Surely, he would not pursue her where they might be spied. But she'd barely slid her grip under the handle when an arm hooked around her waist and he caught her up in the air, swinging her at his side as though she were a child. He held the blackened husk up in his other hand.

She let out a shriek. As soon as her boots touched the ground, she threw herself sideways. Alex held on, but they tumbled. They landed with him partly on top of her, and he used that to his advantage, pinning her while wrestling her into position. His laughter exploded close to her face.

She pushed his hand back. "No! Noooo!" If he smeared the sooty material over her cheek as he obviously intended, she would not get the streak off for weeks.

"*Miss* Lawrence!" The indignant exclamation stopped

Elspeth's wiggling and Alex's threatening. They both looked up at Rosa, who stood with her hands balled and her eyes wide. "Lieutenant Morris!"

By her tone, one would think Elspeth's petticoat had been around her waist. She felt just as censured as if it had. Especially when she noticed the mud stains on her petticoat. Looking equally chagrined, Alex dropped his arm and rolled to his side. Elspeth scrambled out from under him.

"Yes, Rosa?" She ignored Alex's proffered hand—no longer clutching the walnut—as she struggled to her feet.

Rosa's bosom heaved. Her full lips pursed. "Miss Charlotte is asking for you. She done took a turn."

"Oh." Elspeth's heart skipped a beat. She grabbed up her basket, then glanced back at Alex, who still sat beneath the tree with one knee drawn up. "Pray, excuse me, Lieutenant."

She hurried off at the servant's side without a backward glance. But her face and ears burned the whole way to town. She brushed at her dress as they entered the main street.

"Rosa? Um...there is no need to mention, er..." She found she couldn't finish her sentence.

Rosa maintained the dignity of an African queen. Not a sideways glance. Not a blink. "I would not dream of it."

"Thankee. Just how bad is Miss Charlotte?" She'd thought the quinine from the bark of the cinchona tree had finally taken effect. That Roger's mother was on the mend. That was why she'd set off to the trading post, to stock up for her return trip home.

"She took to de bed, shakin' somethin' fierce not long after you left. Moanin' that her head were splittin' open."

Why had Roger not returned from his plantation, at least briefly, to check on Miss Charlotte?

Elspeth quickened her pace to the Bailey home. "Did ye give her medicine?"

"I did, but she would not rest easy till you were by her side.

Sent me out to fetch ya." The servant shot her a sharp glance as she held open the gate. "And a good thing I did."

Elspeth went hot again. Indeed, what might have happened if Rosa hadn't arrived? Would her face be streaked with black, tattooed like an Indian's for the rest of the month as evidence of her personal war with one very stubborn ranger? Or would her lips be swollen from the kiss she'd wished could be her first? Or maybe...maybe she'd just have pummeled the lieutenant to death.

Leaving her basket on the entry table, she rushed up the steps and flung open Charlotte's bedroom door—only to find the woman peering out the window in her dressing gown and mob cap, the curtain drawn back and an expression of intense scrutiny on her face.

"Miss Charlotte! I thought Rosa said ye'd taken to bed."

Roger's mother dropped the curtain, her lips rounding as she whirled to face Elspeth. "Oh, I did! But I had to know where you were."

And had she found out? Just how far could she see from that window?

"I was so worried." Miss Charlotte took a step, then tossed her hand out. "Ah. The dizziness!"

"Dinna fash yerself, Miss Charlotte. I'm here now." Elspeth hurried over to support her. The older woman's skin was cool as a cucumber.

CHAPTER 13

There had been no time to warn Elspeth. Though he'd asked Major Mayson for permission to, he'd been rebuffed. Most testily.

Word had come that the Loyalist forces, triple their own five or six hundred, were marching on Ninety Six. Williamson's militia had retreated in the face of those superior numbers, and Mayson had met him in conference near dawn on Sunday morning, November nineteenth. The two men had decided to amass their troops around the barn and outhouses in a field belonging to a farmer outside town. Alex had scarcely pried his eyes open before being put to work fortifying the camp with outlying earthworks and a palisade of upright logs, fence rails, and whatever else they could find, including straw and animal hides to connect the buildings.

Finishing up hammering a log into place, Alex paused for a drink from his canteen. Already half empty. He cast an eye to town, less than two hundred yards east with the Spring Branch running in the gulch between.

"We're going to need water." Somehow, their troop of

rangers had brought supplies but nothing to drink. "I could take some buckets, be there and back before—"

"Don't even consider it." Lieutenant Wilson dragged the back of his loose-sleeved shirt across his face, leaving rather than removing a streak of dirt. "The major has already made his wishes clear."

"On the lass, not the water."

Wilson gave him a wry look. "We both know you wouldn't be stoppin' at the stream."

One of his men gave a cry. "Lieutenant! Drums."

They all ceased their labor and talking and cocked their ears to the northeast. Sure enough, a rolling percussion cadence carried on the crisp air, undergirding the bright notes of fifes. When the first ranks marched down the street, a chill traveled down Alex's spine. He'd have to trust Roger Bailey to protect Elspeth now...because those rows of King's Men just kept coming.

~

"Elspeth!" From the settee in the front parlor, Miss Charlotte tried to call her back into the house, but Elspeth had to see firsthand what would happen.

She rushed onto the front porch and watched from behind a post as a long column of soldiers entered Ninety Six. 'Twould have been hard to tell which side they were on—as the rangers and officers wore the same uniforms as their Patriot counterparts, and the foot soldiers were garbed in the customary hunting shirts and breeks of any frontiersmen—but the King's Colours floating at the head of the column made plain their allegiance.

Men on horseback led the troops. Elspeth gasped as one with a straight back and a blond queue came into focus. "Roger!"

As if he heard his name, he looked her way. Miss Charlotte's bird-like hand wrapped around her elbow as Roger lifted his cocked hat in acknowledgement.

Elspeth turned to her hostess. "Ye ken he joined the Loyalist forces?"

Miss Charlotte's silence and tight lips gave all the answer she needed.

"Why did ye not tell me?"

"Roger asked me to wait until he saw how things played out."

"Well, it looks as though they have received him with open arms." Elspeth pulled away, queasiness assaulting her stomach. Alex's warnings had born fruit. Could she slip out of town under the cover of night? Nay. She couldn't leave without seeing what happened to Alex and his comrades, packed together in that slapdash fort up on the western hill.

"In light of this confrontation, Elspeth, he had to make a decision. Do you see their numbers? How many more they have than the rebels?"

She did. Elspeth's shoulders sagged. "What will happen?"

"I would think they would attempt to parley first. Perhaps the Patriots will surrender."

"They willna." Though greatly outnumbered, the Patriots were firmly entrenched, and the rangers carried Pennsylvania and Kentucky long rifles perfectly suited for picking off assailants from this distance. They could last for weeks up there.

"We don't know that. Come. We will have a view from your bedroom window."

≈

*B*y Monday afternoon, Alex was fairly certain he'd wounded if not killed two men. It had taken something out of him, the first shot that made contact—unlike the battle with the Creeks. These were men he might have served alongside in former conflicts. Maybe kin. Was Finn among them? 'Twas best Alex did not know. The distance helped, not seeing faces.

Their assailants popped like gophers out of doors and windows in the jail and any other buildings within range on the back of town. They snuck around the other sides of the fort and used the cover of trees to fire on them. The Patriots returned fire with their rifles and two swivel guns.

This had gone on since midafternoon of the day prior, when Major Mayson and a Captain Bowie returned from a conference under a flag of truce. They had been reporting to Major Williamson that the King's Men demanded they deliver their arms and disperse just as the Loyalists captured two Patriots who'd ventured out in search of water.

As for water...Alex crouched on the banquette behind the stockade and dripped the last few droplets from his canteen into his mouth. Even with conserving the precious liquid, he'd run out far too fast. He nudged Wilson, who was preparing to pour fine-grain powder into his rifle's pan. "You got anything to drink left?"

"No one does. But Williamson has a platoon digging a well in the back. They should strike water soon."

What if they did not? How long could they hold out? His tongue already stuck to the roof of his mouth.

Alex repeated the exhausting steps of measuring powder and seating and ramming a bullet, priming the rifle, and preparing to take another shot. He lined up the front and rear sights on a figure in blue peeking around a wagon, but the man jerked back behind cover before Alex could "hold over" enough to compensate for the wind and pull the trigger.

While he waited for the gopher to stick his head out again, he found himself doing something he hadn't done in ages— saying a prayer. For the lass in the golden house, the top of which he could just spy. Was she safe? Had Bailey gotten her out of town?

He almost laughed when a picture of her walnut-hurling fury flashed before his mind. She was right. He had been jealous of that kiss. The possibility that her first one had been stolen by the likes of Bailey almost made him pull the trigger in reflexive anger. He'd like to wring the neck of that sneaky Loyalist. Maybe he would.

~

Though he was staying at the Loyalist headquarters, Roger came to the house Monday night. Hearing his boots and voice, Elspeth stayed in her room. Miss Charlotte mysteriously found the strength to sit at table with him while Rosa served them a full supper—judging by the length of time it took for them to dine. Partway through, Elspeth cracked open the door and ventured to tiptoe down the first flight of stairs. She sat on the landing and strained to catch their words.

"Don't worry, Mother. This will end tomorrow. They will surrender the fort before nightfall."

"How can you be certain?" Miss Charlotte's voice was fainter. "They don't seem to be slacking up in returning your fire."

Roger chuckled. "They have no water. Tomorrow, when we burn them out, they will have nothing to put out the fire with. They shall run out of there like rats."

Elspeth let out a little breath. A moment passed, then a chair scraped. She leapt up and ran on the balls of her feet back to her room. She closed her door as softly as possible while footsteps echoed in the foyer. Then stopped. Oh, thank God.

She stood there, pressed against her door with her heart hammering. What would she have done if Roger had sought her out? If he still did? She could hardly evade him in his own house. Suddenly now, he loomed large and threatening in her mind. The enemy.

She had chosen her side.

Nay, it had chosen her. She had taken it despite not knowing where she stood with Alex. The actual confrontation between the opposing forces had squeezed out her true sentiments. She kept hearing Alex's voice. *Isna our God-given freedom the most important thing?*

She had to do something. Yesterday, all shooting had ceased when darkness had fallen. Under cover of night, could she take the buckets Rosa kept on the back porch, fill them at the Spring Branch, and make her way to the fort? She could cut far upstream. 'Twould be little enough, but she could find Alex and warn him of the Loyalists' plan to burn them out.

Was such a notion foolishness? Aye. She could be mistaken for the enemy and shot. But how could she do nothing? Perhaps, with warning, the Patriots could abandon the fort before daybreak.

She paced, wringing her hands and praying, returning to the window every few minutes as the light faded away. Soon the boom of the swivel guns no longer rattled the windows, and the *pop-pop* of rifle and musket fire ceased.

Thou shalt not be afraid for the terror by night. The verse came back to her clearly.

She went to the clothes press and drew out her darkest outfit—a navy short dress with charcoal-colored petticoat. She slipped into the clothing and covered her hair with a length of black muslin. She fastened the crocheted frog that held her black cloak in place at her neck. Then she sat and waited until

Roger returned to headquarters, Miss Charlotte climbed the stairs for bed, and Poe finally stopped rattling around in the dining room. When the light went out in the kitchen, Elspeth lingered fifteen minutes more, then cracked open her door.

Finding the hall and stairs empty, she crept down. The lock on the back door proved a bit stubborn. She finally got it to turn with a minimum of noise. There were the buckets, stacked on the porch. Could she carry more than two? Not when they were full. She settled for what she could manage and tiptoed down the creaking steps.

"What you doing, Miss Lawrence?"

Elspeth let out a little cry and dropped a bucket. It thudded on the plank beneath her feet and bounced down to the ground.

Rosa's ample form stood silhouetted behind her, hands on her hips. Did this woman miss nothing?

"Oh, I just...I canna stand it anymore. I must have a bath, and I dinna want to disturb ye." Alarming how readily the lie rolled off the tongue of the pious daughter of a Presbyterian minister. *Forgive me, Lord?*

A low chuckle came from the open guest quarters on the back porch. How had she not noticed the door stood ajar? A soft light flickered—a pine knot, burning on a saucer—as Roger came to the threshold, the pungent scent of his tobacco smoke preceding him. "Lord love you, Elspeth, but that is the worst clanker I've heard in quite some time."

Her insides tied into a knot. "Roger. How is it ye came to be there?"

His teeth flashed in the faint light. "Well, you see, I live here. And I decided to enjoy a quiet smoke before returning to headquarters. As you know, Mother does not like the smell in the house."

"Oh. Aye."

"We missed your company at dinner."

"I...felt unwell." That much was certainly true.

"And now you want a bath."

Her cheeks flamed at such a discussion with a gentleman. "I thought it might be soothing."

"Or maybe you want to take your bathwater to Lieutenant Morris up on yon hill?"

"Nay—"

With a sudden lurch forward, he bore down on her, grabbing her forearm before she could stumble backward. "Along with whatever you overheard of our discussion tonight."

"Unhand me!" This was the first time he had ever been rough with her. Indeed, his grip was strong, and she couldn't shake him off.

He shoved his pipe at Rosa and pulled Elspeth across the porch and into the house. "I'm afraid you will be taking no trips across the creek tonight, my dear. Not only could our good townspeople receive the wrong impression of your sentiments, there's a good chance the Patriots might mistake you for one of us and blow your mob cap right off your lovely head."

"Stop, Roger. I dinna wish to—"

"For your own good, you shall remain in your room until the danger has passed." He tugged her up the stairs, still speaking in that imperious tone she'd never heard from him before. "As out of temper as I am with you at the moment, I yet hope you might come to your senses." At the entrance to her chamber, he gave her a little shove.

She stumbled inside but pivoted to face him, putting out her hand to catch the closing door. "Ye canna keep me prisoner. Just let me leave. Let me go home."

"I'm afraid that is out of the question. You will be secure here for now. Think carefully, Elspeth. When this is over, Ninety Six will rest in Loyalist hands."

"Ye dinna ken that."

"Oh, but I do. We will speak again soon." His piercing stare softened. "It will be a fresh start for us. I'm going to attribute tonight's escapade to your deeply held compassion rather than misplaced affection."

A quick tug and he shut the door. A moment later, a key turned in the lock. All her pounding and crying would not bring him back.

~

*E*lspeth had never prayed as hard in her life as she did on Tuesday, November twenty-first. The sniping of rifle shots awakened her from her uneasy slumber shortly after dawn. Were the Patriots taking any hits behind their hastily erected stockade?

She refused Rosa's knock on her door to deliver a breakfast tray. Not long after, a gray haze swirled in the air outside her window. She cracked it for a better view and inhaled a lungful of smoke. Leaning past the sash, she gasped. Small orange flames danced just outside the border of town. The Loyalists had ignited the field and fences near the fort.

Oh, dear Lord, please help Alex and the other Patriots.

The wooden shakes of the back porch rose almost to her window. She could make it down onto them, but what of the drop from the elevated porch? Even if she reached the ground uninjured and unnoticed, what would she do then? She had already ruled out leaving town—which would have required her to steal one of Roger's mounts. Best not to add the hanging crime of horse thieving to her sin of lying. And she could do nothing to help the Patriots in the fort. Nothing except pray. So she stayed put and did just that.

And then she gave thanks because their miserably wet autumn brought a blessing. The wood and grass proved too damp to burn. Elspeth hooted and clapped her hands, not caring if Miss Charlotte and Rosa could hear. They were just as much a party to her jailing as Roger.

Under cover of the smoke in the field, a strange turtle of an object crawled forward. A group of Loyalists had created a shelter of sticks and branches. Elspeth sucked in a breath and started praying again. When the portable shield drew near to the fort, shouts went up. Not because they were in range, but because the wood they carried had caught fire.

Elspeth clasped her hands as they retreated. "Lord, I wouldna be so vain as to think that was all due to me own wee prayers, but thankee just the same."

She refused dinner as well. If they were to keep her captive, let them feel very bad indeed about it. Doubtless, Miss Charlotte was dying of curiosity as to what was happening, since the guest bedroom window afforded the only view of the drama playing out on either side of the creek. But Elspeth certainly was not accepting callers.

Later that afternoon, the Loyalists used a wagon as a rolling shield, again advancing on the Patriot position. This time, the swivel guns in the fort preempted Elspeth's prayers. Ha. Was Roger so confident now? But would want of the most basic resource of all—water—prove the Patriot's undoing?

Finally, a white flag fluttered from the top window of the jail. Elspeth sagged into her chair. "Thankee, Lord. Thankee."

After dark, a lighted candle bobbed its way down Whitehall Road and across the field to the fort. A messenger for peace?

When Rosa knocked on her door with a supper tray, Elspeth called for her to come in. The lock turned, and the stately black woman entered with hot tea, a crusty loaf, and a mincemeat pie.

Elspeth made no move toward the tray as Rosa placed it on the table. "I must ken...what is happening?"

Straightening, Rosa flattened her mouth and surveyed her. "You love him, don't you?"

"Roger?" Elspeth let her hands fall to her sides. "How can ye ask me that after—?"

"The one with the scars. Morris."

Her mouth dropped open. "I *care* about Lieutenant Morris. We survived something unspeakable together. But..." Love? Could she truly be in love with a broken man on the run from his past, a man who might be incapable of loving her back? That would be the most foolish thing she'd done yet.

Rosa huffed a sigh. "He's gonna live—if he's not been shot already. The boys up in the fort done struck water. And they're gonna make peace in the mornin'. What that means for us is, we need to start packing. Mister Roger sent word to be ready to go to Charlestown. He said you need to pack too."

CHAPTER 14

*I*t took Alex until Thursday afternoon to get shed of that miserable fort and his duties. His inner man raged to escape the place his superiors ordered his body to remain. Their leaders had taken most of Wednesday in hammering out an agreement, and only the next morning did the Loyalist troops withdraw. Then there had been the business of leveling the stockade, all but the original buildings.

By the time he was cleared to enter the town, he fairly sprinted across the creek and up the back way to the golden frame house. He thudded the knocker against the front door and received no reply. He pounded with his fists. When that did not avail, he fell to shouting, "Bailey? Elspeth! Open up."

Not a movement came from within. Alex darted around the side of the residence and peered at the upstairs windows, seeking a flutter of a curtain or a curl of smoke from the chimney. Nothing. He picked up a pebble and tossed it at what might be the spare room.

"Elspeth?"

Where were they?

He was circling the house with the intent of trying the back door when a dark-skinned face appeared on the other side of the fence. "They's gone, sir."

Alex stopped and whirled. "Gone? Where?"

"Charlestown. Mr. Bailey, he done joint up with the King's Men. He close up the house and took his mama to her kin."

Alex's stomach squeezed. So the fence-sitter had finally made good on his true sentiments. "And the young lady who was their guest?"

The grizzled servant scratched his chin whiskers. "All I know is, it was about town she was to be his betrothed. I reckon she gone with 'em."

The air left his lungs with the force of a bellows. Elspeth, gone to Charlestown? With no word, no goodbye? He'd assumed her anger the day before the battle held a teasing edge. She'd drawn the same from him, as only she was wont to do. Had he taken what she intended with complete gravity too lightly? Offended her to the point she had pledged herself to his enemy?

God, it canna be. Please, just let me find her.

Why was he bargaining with the Almighty? If God had been silent these many years, did Alex really expect Him to speak now? If the lass was gone, she was gone.

For a moment, he considered finding Charlie and thundering down the Charlestown Road. But interfering with a retreat even to fetch a lass could be considered a violation of the treaty just signed. He closed his eyes a moment, then turned toward the front of the house as his informant disappeared from the other side of the fence.

Alex walked past the front porch with his boots full of lead. What was he to do now? His duty. What he had always done. He paused to rub his eyes, to grind that into his befuzzled brain. When he dropped his hand, a cloaked figure clutching a fabric bag stood at the front gate. He blinked.

"Elspeth?"

He did not wait for her to answer before running to her. The relief in her eyes welcomed him moments before he grabbed her up and swung her in a circle. A breathless laugh escaped her as he squeezed her around the ribs. He set her down, cupped her face, and pressed his lips to her forehead, nearly knocking off her hat. Not caring that passersby might gawp.

"Lass, I thought ye'd gone with them."

Her smile glowed up at him. "To Charlestown? Nay." A frown quickly settled over her brow. "Not after Roger locked me in me room."

Alex's jaw dropped. "He did what?"

"Aye. When he caught me takin' his buckets to the Spring Branch Monday night. I'd heard how parched yer men were for water."

"Lass! Are ye daft?" Before he thought better of it, he covered her face with his hand, as though that might stop the flow of foolish words. But she only giggled under his fingers. He released her. "I think less poorly of the man, knowin' his reasons. I might have done the same. Ye coulda been shot, ye ken."

"I think he was more upset that I was fashed about ye."

Alex reached for her again, holding her by the shoulders. "And I was fashed about ye as well. I couldna get free to warn ye in time."

"I was lookin' for ye at the courthouse just now."

"I came here straightaway."

Their words tumbled over each other. They both laughed.

Alex shook his head. "He just left ye here, all alone?"

Elspeth raised her shoulders. "They packed up their things and loaded a wagon. He asked me to go with them, promisin' a fine life in Charlestown. Indeed, I think he expected I would be too affrighted to decline. But I've made me choice." She lifted her chin. "I am a Patriot."

His heart surged. "Ah, lass." Alex rubbed the side of her temple with his thumb. Then he drew her to him. "Ye always have been."

"I just didna ken it yet..." The murmured words almost got lost in his frock coat and implied a deeper meaning than he could grasp in the moment. "Though it did give me a pain, the way Miss Charlotte treated me. She would not even look at me, Alex. And I counted her me only friend."

"She was actin' on her own hurt, I'd wager." He rubbed her shoulders and then forced himself to step back. The worry about her had left him in less control than normal. "But what are ye to do now?"

"Here's me hopin' ye can help me get home. Roger offered me a horse...well, he offered to let me da *pay* him for a horse."

Alex snorted in disgust. Some gentleman.

"But I wanted nothing from him. I figured, even if something had happened to ye"—her throat worked—"yer major might give me an escort."

Alex straightened. "I am certain he will, and me with it. Our victory has ensured the safety of Ninety Six for the time—"

"Victory?" She broke in, one brow quirked up. "Roger said 'twas a Loyalist win. That they were only withdrawing across the Saluda to give things time to cool down. And takin' yer swivel guns with them."

"Ha! They are to bring those back, once they have paraded them a wee bit. And his commanders are all too aware of the sizeable army Colonel Robinson is raisin' in Camden. They will be here afore long. Nay, the Loyalists are on the run. Roger won't be back in these parts any time soon."

Already, there was talk of linking with Robinson to round up any opposition. Normally, Alex would be eager to join such an expedition. But if given the choice between more shooting at former friends or escorting Elspeth to safety, he did not need to think about his decision.

She surveyed the impressive residence behind him. "That would explain why Roger was so keen to take everything of great value. 'Tis sad, in a way." Her face brightening, she reached for his hand. "So ye can take me home, then?"

"If Mayson will reassign me to Fort Charlotte, aye." The skeleton crew there could probably use another officer.

He told himself the warmth that invaded his chest when he thought of that stemmed from a desire for a peaceful winter. From some comforts of a home nearby that might on occasion extend to him. Those comforts never lasted, but he might enjoy them while he could, no? 'Twas the best he could hope for.

And of course he rejoiced that Elspeth had at last seen her way clear to the Patriot cause.

"Come." Alex picked up her bag. "Ye have no more call to linger here. Let me find ye a place among the officers' wives while I seek permission to leave for Fort Charlotte."

He did not miss the assessing glance she shot him as she slipped her hand through the crook in his arm. He'd take care of her, aye, as he would the little sister he never had. 'Twas a man's nature to notice that her soft curves beneath him when they had wrestled under the walnut tree had felt anything but sisterly. But he was not in a position to offer more than a brother's protection.

~

*P*assing through the rolling countryside around Fort Boone atop the mare the army had lent her for the ride to Fort Charlotte, Elspeth put back her hood and allowed the sun to warm her face. Eagles soared high above on unseen currents that pushed out the long-entrenched dreary weather. The rains had taken down many of the leaves early, but glimpses of fall colors remained, most especially the lobed red leaves of the white oaks.

High spirits prevailed among the company of fifteen men returning to Fort Charlotte, even though they might miss out on the opportunity for glory with Colonel Robinson's campaign. Captain Caldwell and most of his men, save the sergeant reassigned to Fort Charlotte and made a lieutenant, would be taking part in that venture, but these rangers were newer recruits who had fought alongside Alex at Williamson's fort. A snug winter out of the weather would give them a chance to hone their combat skills and strengthen their allegiances. For a time, newly promoted to captain, Alex would be the officer in charge at Fort Charlotte.

That he had given up a military mission to remain near her swelled Elspeth's heart with hope.

A strong tenor from the ranks led off a tune among the men riding behind them. "'I'm lonesome since I crossed the hill, and o'er the moorland sedgy, such heavy thoughts my heart do fill, since parting from my Sally...'"

"Do rangers normally sing whilst they ride?" Elspeth glanced at Alex, astride his stallion named for Bonnie Prince Charlie.

"Aye. But no' that tune."

"What do they normally sing?"

He chuckled. "Dinna ask. 'Twould burn yer ears, sweet lass."

Sweet lass. Such an endearment 'twas music indeed, drawing more of a blush than a bawdy chanty might. And the grin that flashed over his face, carving out new laugh lines! Scars or no, this man's rugged handsomeness seared her like a blade heated in a blacksmith's forge.

"Methinks they have claimed ye as something of a figurehead." Alex sent her a wink.

"Me?" Elspeth put her hand on her chest.

"Aye. The lass who left a Loyalist oak a'pinin'. Now ye ride at their head, inspirin' ballads."

As if to prove Alex's point, the last verse drifted up to them. "'Her golden hair in ringlets fair, her eyes like diamonds shining...'"

He raised his one eyebrow at her. "Seems I coulda stayed in Ninety Six. Something tells me ye will have no shortage of protectors from here on out."

"Oh, nay, ye canna get shed o'me that easily, Alex Morris." From now on, she aimed to make it as difficult for him to forget her as he had been for her to forget—impossible. Betting that he couldn't resist the challenge, she spurred her mare ahead of his stallion down the gentle slope.

Sure enough, hooves thudded and rocks skittered as Alex urged Charlie to keep pace with them. Her curls sprang free of her mob cap. She laughed back at him, pulling ahead, then slackening up, pulling ahead and slacking up, until they reached the outskirts of New Bordeaux. This was the way their youths should have been. There should have been teasing and flirtation and corn shuckings a'plenty. Now she had to show him as much joy as she could while he remained near. Maybe he'd learn how to grasp onto life rather than merely surviving in death's shadow.

At the gates of Fort Charlotte, she relinquished her mount to Lieutenant Rawdon as the troops filed inside. With no regrets, she took the hand Alex offered and climbed atop Charlie behind him. 'Twas heaven, the excuse to wrap her arms around his trim, solid waist. Did he think her forward when she rested her cheek against the blue woolen material covering his broad back? She felt no need to speak the rest of the way home.

Fragrant smoke wafted from the dogtrot cabin as they entered the yard. The children poured out onto the porch, shouting their greetings, but where was Da? Gone visiting, most likely.

As soon as Alex helped her down, Galilani tugged at her cloak. "Miss El, *e-do-da, ga-ga-lo-i!*" Rather frantically as she spoke the Cherokee word for *father*, she made a breaking motion, then pointed low on her deerskin tunic.

Elspeth's heart stumbled over a beat. "Leg? Da hurt his leg?"

Inoli stood back from the clamoring girls and spoke solemnly in perfectly clear English. "Father break leg."

Alex appeared as thunderstruck as she was.

"Nay! How?" she asked.

The boy pointed to a wooden ladder still propped against the edge of the roof.

While Alex secured his horse, she ran up the steps and into the house. Ulisi turned from the hearth, and Da looked up from a book, the curtains that normally concealed his bed drawn back. His one leg stretched out in front of him was wrapped and elevated.

"Elspeth!"

"Da! Whatever happened?"

The girls crowded around her, chattering in a mixture of Cherokee and English, but she shooed them off and went to sit beside her father, kissing his bearded cheek.

He waved his hand at her. "Oh, 'tis nothing but a small inconvenience. I was attemptin' to stop the leak in the roof."

"Da, tell me true." She propped one hand on her waist. "How bad is it?" Before Da could answer, a shadow loomed over her, and she followed his gaze to Alex.

"Well, ye're not the man I expected to see."

Alex smiled, and Inoli peeked around from behind him, then stared up at the newcomer.

"We have much to tell ye, Da."

"All in good time. Thankee fer bringin' Elspeth home."

"My pleasure, sir." Alex shook Da's hand, then stepped back.

"Did ye get the doc to treat ye?" She was already feeling his forehead for signs of fever.

"Aye. The physician at the fort hadn't yet returned, but that

French doctor from New Bordeaux came out. He said 'tis but a wee break that ought to heal well enough if I stay off the leg for some weeks. Unfortunately, it couldna have come at a worse time of year." His wool dressing gown parted to reveal his white shirt beneath as he drew a breath, then released a lusty sigh.

Elspeth nibbled her lower lip. "The shakes will just have to do fer another winter, I suppose. Although I dinna relish slaughterin' a hog without yer help."

Alex moved into her line of vision. "I can help."

"What's that?" Da cocked his head.

The man of few words knit his brow as though reticent to give explanation, but explain he did. "I had a look at the roof before I came in. I hate to say, but there be several spots unlikely to hold if we get a heavy snow. 'Tis no stranger I am to a froe, nor to killin' and smokin' a hog. I can also hunt to lay by venison when I'm out and aboot scoutin'. I daresay ye will need more than a ham with this many mouths to feed."

Elspeth drew a breath and reached for Alex's hand, a gesture which her father's eyes did not miss. But he was practically sagging with relief and in no position to question why she looked to Alex now rather than Roger.

"'Tis good of ye," she said. In addition to agreeing to see to the roof and the slaughtering, Alex had also anticipated the need she never would have mentioned before him—hunting. "But will ye have time, with yer duties at the fort?"

He chuckled, the sound wiping away her worries. "To lend a helpin' hand to 'the girl I left behind me'? I dinna expect arguments."

CHAPTER 15

*A*lex proved true to his word. A few days after his return to Fort Charlotte, he came to help Elspeth round up and slaughter their hog. She boiled water in the cauldron in the yard and then poured it over the wooden trough on the smoke-house floor to ready it to receive the portions for salting.

He returned the next day to make shingles. From the smokehouse door, Elspeth stole peeks of him in his waistcoat and breeks, tapping the froe into a banded section of upright log with a wooden mallet. If only she could stare as openly as Inoli, who watched every move as Alex splintered the log into pie-like sections, then used a side ax to remove the bark, sapwood, and any rough edges.

Alex never once glanced at the boy. Thankfully, he did not glance at her either. When he went to the barn to further plane the shakes at her father's shave horse with the draw knife, she finished the second salting and returned to the cabin.

The girls had completed their spelling lesson and were ready to assist Ulisi with dicing vegetables for the succotash, so Elspeth checked over their work. They had come a long way from learning the English alphabet to reading and writing short words. She would have to give them harder words next time. She praised each girl and released them to prepare supper.

Inoli, as usual, had left his lesson half done, but she hadn't the heart to call him in while Alex was here. If only he would acknowledge the child in some small way. Perhaps he did not realize just how early Cherokee boys learned their way around blades. Even if he did not trust a beginner to make shakes, and even if the language barrier kept them from conversing, 'twould lighten her heart if Alex offered Inoli a smile or at least a nod.

Either way, Alex deserved a reward for his labors on their behalf. She would make a treat—an apple tansey. And she'd set hers beside prim Mrs. Guthrie's from Boonesborough any day. With a quiet smile that anticipated Alex's appreciation, she set to work cutting three pippin apples into thin slices.

She stirred together four eggs, six spoons of cream, and some cane sugar. Adding the nutmeg put her in mind of a request she needed to make of Alex. But how much should she rely on him? They had already asked so much, and his true responsibilities lay elsewhere.

She blew a hair out of her face. On no account would Da let her ride to Londonborough alone. 'Twas much farther than even New Bordeaux, and since learning of all that had unfolded in Ninety Six, he trusted folk less. Maybe due to beholding the disappointing nature of men and maybe due to not feeling as able to protect her himself since his injury.

Before going further with the tansey, she wiped her hands on her apron and went out onto the porch. The roof creaked above her, and she leaned over the side and looked upward. Alex was climbing on the rafters, a small pile of shingles in front of him and several nails in his mouth.

"Dear me." Her breath puffed out in a small cloud on the frosty air. Elspeth hung onto the porch rail with one hand and fixed her other on her hip. "I suppose this isna the best time to talk."

Settling on his rear, Alex removed the nails from between his lips, and they split into a grin that nearly stopped her heart. "As long as I dinna fall in on yer da, we can talk all day. I should be up here a while." He glanced around, and his face screwed up. "Ah, botheration."

"What is it?"

"I forgot the hammer."

Before Elspeth could offer aid, footsteps ran her way. Inoli appeared at her side and bolted up the ladder with her father's hammer in tow.

Elspeth raised her hand to her chest. "Ah, Inoli, good boy."

Alex's initial expression of relief froze when he clamped eyes on Inoli. His face went hard, then, almost as though trained, blank. He palmed the tool without further acknowledgement.

Elspeth's hand snapped back to her waist. "Well, are ye not going to thank him?"

After a brusque nod in the boy's direction, Alex turned his attention to the first rotted shake. "What was it ye wanted?"

"I am not so certain I want it now."

"Suit yerself."

A sharp pain pierced Elspeth's chest as Inoli climbed onto the edge of the roof and settled himself cross-legged there. She briefly considered fetching another tool—her skillet. It might be put to better use atop Alex's head than heating his tansey.

But this was for the children. She drew a breath and made her begrudging request. "I need to go to the Widow Schneider's in Londonborough to pick up the *lubkuchen* and *stollen*."

"The what?" Alex turned and saw Inoli perched between them. He waved his arm. "Tell him to get down."

"Why?"

"Obviously, the child doesna need to be climbin' on the roof."

Elspeth elevated her eyebrows. "Do ye have any idea how often I have called him down from that pine tree yon?" She pointed to the tallest evergreen with wide-spaced branches near the driveway. "He wants to help ye. Why not let him?"

"I dinna need help. This is a one-man job. Now what about Londonborough?" He swiveled back to his work, prying up another weathered shake.

Impatience lessened her concern about imposing on the stubborn man. "Will ye ride there with me, or no? I would be ready tomorrow, though I understand if ye need more time."

"Aye." He positioned a sturdy replacement over the empty spot and hammered it into place. "I will take ye. And the day after that, I thought I would go hunting."

Inoli sucked in a breath and sat up straight. "*I-no-lu-ga*?" *You go hunting?* "I go!"

Alex's dark gaze shot to the boy. "Nay. Ye won't."

Inoli ducked his head and clasped his ankles. His crest-fallen expression hollowed out an aching space in Elspeth's heart.

"Oh, come, Alex. The boy will be no trouble. Da has showed him how to fire the musket, and he has hunted many times with a blowgun and bow and arrows. Ye might learn something from *him*."

His fingers tightened around the handle of the hammer, and he switched his focus to her with such fierceness that the hairs on the back of her neck raised. "I wish to learn nothing from him. I wish to teach him nothing. I am here to aid the family I once ken because they are in need. That is all. And that is all ye will ask of me. Understand?"

She swallowed. Her first inclination was to nod and scamper back inside. But something told her to stand her ground. Her chin went up. "I am not makin' a new request. Ye already put the musket in his hand. Remember?"

He blew out a soft breath. "That, too, was done for you. And now I am askin' ye but one thing...keep him away from me. I willna encourage his handlin' that weapon...him, of all people."

Elspeth looked from Alex to Inoli. Rather than cowering, the child had uncurled and glared at Alex. No doubt, he responded, as she did, to the strangely personal nature of Alex's attack. She held out her hand. "Come, Inoli. Come in the house."

He spurned her touch, though he scampered down the ladder. Rather than retreat inside, he darted off toward the creek.

Elspeth shook her head and stared at Alex. "What did ye mean, 'him, of all people?' Why are ye so set against the boy?"

But he had already turned his back and resumed hammering.

❧

"So, Alex, do ye think the trouble is over, then?"

Reverend Lawrence filled his pipe as they sat by his hearth the day after the shingle-making. He occupied the only Windsor chair in the cabin, his leg propped on a stool before him, while Alex remained on the bench next to the table. Behind him, the women and children cleared away the trenchers used for the pine-bark stew Ulisi had served upon Alex and Elspeth's return from Londonborough.

"With the Loyalists hereabouts? Aye, for now. I hear Thomas Brown was ousted from Charlestown by the provincial government and has fled to British East Florida."

Reverend Lawrence grunted as he took his first draw of tobacco. "From what ye shared of him, I wonder, will he stay there?"

Not until the man had poured his cup of bitter vengeance upon Georgia and Carolina. "I doubt the backcountry has seen the last of him. But Robert Cunningham languishes in the Boston jail. I dinna think the congress will pardon him. And his brother, Patrick, canna evade Colonel Robinson's troops for long." Alex shook his head. Dispatches to Fort Charlotte revealed that the Patriot militia had swollen to the unheard-of number of more than four thousand and were successfully rounding up the remaining Loyalist leaders and their followers.

"Coffee?" Elspeth plunked a mug down on the table behind him.

He turned to her with a raised brow and a smile that usually brought about her instant softening. "Does this mean ye are finally about to open that sweet-smellin' packet ye withheld from me the whole way home?"

Home. Had he really just used that word?

Her blue eyes flickered, but her mouth remained firm. "Ye can sample either the lubkuchen or the stollen, aye."

"But not both?"

"I take it that means ye want coffee." She poured some of the aromatic brew into his mug and raised the pot with a glance at her father.

He gave a dismissive wave and a point at his pipe, then resumed his questioning of Alex. "But ye think the peace won't be permanent."

"Not if the plans of Kirkland, Brown, and Cameron succeed." Alex took a sip of his coffee and stretched his legs toward the fire. Maybe he should remove his boots, let the heat from the flames warm his stockinged toes.

Reverend Lawrence hefted a sigh. "Aye, I fear ye were a sight more accurate than I where Cameron was concerned. I couldna believe how he thumbed his nose at the Council of Safety. I still say he wants the Cherokees to remain neutral."

"We shall see." Alex wouldn't tip his hand to his preference that Cameron failed. And not just to satiate his own appetite for revenge. Yes, it would mean battling two enemies, but peace would never hold with the Cherokees, anyway. Might as well get all the fighting done while the militias were embodied against the Loyalists.

What his notice gravitated to at the moment was Elspeth, unwrapping the treats she'd bought from the German widow. The children also watched with eager eyes. She saved the fruit-cake for another day and instead dispensed the soft, chewy cookies made with molasses and the spices and walnuts she'd contributed. She slid Alex a cookie across the table, not meeting his eyes when he thanked her.

Cookie in hand, he glanced up to encounter unmistakable amusement on Reverend Lawrence's face.

Elspeth delivered her father's treat with markedly greater deference than she'd shown Alex and retreated to the rug with the children.

The reverend asked in a low voice, "Still out of countenance with ye, is she?"

"I'm afraid so."

Though he'd apologized for his stern tone with her even before leaving the day prior, Elspeth had remained guarded on their outing today. He had even asked her to tell him about her sister, and she had, sharing her memories of happy, dark-haired little Leana before she was whisked from her mother's arms by a Cherokee brave moments before another warrior set upon Bridget Lawrence. The man had surely saved Leana, though he'd taken her far away. And this man beside him, Duncan Lawrence, had watched it all unfold from the wagon stuck in the bog where he had fled to fetch his musket—powerless to intervene in time.

Alex's hand tightened around his mug. It tremored. The coffee sloshed, and he set the drink back on the table and leaned forward, massaging his hand.

"Are ye all right, lad?" Reverend Lawrence's gaze fixed on him with compassion.

Such compassion. How could he fill his home with the very spawn of the people who—

"Elspeth told me the boy asked to go huntin' with ye. I can understand why ye might refuse."

Had refused. "Aye." Alex let the word out on a breath. The walls that had provided such comfort seemed to close in around him. This was why he'd taken a harsh tone with Elspeth the day prior. The Lawrences presumed on their former association with him, asked him the outlandish. He had to be harsh to maintain any boundaries at all.

"Ye ken, Inoli grew up without a father, much as ye did. While that is not as much a hardship in their culture, where their mother's kin step in to raise a child, ye can imagine what sort of uncle Split Ear might be." Reverend Lawrence puffed his pipe, but his eyes did not waver from Alex's face.

"'Tis not a position I am qualified...or desiring...to fill." He forced the response out from between his teeth.

Elspeth's father nodded. "And yet, someone must fill it. The braves will have considered the gift of the musket in exchange for their leavin' the boy with us a bindin' agreement. They must find him skilled in the pursuits of a man as well as in English and arithmetic when they return." Reverend Lawrence sat back, nursing his pipe and watching the fire, letting his words settle.

Alex reached for his coffee. Best finish it and be on his way. He would not be cornered into another commitment, not when he fully intended to dispatch Inoli's uncle to the happy hunting grounds the first opportunity he got. Reverend Lawrence, of all people, ought to understand.

Elspeth had taken a mysterious little box Widow Schneider had given her upon her lap. The children inched forward on their knees as she opened it and showed them what was cradled in the straw inside. They put out fingers to touch the tiny figures and questioned her in their language.

Reverend Lawrence chuckled. "They are askin' what it is. This should be interesting."

Elspeth said, "'Tis a nativity." As they struggled to echo the strange word, she smiled and lifted out a painted clay baby Jesus in a manger. "Remember the story I told you about how the Creator's son was born as a human child?"

When the discussion fell into the native language, Alex could no longer understand. He'd been mystified himself by the displays in the German widow's house meant to welcome the Christmas season. "They call it *putz*, these nativity scenes they make." He shook his head, his heart lightening at the change of topic. "And they decorate their homes with greenery."

"Aye, their churches too." Reverend Lawrence rumbled another laugh. "'Tis strange enough, but I own, the joy they take at Advent has softened my heart over the years. Like most Presbyterians, I used to think Christmas a popish holiday invented by those seekin' an excuse to wassail and fire off their guns. But now, well...I see no harm in a good Christmas puddin' and the singin' of a Watts song or two."

Setting up the nativity on a side table, Elspeth chattered in Cherokee. Then she spoke in English the word *sacrifice*. She had come to the part where Jesus went to the cross to atone for the sins of all men. The children knelt on the braided rug, their attention fixed on her every word and gesture.

Something in Alex's heart twisted. "Do ye really think it will make a difference? What ye teach them?" he asked Reverend Lawrence softly. For a moment, he grasped the concept behind the Lawrences' hope for change, for harmony.

"Think back to yer own childhood. Did ye not learn the most about God when ye were of tender years?"

Alex lowered his mug, swallowing hard. "We went to church in Darien."

"And did yer ma not teach ye at home as well?"

Inoli's exclamation broke into their conversation. "Like Selu."

Elspeth smiled and laid her hand on his shiny, dark head. "Yes, rather like Selu, in the story of the grandmother of your people who gave up her body to give the gift of corn. But Jesus gave us *life*." She sent a look of intense excitement her father's way.

He nodded, and she leaned forward, continuing in Cherokee. Reverend Lawrence prompted Alex. "Ye were saying, about yer mother..."

The sound that shook loose from Alex's chest was too rough to be called a laugh. "Me mother was content to send me out with the men of her clan. And I to go. Me scars were a badge of honor to them, rather than a reminder of all that had been lost." Now, why had he said that? The warmth of the fire, a bit of human kindness, and the Lawrences had scaled his defenses.

"I'm sorry to hear that, lad." The reverend leaned forward and put a hand on his arm.

The touch burned through Alex's sleeve. "'Tis of little regard."

"On the contrary, 'tis of the utmost importance. Yer mother had a duty to nurture ye past yer hurt. It grieves me heart that she might not have done so. That ye had to wander far from home seekin' peace." He sat back, his brow winkled.

"Home...I dinna ken what that is. I thought if I had me own place, but..." His acreage in the Ceded Lands had felt far emptier than the barracks at Fort Argyle. At least there, comrades had needed and surrounded him, and in South Carolina, kin had welcomed him. Kin who now fought on the opposite side. The ache yawned wide in Alex's heart, and he spurned the moisture that threatened to leach into his eyes.

"Home is where the people ye love are. Maybe ye just hadn't found it yet." Reverend Lawrence watched him carefully.

"Aye. Well." Alex thumped his mug onto the table. "Ye may find peace here, in this way. There will be no peace for me until after this war." He stood, drawing Elspeth's gaze.

"Are ye leavin'?"

Did she sound disappointed? His heart surged, but he refused to look at her, not under her father's careful assessment. She struggled to her feet, nonetheless, while Alex shook the reverend's hand, and she trailed him to the door.

"Thankee for ridin' with me today."

Now the lass thawed?

"Thankee for supper. Goodnight." With a nod, he slipped out the door, but Elspeth followed him onto the porch.

She paid little heed as Inoli slipped past her, presumably to private business in the woods. Her breath became a white cloud on the chilly December air. "Alex, I...I was wrong to ask so much of ye. Ye have done more than enough." Her fingers wrapped around his arm. "I only want ye to feel welcome here."

"I do, but it may be a while before I see ye again."

"Of course." She ducked her chin. When she raised it, hope flared in her eyes. "But say we will see ye for Christmas."

A smile tugged one corner of his mouth. "Will ye give me stollen?"

"Aye." Her grin answered. "I might even make ye a syllabub."

He risked more than going soft under such ministrations, but how could he refuse the offer? Her father's words about home circled in his mind. He had once dreamed of a place like this. The officer who had trained him at Fort Argyle during his first stint in the Georgia Rangers, Ansel Anderson, had made him long for such. A second son without land or inheritance, Ansel had navigated the intrigue in Savannah when the Stamp Act had been passed to win the favor of a member of the Governor's Council for the hand of the man's daughter. The story of his transformation from King's Ranger to Patriot had gone far in molding Alex's views. As Ansel's obvious bliss with his new wife had in making Alex wonder if one day, even he might find home at the side of a good woman.

Would there be that much harm in enjoying it while he could? In pretending the Lawrences were his family?

A strange, high-pitched chanting stole the words of his reply. "What is that?"

Elspeth blew out a soft breath. "Inoli. I will have to go fetch him."

Alex frowned into the darkness. "From the woods?" Wild creatures prowled amongst the trees, even more so now with the cold season upon them, and the boy had gone out unarmed.

"From the creek. He prays to the gods of water and fire. Last night, he did the same...and came in dripping wet and half frozen." She shook her head. "'Tis the way of his people."

Alex gaped at her. "To what purpose?"

"To receive favor for when he goes huntin' with ye."

CHAPTER 16

*I*n a gray sky sprinkled with high, filmy white clouds, the January sun struggled to burn off the haze before midafternoon. Even the faint breeze from the wide brown waters of the Savannah River touched Alex's skin with the mildest of dampness. The scent of roasting venison promised a hearty dinner after Reverend Lawrence's sermon. Alex had sent a wagon to bring him to the fort. The Sunday preaching and meal offered a good opportunity for the men to bond.

Aye, all was well as the minister began his sermon. Loyalist Colonel Fletchall had been found hiding in a hollow sycamore at his plantation, Fair Forest. Patrick Cunningham's men had been surrounded in late December at the Battle of Great Cane Break. Though Cunningham himself had fled, 'twould not be long before he, too, sat behind bars. Colonel Richardson's militia had made it home starved and half frozen by rain, then a blizzard. Heroes, all. And somehow, Alex had made it to the mission on Charlie through two feet of snow for Elspeth's Christmas feast.

Oh, and he had taken Inoli hunting. Though he hadn't

resigned himself to the sight of a firearm in the small brown hand, 'twas needful for the Lawrences to fulfill their bargain with the Cherokees. Thankfully, skulking through the woods on the trail of wildlife required little conversation. Inoli had even shot their Christmas turkey. He had looked to Alex with such obvious need for approval that Alex had smiled and congratulated him with a thump on the back.

After supper that evening, he had ventured an inquiry about Alex's dragoon pistols. "Shoot them, Cap-tain?"

Somehow, he'd found himself doing a firing demonstration from the porch.

Following a rather lengthy prayer, Reverend Lawrence opened his huge leather Bible. "Job 31:29-30, 'If I rejoice at the destruction of him that hated me, or lifted up myself when evil found him: neither have I suffered my mouth to sin by wishing a curse to his soul.'"

Alex stiffened on the makeshift bench and peered out of the corners of his eyes at Elspeth. She offered not so much as a blink.

Seated on a platform before them so as not to tire his leg, her father spread his hands open. "Men, this season past, ye have engaged in a great struggle...a struggle which has caused some of ye to call yer neighbors, yer friends, and sometimes yer kin, enemies. As followers of Christ, we should do all we can to mirror His example and seek peace. Betimes, we still must raise arms to defend our homes and families, the values we hold most dear. And when that time comes, with a clear conscience before yer Maker, fight not for hate of yer enemy, but rather, for love of yer cause."

Murmurs of agreement rippled among the rangers assembled on the parade ground—most of the company. Had Reverend Lawrence finally come 'round to the cause of freedom? Alex's many fireside conversations with him this winter indicated it might be so.

The preacher flipped pages and consulted another text. "The Lord tells us in James chapter six, 'But I say unto you which hear, love your enemies, do good to them which hate you, bless them that curse you, and pray for them which despitefully use you....For if ye love them which love you, what thank have ye? For sinners also love those that love them. And if ye do good to them which do good to you, what thank have ye? For sinners also do even the same.'"

Alex focused on Elspeth's hand stroking Ayita's head. So calm. Why this fluttering in his own heart?

"'But love your enemies, and do good, and lend, hoping for nothing again; and your reward shall be great, and ye shall be the children of the Highest: for he is kind unto the unthankful and to the evil....Judge not, and ye shall not be judged: condemn not, and ye shall not be condemned: forgive, and ye shall be forgiven.'" He looked up, his gaze sweeping the crowd. "Some of us may have lost much or may yet lose much to our enemy. Many of ye ken, I speak from experience. Even so, our enemy is our brother."

Beside Alex, Elspeth dipped her chin, her fingers tightening around Ayita's braid.

Alex faced forward and stared straight ahead. Surely, this sermon fixed on him. Reverend Lawrence had betrayed his trust by turning his confidences on him in this public manner. He had taken Inoli hunting, had he not? Even now, the boy sat at his feet, a fixture in Alex's shadow. He held up the bear he was carving for inspection, and Alex managed a small nod and smile.

"This spring, ye may again face yer enemy on the field of battle. When ye do, remember what Christ has forgiven you. If ye have hated, even the men ye feel justified killin' in battle ye have murdered." Reverend Lawrence closed his Bible. Indeed, his gaze settled on Alex. "Ye may have heard it said that to forgive frees the one wronged. May I add, ye can only hold one thing in yer hand at a time—hatred...or love. Won't ye release the hatred so there be room for blessings the Good Lord would give ye?"

Surely, his scars branded him the recipient of this chastisement before the entire assembly. Not a man here did not ken him as the boy who'd survived the Long Canes massacre.

As soon as the minister had them bow their heads in prayer, Alex shot up from the bench and strode away.

In the officers' quarters, he threw his hat across the room, poured himself a cup of cider, and paced before the fire yet spluttering on the hearth. With a *thunk*, he added another log and used the poker to stir up the flames. His chest burned just as hot.

The door opened behind him, and Elspeth slipped inside, pushing back the hood of her cloak. Her blond curls tumbled out from beneath her mob cap.

He did not wait for her to make inquiry, but rather, fired a volley at her. "Did ye ken he planned this...this *ambush*? I'd have rather ye saved me his canting and told me straight yerself that ye find me in need of repentance."

"If ye feel in need of repentance, Alex, 'twould not be me doin'. Or me father's."

He plunked his cider down on the nearby table. "There has been one thing, Elspeth, one thing, which has kept me going all these years. Kept me from curlin' up in a ball as I did that day and dyin' inside. And that has been the promise I made to meself that I would settle the score with those who took everything from me. *Everything*, Elspeth."

She took a few steps toward him. "But there is life and there is death. We must choose, and that which is feeding ye isna of God."

"Wherever it comes from, it will achieve the intended result. For I willna have peace until the man who killed me brother lays dead. Him and as many of his brethren as I can fell. For even if I dinna remember the details of that attack on our families, I saw the results. Every day." He pointed at himself with his first two fingers. "*In me own mother's eyes.* In the eyes of everyone who looks at me."

"Not in my eyes." Elspeth came forward and ran her hand softly down his arm. "Da told me what ye said about yer mother. How she pushed ye away after the attack. All I ken is, she had scars, too, only where ye couldna see them. And they made her touched in the head, because where she saw pain and loss, she should have seen honor and courage."

Her words cut the legs right out from beneath him. He collapsed on the bench. "If I had been courageous, me brother might still be alive. But I told her, right after, that he died savin' me."

"He died savin' both of us, and ye might have as well had the Indians not been driven back. But 'twas not for a lack of courage." She knelt before him, her cape puddling about her. "Ye fought the warrior that came at ye, Alex. Ye both did. And the reason he came was because of me."

"Nay." He reached for her face, fingering the side. "Ye stayed in the canes where I put ye, did ye not?"

A sudden flash of her came as he had seen her then, fifteen years younger, just a glimpse through the stalks. Her eyes wide with absolute terror and her knees drawn up to her chest. That chest heaving with silent sobs as tears ran down her face. The suddenness of the memory almost tore a groan from his throat. He dropped his hand to her arm, squeezing the fabric of her cloak so he would not hurt her with his desperate grasp.

She nodded. "Aye, but I couldna hold back me cryin' from fear. If I had been silent as ye bid me..."

"Elspeth, nay." He couldn't bear the intense sadness, the self-reproach that shuttered her expression.

"How do ye ken? Ye still dinna even remember." Her lips pursed. Tears glistened in her eyes, and she sniffed. "But can ye not see how I could never look on ye with anything but love?" She reached up and drew his head down toward her, her small fingers questing beneath his hair. Sudden vulnerability pierced him. He'd forgotten he had thrown his hat across the room. "Can ye not see how ye are the walkin' embodiment of sacrifice? For each of these blows, ye took for me."

When her lips touched his forehead, first in one place, then another, he gasped. Such tenderness he had never known. Not just acceptance, but admiration. And had she said...love?

"I would do it again."

She pulled the whispered truth right out of him. She pulled him to her like a magnet. He stared into her blue eyes, their breath mingling. His came faster. Inches away, her lips beckoned. Tenderness of this sort might salve his wounds as nothing had before. He could drown his pain in her sweetness.

She laid her forehead against his. "Alex, ye must forgive her."

Still, he struggled for breath, barely resisting the urge to kiss her. "Who?" He cared not. She could make him forget every other woman on the planet.

"Yer mother."

The words froze him, breaking the moment.

"Not just the braves." She moved back just an inch, her whisper intense. "Ye have to forgive her too. Only then will ye be free."

What she asked stabbed straight to his heart, right when he'd laid it open to her. Before he could withdraw, the door opened, and Reverend Lawrence stood silhouetted in the bright light, leaning on his cane. "Elspeth." His voice thundered through the cabin, in no wise weary after his sermonizing. "'Tis time to go. Come, daughter."

The request left no room for argument. Though she flushed and created a larger space between them, she did not jump to her father's bidding. "Aye, Da," she said, but she reached for

Alex's hand. She uncurled his fingers, speaking softly. "Will ye open it? Let the hate go and receive what God would give? 'Twould be more than ye could imagine."

"Lass..." How could he do that? How could he tear down every defense he had built up, all at her mere request? Who would he be without his quest for vengeance? It had been the fixture on his internal compass for as long as he could remember.

"Come Thursday." She kissed his fingers before rising from her knees. "I have something I want to show you."

Did he even want to know what that was?

~

E lspeth and her father did not speak as the wagon lumbered away from the fort, driven by a private who worked with the horses. She couldn't ignore Da's silence as he sat beside her in the back with his leg pillowed. But neither could she dwell on it, for most of her remained back in the officers' quarters with Alex.

She closed her eyes, feeling again his dark locks sliding over her fingers, the firm scars beneath. Picturing the need in his eyes. Much as she had longed to let emotion take its course, she had been compelled to speak the truth to him. The full truth. And it had not shattered the bond between them.

"He is not ready."

Her father's statement did shatter the silence, though. "What?" She opened her eyes and turned her head.

"To give whatever ye need from him, Elspeth." His light-blue eyes bore holes through her, unwavering even as the wagon jostled them. "The things I have learned from him these many weeks, the way he stormed away after the sermon today, all support it."

The cold draught of air she took inflated her lungs. "I dinna agree. Ye didna hear the things that were said between us today."

Da puffed out a frosty breath. "And *not* said. To find ye in such an improper position, alone with a man..." He let out a moan and rubbed his face.

"Oh, Da, ye act as though we dinna ken him, when ye ken well enough I have been waitin' for him me whole life." And finally today, he had let her past his walls. In her gentleness, he had glimpsed what was possible when he allowed love in—she was sure of it.

"His anger drives him, Elspeth, and he is not ready to release it. If ye get close to him, he will only hurt ye. I had hoped it would be otherwise, but it seems my hopes were misplaced."

"Nay. They were not." She grasped her father's mittened hand and patted it between hers, rather frantically. "Ye will see." After she saw Alex on Thursday, the dam would break at last, and he would be able to give her back the love she longed for.

CHAPTER 17

*A*lex grumbled to himself as Elspeth led him on a merry chase along bridle paths northeast of New Bordeaux, staying just far enough ahead that he couldn't ask her their destination. The cold, wet season, which seemed to stretch on forever like the forest around them, ensured that no bud or shoot yet dared to put forth. Damp leaves in various shades of brown carpeted the forest floor, while the drays of squirrels wedged into bare branches above, reaching to an equally dull sky. The deep green of the fir and pine and the light-bronze leaves of the beech provided the only relief to winter's monotony.

He must be touched in the head to follow the lass so blindly. She'd bewitched him with her sweetness. Having tasted of it, he longed for more—against all reason. He'd even thought on what she said about his mother. Elspeth's words rang true. If forgiveness were only a logical decision, he might could forgive Leah Morris. Leah Bane now, married to one of her distant cousins there on the coast. But then one of what must have been a hundred small rejections over the years would rise before his eyes, and the pain would immobilize his will.

His will. His will had always prevailed. Was Reverend Lawrence right? He was not free, but a captive?

Finally, they turned onto a little-used wagon road, and he was able to trot Charlie up beside her father's gelding. "Lass, where are we goin'?"

She peered at him from the side of her hood. "Ye will see."

"Why are ye bein' so mysterious? And why did ye ask me to come on a Thursday?"

"Do ye not ken what today is?"

Did she not remember what he'd said about games? He grunted his frustration. "Thursday."

"Aye. Thursday, February first, 1776."

"Me felicitations. Ye keep track of the calendar." And what significance did today hold?

Up ahead, the narrow lane approached a sizeable creek that had flooded its banks. Brown water stood in the boggy hollow, obscuring the trunks of trees and the ground on either side of the road for many feet past the creek bank. Elspeth slowed her mount.

Alex scoffed a bit triumphantly. "But apparently, not very good track of the local trails. I dinna think we will be crossin' that today."

"Nay." She stopped and swung her leg over the gelding. "We willna. For this is our destination."

Following her lead, Alex dismounted and led Charlie toward the creek. No people or buildings were anywhere in sight. The rushing of water and the whisper of the damp breeze through the evergreens were the only sounds. Eerie sounds.

Something uneasy turned over in his gut. "Lass, what are ye aboot?"

She turned to him. "Do ye not recognize this spot, Alex?"

"Ye ken I have been gone from these parts many a year, Elspeth, and I have no call to scout this ground from the fort."

Despite his words, his midsection tightened. This place felt like the end of the road in more ways than one.

"This is where it happened." Holding her horse's reins, she stared at him with unwavering blue eyes. "Sixteen years ago, on February first, 1760, you and I were here. Leana was here. Ethan was here. This was the last place we saw them."

The tightening became a wrenching, as if someone wrung him out like a shirt on laundry day. On "execution day." His knees went weak, and for a moment, it seemed the ground might swallow him whole. "Ah, lass, what have ye done?" The betrayal of her trickery pained him almost as much as the place did.

Her expression pleaded for his understanding. "I have brought ye here to remember because this is where I had to come to stop me own nightmares. Da brought me here. To be free."

The breath he drew whistled in between his teeth. "But I wager he asked ye first."

Her face twisted. "Would ye have come, had I asked?"

"Ye ken the answer to that." He couldn't look at the place. The trees closed around him, silent witnesses to the unspeakable, forcing him to hear their testimony. The ground itself seemed to cry out. He placed his hands on Charlie's saddle and raised his foot for the stirrup.

Elspeth smacked the stallion's rump, and Charlie turned in a circle, snorting. As Alex followed his horse, she pointed. "There is the bank where I showed ye the panther tracks. The canes are still there, though they have been eaten or cut back."

His attention wavered, making his second attempt to mount as clumsy as the first. Or maybe 'twas because his legs had turned to jelly. Charlie sidestepped, and Alex let him go.

Elspeth released her mount and extended her hand.

He froze in place as a voice he hadn't heard in sixteen years echoed in his mind.

Alex, what are ye doin'? Get over here and help us with the wagon.

His lean, dark-haired brother had been twelve at the time, his voice just deepening, but it had cracked in the middle of the summons. "Ethan came to get me. I wasna helpin'. That was why he was with us when the attack started."

Alex hadn't moved, so Elspeth took several steps in his direction and took his hand, anyway. "That was my fault, not yers."

The gray woods echoed with the memory of gunshots and war whoops, that spine-chilling portent that all of life was about to change. Or end. A shudder ran down his body. "Ye shouldna have brought me here." He barely registered her squeezing his fingers.

"Nay. I believe ye can only release the past if ye face it head on, like the enemy it has been. Ye dinna turn yer back on yer enemies, do ye, Alex Morris?"

Panic clawed its way up his spine, the same sensation that had driven them into hiding. "He couldna get into the canes as far, could he? Then when the brave came near..." *Swish, swish, swish.* The memory of the sound of the tomahawk cutting through the canes buckled his knees, and he knelt in the dirt beside the road as his brother's warning whispered from the past. *Get down. Dinna move.* "I had to do something. I drew me knife."

Elspeth huddled beside him, an arm encircling his back. "Ye drew it because he heard me cryin'."

"Nay." Alex shook his head. The scene played as vividly in his mind now as if it happened in real time, the flashes coming fast and hard. "He never turned his head. But he was gettin' too close."

"Is that true?" She gasped. "I always thought I brought him over. I have been so sorry for that." She began to weep softly.

"I can see his face." Split Ear...years younger, a warrior

fierce and painted red and black, his hair hanging in a scalp lock. Terror tore at Alex's chest, and he bent forward, breathing fast. He covered his eyes, attempting to rub the snatches of vision away.

He must stop this. He tried to get up, but the weight of the past sat upon his shoulders, as immovable as a boulder.

"Oh, my darling…" Elspeth's hand stroked his neck.

Her touch there brought another memory. "Ethan jumped on his back." His knife, flashing. The brave roaring in rage. The next things Alex remembered bowed him to the earth with a primal cry of horror and loss. Even now, he had to shut it off. "Oh, God. God, help me."

Mercifully, God answered, or perhaps memory did, as the recollection of the blows that fell on him and his brother as Ethan had attempted to shield him faded to blackness. Alex had no idea how long he crouched there before the call of a mourning dove and Elspeth's gentle keening reached his ears.

It had been so that day, too—the next thing he heard, the crying. When his eye had finally cracked open, she had scooted toward him, her little face tear-streaked and terrified, reaching for his outstretched hand.

He raised his head a fraction now. "Ye came to me."

A soft gasp, and the weight of her crouching over him lifted from his back. "Aye. I thought ye were dead. And then I saw yer finger twitch. And I ken I wasna alone."

"Ye cut yer petticoat with me knife and used it to bind me wounds."

"And ye took me upstream."

Aye. Away from the horrible scene, by then deserted of both family and foe. They had huddled together beneath a rock overhang for countless hours, for days, until they finally heard English voices calling and boots tramping through the forest.

Alex pushed himself to a position on his knees, which had gone numb beneath him. "Why so long?" he whispered. "Why did they not come back for us?" The sense of abandonment...it had started before his mother ever failed to meet his eye.

"I suppose in their panic and fear, they took ye for dead and me for stolen." She reached out to wipe the tears that wet his face. "We werena the only ones rescued, ye ken. They found nine children alive when they returned to the area with help."

Alex turned his face toward Elspeth, staring at her even as he seemed to hover above both of them crouching there. If only he *could* leave his own body. Fly far from this place. Never remember again. His lips were so numb he could barely get them to move. "What have ye taken from me?" The question came out ragged, croaking.

She sucked in a quick breath. "What?" Her damp eyelashes blinked rapidly.

"Ye forced me here against me will, bowed me to the very earth, and stole the one thing that kept the pain at bay. The forgetting."

"Alex." Her fingers grasped his waistcoat. "To heal, ye must face the pain. But ye dinna have to do it alone. God gave us each other to cling to. He did so then, and He does so now."

"That makes it all the worse...that ye couldna leave well enough alone. Ye, who should of all people have understood."

She grabbed his hands. "'Tis because I love ye that I canna leave ye alone. Remember Da's sermon?" She pried open his fingers. "Ye must give up the pain and anger, but how can ye do that if dinna ken what ye're givin' up? Now ye do. Give it to Him, Alex. He will heal ye. Ye may have survived all those years ago, but ye have never been whole."

"I allowed me brother to take the blows meant for me." Self-loathing gave force to his words as the pain of it threatened to rip him in two. "Now I ken exactly what he endured. How can I ever forgive meself, much less give that to God?"

"The same way I did, for the blows ye took for me. And who better to understand than one who took the punishment for us all?" Leaning forward, she held onto his hands as though they were her lifeline. Her face lit with a fierce inner light. "Oh, my love, can ye not see the beauty in it?"

"Beauty?" He spat the word as though it was poison from his mouth. He jerked his hands away. "Nay. All I see in this place is blood and death. Pain and evil. And the face of my enemy, who I will hold in reckoning if it is the last thing I do." The resolve hardened in him, satisfying in its solidity, restoring his focus.

Elspeth shook her head. "But how? The man who attacked us is long gone, Alex."

"Nay. He is near at hand. He is Inoli's uncle." He took a grim satisfaction in the horror that swept across her face. "The man who earned his name from me brother's blade—Split Ear. Ye wanted to ken why I avoided the boy. Now ye do. Someone must pay for what happened here. I will make certain he does."

~

Elspeth had followed Alex from the woods rather than the other way around. At the turnoff to the mission, he had left her, and she hadn't seen him since.

Two weeks later, she sat at her spinning wheel, attempting to teach the girls how to pull a fiber directly from a clump of flax and spin it onto the loose end of roving wrapped around the spindle. She intended to push the treadle only enough to pull the roving taut, but with the thud of one of Inoli's arrows hitting the target outside, her foot thudded down, too, and the thin thread snapped.

Like her patience. Like her composure.

With a soft moan, she leaned forward and let the tears almost always just behind her eyes escape. What had she done? How had her carefully laid plans backfire so horribly?

Watching Alex face his demons had nearly been as difficult

as facing her own on her first trip back to Long Canes Creek. But it had been a needful part of the cleansing. When he had remembered, she had been certain her decision to return him to the site of the massacre had been the right one. But instead of finding a cleansing by the water, he had accepted a second baptism in revenge. And to think that the man he sought had been so close this whole time. Now his reactions to Split Ear and Inoli made so much more sense.

"Cap-tain!" Inoli's jubilant cry brought Elspeth's head up from the spinning wheel.

She knocked her stool over in her haste to run out of the room. Indeed, a figure in blue and white approached on horseback. Her heart thundered, and she lost her breath. Inoli capered about, waving his bow. He had asked about Alex every day, wondering when they might go hunting again.

But as the rider drew closer, Elspeth clenched a hand to her chest. The horse was dark, not bay. And the man atop it, while possessing the same upright bearing, was broader and shorter. She called Inoli over to her and held him against her, as if the nearness of his firm little body could staunch the flow of disappointment from her heart.

"Miss Lawrence." Their caller lifted his hat when he drew up before them. Ah, yes—Alex's new lieutenant, Rawdon. She recognized him. So did Inoli, whose shoulders sagged. "Captain Morris asked that I stop by and see if you and your father might be in need of anything."

She still couldn't get used to Alex being called *captain*. She swallowed past the lump in her throat. "Where is he?"

"He has gone on a long scout, miss, but he wanted to make sure you were not in want of anything."

His choice of words stole her ability to reply. *In want of anything*...yes, of sight of Alex. Of the sound of his voice. Of his forgiveness. His understanding. For him to look upon her with tenderness again. She wavered in the yard, and only Inoli held her up.

Da had limped to the door behind her and was able to answer where she could not. "Thankee, Lieutenant. We are doing just fine, but we appreciate ye checkin', all the same."

"Very good, sir. If that changes, just send word to the fort." He made to wheel his stallion around, but Elspeth's breathless request stayed him.

"When Captain Morris returns..."

"Yes, miss?"

"When Captain Morris returns, will ye please tell him we would like to see him?"

"Of course." He tipped his hat again and galloped away.

The disappointment was twice as painful as the waiting. Elspeth released Inoli to return to his target practice, but he slunk off toward the creek. She made it back to the steps before tears blurred her eyes, causing her to stumble over the first one. Down she went, in a heap of petticoats and unchecked sobs.

"Oh, lass." Da stumped forward until he could ease himself down onto the steps next to her. He slipped an arm about her shaking shoulders. "Do ye want to tell me what happened when last ye saw Alex?"

She covered her face with her hands. "I took him to Long Canes Creek."

Da went still beside her. "Ye did? Ye *didna*..."

Miserably, she nodded. "He didna take it well."

"Well, surely...surely, ye asked him first."

Elspeth moaned and scrubbed her eyes. "Nay. I ken he wouldna have gone."

"Then ye shouldna have taken him." The indignation in her father's response brought on a fresh bought of weeping. "Lord have mercy, lass. What were ye thinkin'?"

She lifted her sticky face. "That seein' the place again rid me of me own lurid imaginin's."

"But how many talks did we share before that, how many prayers, how many Scriptures? Did I not tell ye the lad was not ready?" His hands on her shoulders vibrated her ever so slightly.

She deserved this chastisement. 'Twas a relief to have spoken aloud what she had been telling herself for days. "Aye. Ye did. But I thought I saw different. He was respondin' better when we spoke of it. And to Inoli." She opened her hands in front of her. Empty. They were so empty. Worse than before.

"Aye, he was makin' progress with the boy, and now that may be ended as well."

How could Da blame her for trying to do what he himself had aimed to? "I wanted him to remember and forgive as ye said in yer sermon, so he could be free to receive blessings."

"And ye were certain that blessin' included ye. Am I right?" He thumbed her chin.

"Can it not?" Elspeth's lower lip trembled. Surely, God had brought Alex back into her life for a reason. He had heard her prayers. Why would she, of all people, not be used to help Alex find healing?

"Tell me, when ye contrived this plan, did ye do so for him... or for yerself?"

The awful truth struck her like a falling oak branch, and she released a little puff of air. "I wanted him...I wanted him to be able to love me back." The groan tore out of her, and she covered her face again. She had told Alex she loved him, and not only had he not responded in kind. He had left her.

"Oh, lass." Da drew her head onto his shoulder, where she cried while he smoothed her unruly hair.

"I'm so ashamed. Ye warned me, but I didna listen. And now I've ruined everything."

A soft chuckle rumbled from her father's chest, and she drew back a smidgen. "There ye go, runnin' ahead of the

Almighty again. Who's to say how this will end, Elspeth? Alex has heard the truth. He needs to digest it."

"But will he digest it, or will he spit it out?"

He firmed his mouth, angling his face to one side. "That is not under yer control, now, is it? We none of us are meant to be another's savior. Let God do His work. Let Alex make his choice. Do ye think ye might give the lad time this go-round?"

Elspeth peeked at him. "How much time?" Perhaps she showed she hadn't learned her lesson, but for six months, she had known the satisfaction of an almost-whole heart. Bearing its rending again was more than a body could stand.

Da shook his head. "Maybe he will come when I next preach at the fort."

She pressed her lips together. "Dinna take this wrong, but I doubt ye have more ground to stand on than I do, where yer sermonizing is concerned."

Da laughed, then he took her hand in both of his. "Then we will have to pray, Elspeth. Pray as never before." He peered at her with the discernment of all the Scottish ministers who had gone before him. "But target yer prayers for his freedom, not the meetin' of yer own desires."

Elspeth blinked, and another tear rolled down her cheek. Would it come to that...God asking her to give Alex up? Could she countenance that?

A movement behind her drew her notice. Galilani stepped onto the porch, Leana's ragged doll clasped in her hands. She lowered it onto Elspeth's lap and patted her head much as Elspeth had often patted Galilani's.

"Thankee." Elspeth touched the sweet child's hand and then hugged the doll.

Nay. God would not ask her to put Alex on the altar. She had already given up too much.

~

On the Sunday in February that Reverend Lawrence was to preach at Fort Charlotte, Alex crossed the shallow ford of the Savannah River on Charlie and made a visit of goodwill to their neighbors at Fort James. The palisade covered an acre on a plateau overlooking the shoals at the fork of the Broad and Savannah and was now manned by fifty Georgia Rangers. Though they were mounted and well-equipped, they lacked the smart appearance of the Third South Carolina. Many had married Creek women and wore deerskin hunting shirts and leggings in lieu of a uniform. But they welcomed a former comrade and vowed aid when needed in the spring.

That aid might become needful they all ken well. England had declared the colonies in a state of rebellion. British warships had arrived in the mouth of the Savannah River in January. But Captain Caldwell wrote that the Patriots were constructing a stockade of almost impenetrable palmetto wood on Sullivan's Island. Under Colonel William Moultrie, the new fort with its thirty-one cannons would offer Charlestown's first line of defense.

They would be equally ready to repel any attack in the backcountry. 'Twas but a matter of time before Cameron and Stuart roused the Cherokees against the Patriots. The wait ate at Alex like a hungry parasite. The nightmares and waking memories that now plagued him fed his impatience.

Sometimes, when he lay on his cot at night or rode through the greening woods, he would hear Elspeth's voice in his head, speaking of love. He should not have opened himself to the possibility. She might make him laugh. She might stir his desire. She might even at times breach his walls with her tenderness. What man would not want more of all those things? But could he, in truth, give her back what she offered him?

He could never allow himself to need Elspeth as much as she needed him. How many times would she push and he would pull, would she pry and he shut down, before she realized he could not satisfy her? That all that lay at his core was emptiness?

When that happened, the rejection would be worse than never having had her. And Alex had spent his entire life preparing for the worst.

His mother had been right. Some things from the past needed to be blocked out. And the Lawrences were his reminder.

CHAPTER 18

The redbud trees still vied with the dogwoods for glory when Ulisi told them it was time for their first spring ramble in the woods. In the past, Elspeth had relished their outings, which usually took most of the day. They would set out while the dew clung to the morning glories and later have a picnic along a burbling brook, not returning until well into the afternoon. 'Twas rather like a treasure hunt, pushing back winter's deadfall to reveal the arrow-shaped leaves of the ginger plant or sending forth a cry of triumph when someone discovered a new patch of ginseng.

Today, however, Ulisi's explanations about the uses of the plants seemed endless. The Cherokees employed literally everything to some purpose—roots, shoots, stems, leaves, flowers, and bark. And their stoic grandmother surely ken them all. Their baskets filled before noon, both of herbals and edibles. They had plenty of cleaver shoots, chickweed, and fresh curly dock leaves to cook up with the salted ham and corn pones for supper.

While Ulisi helped the girls harvest yarrow and plantain nearby, along a more northerly part of Russell's Creek, Elspeth sat on a rock and fingered a clump of lavender spring beauty blossoms on the bank. For the hundredth time, the notion of riding to Fort Charlotte tickled her mind. What would Alex do if she just showed up at the gate this evening and demanded to see him?

She could put an end to the not knowing once and for all.

Nay. She could not do that. If Alex wanted to see her, he would have come long before now. Not only had they sent the message by Lieutenant Rawdon bidding Alex visit, but her father had followed it with a written missive. An invitation to sup. No reply had been received. If she forced a confrontation, as she had before, it stood a better chance of ending badly than the way she might wish.

Sacrifice—Alex had made a huge one for her long ago. Now it seemed God asked her to do the same for him...by letting him go. Most days, she had nearly made her peace with it. But times like this, when the earth broke forth with new life and promise, the longing returned deep in her belly, followed by the ache that throbbed with the fierceness of a rotten molar.

At last, Ulisi deemed they had collected a sufficient assort-ment of the earth's bounty—always leaving enough for that which was diminished to regenerate—and they started the long hike home. When they entered the clearing, Elspeth frowned. No curl of smoke came from the chimney. No figure in waistcoat and breeks strolled out onto the porch to exclaim over their finds. And no one chopped wood at the block where she had left Inoli at work. Da must have taken him for a ride.

She set about cleaning dirty hands, faces, and moccasins, followed by overseeing supper preparations. By the time horse hooves sounded in the yard, they had set the board and heated the food.

Elspeth turned from the hearth with a long-handled spoon in her hand as Da entered alone. "Is Inoli seein' to the horse?"

Her father's cheerful greeting faded to a bewildered frown. "I thought he was with you."

"On an herb hunt? That is women's work." No Cherokee male worth his woven belt would be caught doing such. What was Da thinking? "I left him choppin' wood."

"He was gone when I set out. I figured he had followed ye for some reason."

"We did not see him all day." Had he been about some prank, he would have revealed himself during their foraging. "But then...where is he?"

Their eyes turned toward the door at the same time. Da's Brown Bess now sat there, but Inoli's musket was missing, along with his powder horn.

Elspeth let out a gasp. "He has gone hunting."

Her father extended a hand as if to stay her. "There is no cause to panic, now."

"But he should have been back already."

"Not necessarily. Cherokee men often hunt all day, even for several days at a time."

Elspeth's eyes rounded. "But he is alone! He canna spend the night in the forest. Even when the boys go off to prepare for manhood, the men look out for them." And Inoli was not old enough for even that.

Her father reached for his musket. "I will look for him."

"Thankee." She faced the flames again, composing herself. She would not rest until the boy was safely returned. If they allowed something to happen to him...

A few moments later, horse hooves clattered away from the house. Elspeth took a breath and turned to face four sets of wide, unblinking, dark eyes. "Dinna fash." She waved her hands out. "*Hi-ga.*"

Though they doubtless did not ken the meaning of the first instruction, they certainly understood her directive to eat. Their little tummies had to be rumbly after a day of traipsing over root and rock. Ulisi hastened to serve up the supper, and Elspeth accepted her plate but found she could only pick at the meat, bread, and greens. At last, she slid the remains onto the hungriest child's empty plate and went out onto the porch.

Through the budding trees, evening painted the sky in tints of red and orange. A cool breeze caressed her cheek, bringing with it the loamy scent of freshly turned earth from her garden. Peep frogs started a chorus down by the creek. She shuddered, for despite the beauties of spring, a young boy was facing the gathering darkness alone.

Was he hurt? Lost? Even though Cherokees were expert trackers and canny with directions, Inoli's world had remained small during his time here. He was unfamiliar with the lay of the land. He only ken the way to his village and to the fort. And the places Alex had taken him hunting.

Elspeth stiffened. That was it. If Inoli hadn't headed back to his village, he would be wherever he had gone with Cap-tain.

She paced the porch and prayed, stopping every so often to cock an ear for the return of her father. At last, he trotted on his gelding back into the clearing—with no smaller form astride, before or behind him. Elspeth's heart sank.

Da called out to her. "Is he here yet?"

She hurried down the steps. "Nay! Where did ye go?" Reaching for the bridle, she held the horse while her father dismounted, moving stiffly from his injury. He had probably been too long in the saddle.

"I made a thorough sweep around the house and rode a good ways both north and south on the Fort Charlotte and Old Cherokee Road."

Elspeth closed her eyes and let out a soft breath before she jammed her foot into the stirrup. She answered her father's startled expression as she swung up onto his gelding. "I think I ken where he is."

But she couldn't find him alone. She finally had her excuse

to ride to the fort...and it was not one she would have wished for.

Elspeth did not stop to respond to her father's question before digging her heels into the horse's sides.

~

*T*he sky over the Savannah River burned a brilliant orange when a commotion at the gate raised Alex's head from his chiseling of a rifle flint. A slight rider in petticoats conferred with the guard on duty, who pointed in his direction.

Elspeth.

He straightened, his pulse up-ticking. A moment later, she rode toward him, her horse's trot telling him this was no social call.

But of course it wouldn't be. Not after he had ignored her last two invitations. He could think of no other way to sever the connection between them before it became even more painful. His stomach twisted with both guilt and dread. He set aside his chisel and rose from the porch of the officers' quarters.

"What's wrong?"

She turned the gelding to one side of him. "Inoli. He is missing. We think he went huntin'. He took his musket."

"Alone?"

"Aye." She lifted herself in her stirrups, clearly impatient.

"How long has he been gone?"

"Most of the day, we fear. We were out that whole time and came home to find him gone. Da already searched around the cabin and up and down the road." She dipped her chin, avoiding his gaze. "We thought...maybe he went huntin' where ye took him. I canna explain it, but I just...I just feel as though he could be in danger."

Alex glanced at the setting sun. Aye, the boy was unfamiliar with the land and too young to overnight in the forest without supervision. Surprising, the shiver of fear that purled through him. Fear for the child of his enemy.

"Alex, I would not have come here if there were anything else...anyone else who could help."

She had taken his reflection for hesitation. He reached for the gelding's bridle and stroked the horse's nose. "Ye came to the right place. I'm in mind of the big ridge where he killed the turkey, a couple miles from here."

"Good. Let's go." Elspeth extended her hand down to him, but he shook his head.

"I go alone. Charlie is picketed in the meadow outside the fort. And I will need to get me things."

Her face flushed. "Are not two sets of ears, eyes, and hands better than one? Ride with me and there will be no delay."

"No offense, lass, but we are fast losin' the light, and I can move quicker on me own. If I need help, I will come get ye."

She hesitated, then nodded. "Verra well." As she turned her horse, her lack of argument testified to the seriousness of her concern.

Alex dashed inside the cabin for his weapons, powder, and possibles bag, then fetched the heavy saddle from the fort's tack room. By the time he located Lieutenant Rawdon to inform him of his departure, many precious minutes had slipped by.

He found Elspeth waiting just outside the stone walls. He did not have it in him to be irritated with her. "There's no need for ye to follow me, lass. All will be well."

"Will it, though? I dinna feel good about ye goin' alone."

Despite looking to him for help, she would not look at him. A shaft of regret pierced his gut. She deserved far better than him, and one day, she would realize it. But she should not hang her head for calling on him for this. He would have touched her boot in the stirrup to reassure her, but his hands were full. Words gently spoken would have to do.

Alex shifted the weight of the saddle to his right hip, quirking one side of his mouth up. "The boy likely had some notion of proving himself." Or gaining attention, seeing as how Alex had deserted him. "He is probably sitting by a fire in some clearing even now, debating his bravery in sleepin' under the stars."

Elspeth's fingers flexed around the reins. "Oh, I pray that is so."

"Go home and wait there. I promise, I will bring ye a report posthaste."

Her face hardened. "Nay. Dinna bring me a report, Alex Morris. Bring me a boy." Never was a command spoken with more expectation by a general.

He gave her a nod. This, at least, he could do for her. He was a scout. How hard could a boy be to find? Finding him before dark would be the challenge. And Alex did not dare arrive at the mission without him.

Elspeth kept him in sight as she turned the gelding, then clicked her tongue. Her horse trotted away.

Within minutes, Alex rode in the same direction. As he cut off on a bridle path that wound up the ridge between Fort Charlotte and Russell's Creek, a shot sounded ahead. 'Twas a good time of day for the boy to take down a deer if he had been lying in wait. Alex urged Charlie to pick up his pace, but the peace of the hills contradicted any concern.

Studded with pink and white blossoms, the forest glowed with soft golden light. Birds called their goodnights from the branches above, and faint rustlings in the thickets signaled small game nestling into their dens and holes. As the land climbed, rolling vistas spread on either side, obscured in the east by purple and gray fingers of night. Silence settled with the dark.

The game trail that led down into the ravine lay mostly in shadow. A tributary of Russell's Creek ran at the bottom, offering a hunter advantage with a view of both ridges through generously spaced trees.

When Alex urged Charlie down the path, he snorted and sidestepped. "Come, boy. What is it?" Alex patted his neck. He pulled his rifle from its sheath and held it upright with one hand while tugging the reins with the other. Slowly, the stallion moved forward, his ears swiveling. From the lip of the ridge that butted out over a series of boulders just ahead, anything out of place would become obvious.

As they skirted a tangle of mountain laurel in full leaf, a snorting, shuffling sound came from the trail ahead, maybe forty yards below and to the right, where it became visible as it passed before the rock overhang. Alex raised himself in his stirrups and narrowed his gaze. Was that...yes, a powder horn. Lying on the ground. He drew breath to call Inoli's name. And then his brain registered the rest of the scene.

A few feet from the remains of a deer carcass, a massive black bear paced the level area in front of the boulders. The creature's ears lay back. It huffed and pawed the ground. And then it galloped toward the second rock, where a patch of deerskin clothing could be seen in a crack just big enough for a boy to wedge himself into. A boy who gave a keening cry. This was no bluff charge.

Alex whipped his rifle up to this shoulder, but Charlie let out a scream of a whinny and spun in a circle. Alex's broadside shot entered the bear's sinewy shoulder. It let out a roar, stumbled, then pivoted, turning their way. Alex jammed the rifle into the sheath and drew the dragoon pistol on his right hip. He raised and cocked the loaded weapon as he saw what he hadn't been able to before—the blood streaking the bear's other side, where Inoli's earlier shot must have gone awry. The reason a normally timid creature had attacked. And now, it barreled up the hill straight toward them.

Charlie spun, bolting. The sudden movement laid Alex

back in the saddle...but not back far enough. A tree branch whacked the side of his head. His finger tightened on the trigger and fired the pistol into the air as he tumbled from the saddle. He landed partly on his side, partly on his back. He dropped the weapon.

Branches cracked. Grunts punctuated heavy breaths. Feet pounded the earth.

He raised partway up and reached for his left dragoon pistol. A bellow blasted hot air into his face, and equally hot knives sliced upward across his ribs, spinning him around. A blur of black fur ran past him. Turned. Beady eyes fixed on Alex. Teeth clacked, a sound like bones breaking. The first swipe had intended to disadvantage him. This would be the pass that would kill him—or at least maim him for life.

He had one shot. Alex raised his shaking hand and aimed just above the pointed brown snout. He cocked the weapon.

The bear lurched forward.

Alex pulled the trigger.

CHAPTER 19

*D*arkness had long since fallen when steps thudded on the front porch, stumbled, and thumped.

Elspeth ran and flung open the door. Alex knelt on the top step, hatless, his dark hair trailing over his face, Inoli clutched in his arms. From the looks of it, he had narrowly saved them both from a tumble.

The lamplight illuminated ragged tears in the boy's leggings, soaked with blood. Elspeth breathed out a prayer and hurried forward, calling for her father. "What happened?"

Alex rose with Inoli still in his arms but relinquished him with a grunt when Da appeared at Elspeth's side.

Inoli's eyes glowed as big and round as the full moon. "*Yo-nv!* Cap-tain shoot."

The air whooshed from Elspeth's lungs, and her gaze swung to Alex. "A bear?"

He gave a nod, bracing on the porch post. "Inoli startled it from feastin' on a deer. He winged it, and the beast had cornered him in some rocks when I came upon them." He followed them into the house as Da bore Inoli to his Windsor chair, deposited him there, and draped his wounded limb tenderly over the stool. Alex tilted his head toward it. "He couldna quite get all of him hidden."

"Praise be that ye came in time." Elspeth handed her father a clean rag and whirled for the door. "Remove his legging and staunch the bleedin' with this. I will fetch Ulisi."

"I must go back out...for Charlie." Alex followed her.

"Is he hurt?"

"Nay, just spooked."

Elspeth tossed him a gawping glance. "Ye mean ye carried Inoli all the way here?"

"Aye."

The realization and the faltering of Alex's steps turned her around. She gasped. For not only was his waistcoat streaked with blood, 'twas also torn...in the same pattern as Inoli's leggings. "Ye are hurt!" Her lungs refusing to inflate, she drew him back toward the lamplight to inspect the damage.

Inoli lifted his head from watching Da tend his leg. "Bear run at Cap-tain."

"Must go for Charlie..." Alex attempted to cover the wound, but she pushed his hand away.

Elspeth swallowed. "Ye are going nowhere. These claw marks are deep." Even as she spoke, a rivulet of blood gushed from the darkest gash. She raised her voice to call the Cherokee woman from across the breezeway. "Ulisi!"

"Me rifle..."

"Wheesht, man." It provided some comfort to give back the same chiding he had given her on more than one occasion, but precious little. She fumbled with his waistcoat buttons.

He took an almost inaudible breath when the material pulled taut about his ribs. "Do ye ken how much a piece like that costs?"

"Do ye ken how much yer *life* costs?" Shooting him a silencing glare, Elspeth unbuckled the belt that held his pistols. One was missing. She eased the other from his waist and his waistcoat from his shoulders, laying both on the bench next to the table.

Ulisi appeared in the doorway, took one look, and whisked out again. She shooed the girls who had followed her from their sleeping chamber back the way they had come.

Elspeth reached for Alex's stock.

"I can do it, lass." But when he began to unwrap the long strip of fabric, he paused, wincing, and fresh red soaked the tattered white cotton shirt.

Gently pushing his hands down, she firmed her mouth and unwound the linen. The intimate gesture brought heat to her cheeks, but her stomach churned with unease. They could stanch the bleeding, but had the bear's swipe injured anything vital? Would Inoli walk with a limp? What dirt and fabric might have penetrated Alex's wound? If infection took hold...

She allowed herself to be nudged away, still holding Alex's gaze, as Ulisi arrived. The older woman plunked her herbal box on the table, speaking firmly in Cherokee. As Ulisi helped Alex shrug out of his shirt, Elspeth turned to the box, opening it and locating the crushed, dried geranium root and yarrow leaves used to stop blood flow. She mixed the two together in two small earthenware bowls while Ulisi pressed a folded rag to Alex's ribcage. He clutched it in place as she spread a blanket in front of the hearth and pointed imperiously to it.

Under other circumstances, Elspeth might have chuckled at how the proud man meekly lowered himself to the floor. But at the moment, the sight of the bloody gashes wrapping around Alex's side and well-muscled chest set her knees all atremble.

She couldn't do this. She could not allow him to see how much she feared for him. She had already shown him far too much. She had been an open book whilst he had held his secrets. Elspeth fetched the whiskey Da kept for medicinal purposes and went to tend Inoli while leaving the other bowl of herbs to Ulisi.

"Hold the cloth under his leg while I cleanse it," she told her father. Then she met Inoli's wide eyes as she held the bottle aloft. "This will sting." She repeated the warning in Cherokee.

Though his one eye twitched, he gave a single nod. Elspeth angled the tip just over his wounds and tilted the bottle. The boy showed the bravery of his people, not making a sound as the liquid splashed on raw flesh or as she patted his leg dry.

Alex was not being so cooperative. Though he issued only a tight hiss when Ulisi similarly washed out his gashes, he attempted to wave her away as she applied the herbs. "Bandage me and let me go, woman. Charlie is out there God kens where."

With a grunt, Da shot to his feet. "I will go find the bloody horse." His exclamation drew Alex's stare as well as Elspeth's. Da blew out a breath. "Only lie still, man, and let the women tend ye. Aye?"

Alex went limp, lowering his head back to the floor. "Aye. Thankee. Check the ridge between here and the fort."

Ulisi continued her efficient ministrations.

Da stomped across the room and laid on his coat, hat, and musket. "Yer horse likely cantered back to Fort Charlotte. I will fetch him and also let yer lieutenant ken where ye are." He directed a threatening stare at Alex. "Ye are in no condition to go anywhere this night."

Alex made a sound that resembled a soft growl, but he did not argue.

After Da left, Elspeth and Ulisi consulted. The grandmother prepared a poultice with the plantain leaf they had just collected at the stream and applied it to Inoli's thin leg while Elspeth poured him a cup of cider. He gulped it down and made a request in Cherokee that stole the chuckle she had stowed earlier.

Alex turned his head their direction. "What does he say?"

"He says that you and he must go tomorrow to the fallen bear."

"For the meat?"

"To take his claws as a memento of yer bravery." Elspeth accepted the cup back from the boy and informed him in no uncertain Cherokee terms that he would not be going anywhere tomorrow. Then she ruffled his hair to dispel the disappointment that clouded his bright eyes. "Ye may be Bear Hunter now, but first, ye must heal."

"Bear Hunter." Inoli grinned. "Yes."

~

The old Indian woman had laid a sticky poultice across Alex's ribs, cooling the burning slash marks somewhat, and departed with her herb box by the time Elspeth came to his side. She knelt and lifted the leaf to gaze with brow knit at his wounds. His bare skin tingled beneath her perusal, and he resisted the urge to cringe out of the firelight. As if he did not already have scars aplenty, here he was, flayed up again, and laid before her like a trout for the skinnin'.

"We will decide in the mornin' if that deepest cut has need of stitches." Lowering the leaf back into place, she reached for a strip of linen she had laid by. "Can ye sit up just a wee bit? We need to hold the poultice secure as ye sleep."

"Aye." Setting his jaw, Alex slid his elbow beneath him. He held his position while Elspeth wrapped the bandage around his torso. She aided him in lying back down, then tied off the ends of the bandage. With a feather-light touch, she ran the tips of her fingers down his chest.

His skin rippled, and he sucked in a breath. Why had she done that? He sought her eyes, but she only met his for a moment before she rose and moved to the table. The cold draft that swirled around Alex came more from loss of her nearness than the swish of her petticoat. But she was back before he ken it, kneeling again, sliding a pillow beneath his head and raising a small glass of whiskey to his lips. It burned better going down on the inside.

"Thankee, lass."

Her warm fingers slid out from under his neck. "Thankee for savin' the boy."

"I did what any man would do."

"Did ye?" She placed the whiskey on the bench and settled next to him, folding her knees to one side. "I saw yer reaction when I fetched ye. Ye werena only calculatin' the odds, were ye?"

"What do ye mean?"

Elspeth cocked her head. "Tell me, what did ye feel, when I first told ye the boy was missin'? Nay, when ye saw him pinned by that bear?"

Alex took a shuddering breath and slid his good hand beneath his head to better keep her in his sight. "I took the shot, o'course."

"Aye, but had the bear seen ye when ye took it?"

He blinked and lowered his arm. How had she guessed that? "What decent man would not do the same?"

"Ye had a choice, whether ye will admit it or no, and ye chose to put yerself in danger to spare Inoli. Just as ye did at Long Canes Creek for me. That is who ye are." Her eyes glistened and suddenly swam, and she blinked hard. "I ken who ye are, Alex Morris, whether ye do or no."

Something in his chest caved open when a tear spilled over her lashes. He eased forward to catch it with his knuckle. "Lass, why must ye always see the good in me? I will only disappoint ye."

Her lower lip wobbled. "Every time I set meself against that very thing, ye do somethin' to give me hope. But I ken I have pushed too hard. I should never have taken ye to that place without askin' ye first. Can ye forgive me?"

"Can I forgive *ye*?" He wrapped one of her curls around his finger. So soft. He longed to pull her down next to him, but the very words he'd just spoken contended with that desire. "Ye acted rashly, 'tis true, but for me good. Nay, can ye forgive *me*?"

"For what?" She whispered it, and her throat bobbed.

"For not respondin' as ye wished." He released the curl, and it sprang back. "If anyone could break this heart of stone in me chest, ye could, lass. But it has been hard for too long."

She blinked again, her gaze focusing beyond him. "'A new heart also will I give you, and a new spirit will I put within you: and I will take away the stony heart out of your flesh, and I will give you an heart of flesh.'" Her eyes settled again on his. "What me da said was true. I canna save ye, Alex. Only God can."

He clenched his jaw, unexpected anger sweeping him at her words. "And yet, God did not save us. He let many of us die at that creek and the rest carry the witness of it all our days. I dinna want savin' by a God like that."

"God is not to blame for the pain in the world. For man's battles."

"And yet He does little to ease them."

She made a scoffing sound. "Must ye persist in seein' only the fearsome? Never the good? Think how much He has given us. Did He not preserve us for three days in the wilderness, as His very own children? And now He has brought us back together, offered us a second chance."

"Elspeth..." It wrung his very heart in his chest, having to tell her this. "Something in me is not right." He could pretend all she wanted. He could even bind her to him and act on his need for her. But he would not cheat her in that way, rob her of her trust and joy.

"I can see that now." She nodded slowly, catching her lip between her teeth. "Somethin' in ye that was meant to trust is broken. Somethin' that God would heal, if only ye would let Him. Can ye not see how much He loves ye, Alex? When the nature of His sacrifice is writ in yer very bones?"

She thought his actions on her behalf, and now on Inoli's behalf, should serve as some sort of mirror. He puffed out a breath. "Maybe there is hope for some of them." Especially the children. He eased back onto his pallet, shielding his face with his good arm. "But what I did today doesna change what I will do tomorrow. Not where his uncle is concerned."

Only wiping his enemy from the earth would assuage his brother's blood and put an end to his nightmares. Only then could he think of having a normal life.

~

*A*lex had lain awake long after Elspeth made her silent retreat to the loft. Long after Reverend Lawrence returned and assured him his horse was in the stable and his lieutenant was apprised of his whereabouts. And not just due to the searing and throbbing of his side. The pain echoed his every heartbeat, and his heartbeat echoed Elspeth's words. Those strange, ancient-sounding words...

I will take away the stony heart out of your flesh...

How was that possible?

How was he to fight the war ahead without a warrior's strong heart pumping the fire of retribution through his veins? He would have no taste for it. If he listened to Elspeth, he might as well lay down his arms just when his country needed him most.

"'*With a clear conscience before yer Maker, fight not for hate of yer enemy, but rather, for love of yer cause.*'"

If that were to be true, this struggle lay between the colonies and England and had aught to do with the Cherokees. But it would not remain that way. Even now, the Loyalists planned with the English Regulars how best to use their Indian allies in the moment of invasion.

Finally, Alex drifted into a fitful slumber where he faced the jaws of a bear, replaced by the worshipful look of a child as he pulled him from the cleft of the rock. Inoli spoke in Cherokee, crediting Alex with his salvation.

"Cap-tain. Cap-tain..."

Alex's eyes flew open. Something tickled his chest. He jerked, and pain clamped in a vise around his ribs, drawing a gasp. Red splotched his bandage. Besides the open wounds, one or two of the bones might be fractured.

But of greater import in the moment, Inoli dangled the eagle feather over him that had yesterday been attached to a lock of his hair. "You take. Brave. *Wa-do.*"

Alex understood the Cherokee word for *thank you*. But the phrase that followed made no sense.

"*Di-na-da-nv-tli.*"

"Nay." Rising on his elbow, he gently pushed the boy's hand away. "I canna take that from ye."

Inoli stressed the phrase again. He rested the feather on Alex's stomach and pushed himself off the bench with Reverend Lawrence's cane, clumping away before Alex could again reject his present.

He held the soft tines between his fingers. Something cracked open that was not a rib. Before the hot emotion demanded release, he jerked upright. The pain served as a good reminder that his mission remained unfinished.

He found his torn and bloodstained clothing on the bench, struggled into it, and let himself out the front door into the cool dawn. But only after tucking the eagle feather into his waistcoat pocket. Inoli had shown Alex more forbearance than he deserved, despite all Alex's growling and barking—even if he'd not been caught unknowingly in the middle of a blood feud.

With his mouth overstuffed with hay, Charlie looked up from the trough in the stable.

"'Twould seem I am forever interruptin' yer meals. Sorry, old boy."

Hefting the heavy saddle summoned a groan, but Alex managed to prepare his stallion for the ride back to Fort Charlotte. He was leading Charlie into the yard when Elspeth appeared on the front porch and ran down the steps. Lightly, like some fairy. Long blond waves of hair bounced unbound about her shoulders and slender waist. In the folds of her knit shawl, she clutched something—maybe a book. The panic in her eyes took him back to their childhood.

"Alex, ye must not ride yet. Yer wounds are too fresh."

"I must find me pistol and see to the bear. Then get back to the fort."

She stopped on the other side of Charlie, petting him for a moment. As she came around the horse, her attention fixed not on the bloodstains Alex bore, but on his breast. "What is that?"

Alex raised his fingers to his pocket. The feather. "Inoli insisted I take it." He dropped his hand to his side. "A sort of present, I suppose. What does *di-na...di-na-da...*" Shaking his head, he failed to recall the rest.

Her brows flew up. "He called ye his brother? Oh, Alex."

The sob she choked on seemed to lodge in his own throat. Then fear of something unknown, of yielding to that something unknown, hardened his resolve. He ken well the sense of being pursued, even if the stalker remained unseen. And it was here, strong. He tossed the reins over Charlie's shoulder. "I must go. The physician at the fort will tend me."

She surveyed him a moment, then ducked her head. She spoke to the ground. "I realize I have to let ye go, much as it pains me."

It pained him, too, because he would be going farther than the fort soon enough. And the road he traveled led him away from her. She seemed to sense it. She saw all he attempted to hide...all except how much he loved her. But if he spoke that, she would expect promises he could not keep.

He could think of but one way to show the regard that welled like an ever-flowing spring from his heart. He dropped the reins and took several quick steps forward, cupping her face with his hands, turning it up to him. Her blue eyes went wide.

How delicate were her bones in his grip as he lowered his mouth to hers. How soft and tender her lips. A tiny gasp escaped before he sealed them with his. Instantly, he wanted more—needed to show her this was not a brotherly kiss.

But she planted her palm on his chest and pushed him away. "Nay, Alex. Ye canna do that. Not like this."

Like what? What did she mean?

"Ye *should* go...and dinna come back until ye have settled things with yer Maker."

He dared to show his true feelings, and she made this about God? He stared at her a moment, then pivoted and mounted Charlie. He did not look back as he rode from the yard.

It was not until he unloaded his gear inside the fort that he found the book in Charlie's saddlebag—the Bible that had belonged to Elspeth's mother.

CHAPTER 20

empers ran short as warmer winds blew across the Savannah River. Spring descended in all its beauty, calling them forth to campaigns of glory and freedom, yet still they waited. Waited for what, they did not know. But too long of a confinement in the cramped quarters tested discipline.

Target practice in the field outside the fort, both mounted and dismounted, coupled with scouting rotations, somewhat alleviated the monotony. Rangers were trained to travel on horseback and fight on foot, but a foe could always set upon them unawares. Still, there was only so much riding and shooting one could do, especially with limited stores of powder.

For almost a fortnight, despite the recovery time his wounds required, Alex did not touch Elspeth's Bible. He would return it when Reverend Lawrence next came to preach at Fort Charlotte. He had been right about Elspeth...only it had taken even less time than he had anticipated for her to find him wanting. Her words about a heart of stone haunted him.

Finally, he asked Lieutenant Rawdon, known to be a religious man, where the reference came from. The passage in Ezekiel spoke of cleansing from old ways and strengthening through God's Spirit. So did many Psalms, which he remembered reading in his youth. David had been a warrior king of Israel, a man he could understand. The military terminology resonated with him. Before he ken it, he was reading from the Bible every night.

By the time Reverend Lawrence arrived, Alex no longer wanted to return the strangely captivating book. And his heart sank when the man entered the fort alone. While Alex could never seek out Elspeth after she had sent him away, something stubbornly foolish in him had hoped she might come and make amends.

Alex stood at the back of the crowd while the reverend preached from Isaiah on a passage about God's desire to exchange beauty for ashes, a garment of praise for a spirit of heaviness. Ashes and heaviness. Did that not describe his life? And well the canny preacher ken it.

"'Whereas thou hast been forsaken and hated, so that no man went through thee, I will make thee an eternal excellency, a joy of many generations.'"

The verse the man read in his ringing tones was the last Alex heard before letting himself out to the meadow. He took a nip of cane sugar to Charlie on the picket line.

A joy of many generations...

Promises he could never believe filled the Good Book. They were for other men, favored of God. Not for men like him, for whom no good thing ever lasted.

The green woods called, his place of comfort. His sanctuary. Maybe this afternoon...

"Alex, did ye find me too long-winded?" The hearty question wrapped in a chuckle came from behind him. Reverend Lawrence approached, leading his gelding. "Tell me, man, do I find ye fully recovered from wrestlin' that bear?"

"Aye." He rested a hand over his waistcoat. With limited physical activity, the flesh had knit back together nicely. What were a few more scars? "But how did ye get away so quickly? Are ye stalkin' me, sir?"

"Not I." The satisfied smirk on the minister's face did not set well with him.

Alex rubbed Charlie's nose. "And yet ye have a way of bein' oddly specific when ye wish to get a point across."

"I find a direct approach works best, don't you?" Reverend Lawrence cocked his head, his wide-brimmed black hat shielding his eyes. Eyes much like Elspeth's, only lighter.

"Then maybe ye can explain me this..."

"Aye?"

"Ye are so fond of cantin' about God's marvelous transformations. Just how is this mystery accomplished?"

Reverend Lawrence dropped his gelding's reins, allowing the horse to graze in the flower-studded field, and rubbed his chin a moment. "Well, bein' the military man that ye are, I suppose I would liken it to how a soldier signs up in the army. He might come with nothing. He might come with much. But just the same, the army will take him in and make him a brother in arms. It will give him a fine suit of clothes, something to fight his battles with, victuals, and a place to lay his head. In much the same way does the Almighty provision us. And not only provision us, but offer identity. Purpose."

"A good example." Alex had certainly found those things in the army. He stared across the tender young shoots of corn breaking through the rich dirt in the neighboring field toward the river as the verse from his own morning Bible reading came back to him. "'The Lord my strength which teacheth my hands to war, and my fingers to fight: my goodness, and my fortress; my high tower, and my deliverer; my shield, and he in whom I trust...'"

"Why, yes, my son." The reverend's brows flew up, and he clamped a hand on Alex's shoulder. "There is no greater power against the forces of evil than our God."

Alex stared at Elspeth's father but hardly saw him. Could it be possible to battle even more effectively from a place of righteousness...right standing with God? Would God be the source of strength he could exchange for revenge? And would that lift the heaviness that had followed him for sixteen years? He could not imagine breathing free.

"What do I do?" The exhaled question was the most frightening he had ever asked. "To effect this exchange ye preached about?"

"Why, you tell the Lord you are ready to join His army. The exchange has already been made for us. We simply lay claim to it." Reverend Lawrence took a step toward him. "Would you like to do that now?"

~

*E*lspeth had been chasing Alex for sixteen years. In mind, if not in body. And when she found him, she had determined that he would feel the connection between them as strongly as she had. But his refusal to surrender to God and relinquish his quest for revenge meant she must give that up.

God had been working on her as well. When Alex kissed her, she'd realized that if she surrendered, she would forever look to him for her filling. But did that mean she couldn't ask about him? She still cared, though she wrestled that caring into God's hands every single day. Still wanted to ken if her mother's Bible was doing its work...or if Alex had returned it.

Elspeth held herself back all Sunday, hoping Da would volunteer a report about what had happened at the fort when he went to preach. After all, he had agreed with her that she ought to remain at home. But he hadn't spoken a word.

Monday morning, Da told them he would be riding out to Boonesborough to call upon the sick. She couldn't take it anymore. Not another whole day of waiting and wondering. She served up her question with his porridge.

"How did things go yesterday?"

He sighed as if disappointed in her weakness. "Things went verra well."

"Did anything of import occur?"

"Aye. Something of import always occurs when God's Word is preached."

Elspeth wiped her hands on her apron. So this was how he would be. He already disapproved of her inquiry, so she might as well be direct. "Did ye see Alex?"

"I did. He heard most of the sermon."

That was something, then. She had seen Da laboring over the Scriptures the week prior and ken his chosen passage. She leaned forward a bit, peering at her father as he spooned a bite of gruel to his mouth. "And did he say anything?" If Alex had not attempted to return her mother's Bible...

Da lowered the spoon back to the bowl and gave her a look of exaggerated patience. "He and I had a good conversation, but the nature of it is not for me to impart. When he is ready, he can tell ye himself. Until then, daughter, ye would do well to look to the keeping of yer own heart, for out of it flow the issues of life."

"Of course, Da." Her shoulders slumped. How many hours of prayer and soul searching might be required before she could content herself in the Lord?

He caught and squeezed her hand. "Ye dinna need a man, Elspeth, to fill the hole in yer heart."

"I know, Da. But does that mean I canna want one?"

"No, sweet girl. It merely means he must never come first."

Seated at his desk in Fort Charlotte's officers' quarters, Alex crumpled the missive sent by courier from Ninety Six. The words it contained threatened to devour the peace that had settled over him since he had prayed with Reverend Lawrence after the Sunday service just past. The man had not pushed him past the prayer nor spoken of forgiveness again. But for the first time since Alex's childhood, the darkness had lifted, allowing him to glimpse the world in its freshness and beauty. The nightmares and debilitating flashes of memory that had plagued him since Elspeth took him to Long Canes Creek had stopped. And not only that, but slowly, bit by bit, memories of a heartening nature began to seep in. He'd blocked out the simple, wholesome time with his family and even Elspeth from just before the massacre. And now, those recollections made him stop and smile.

He wanted to rush to tell Elspeth. But fear held him back... for nothing good in his life had lasted thus far. Why shouldn't this peace, too, this hopefulness, dissipate like the morning mist over the Savannah?

He stared at the missive, the very thing to test his newfound peace.

"Sir?" Lieutenant Rawdon spoke from behind him. "What does it say?"

Framed by a window with its shutters open to the parade ground, the courier, a young lad with roses still in his cheeks, waited at attention.

Still, Alex searched for the anchor of his soul. He did not ken how to pray yet and 'twas not disposed to believe the Almighty sat with an ear cocked his direction, but every now and again, Alex sent up a word or two. Fragmented-like. *My fortress, my high tower...*

He glanced up at the messenger. "Dismissed, Private. Go victual yerself and yer horse." Once the boy scurried down the porch steps, Alex met Rawdon's eyes. "We are to set the fort in order to receive a party of commissioners headed by majors Mayson and Williamson...and, shortly thereafter, a delegation of Cherokees."

Rawdon's already long jaw gradually extended. "Cherokees? Coming here?"

"Aye, to be courted as our allies." Alex's stomach seized.

"What think you of that, Captain?" His lieutenant no doubt watched for flickers of the rage that had driven Alex for so long. It had been no secret in Ninety Six that Alex Morris served for the opportunity to settle his score with the Cherokees. "Are we holdin' a candle to the devil?"

The red haze of hatred had diminished, allowing him to assess things with a more logical eye. Just because he no longer might choose to act out of his baser emotions did not mean all his opinions had altered. "Brethren or no..." Spiritual or military... "I dinna trust them to keep their promises. I will do all I can to advise Major Mayson so. But I dinna believe he will listen. He is too worried about fightin' a two-fronted war."

"True enough." Rawdon nodded. "But if you are right, we may find ourselves fighting it from a disadvantage rather than with the element of surprise and planning on our side."

Alex rose. The lieutenant's methods of reasoning closely aligned to his own. He had also organized a well-disciplined company whose loyalty to Patriot ideals—and to Alex—was not likely to be called into question. "If that is the case, I hope ye will ride with me, Lieutenant Rawdon." He extended his hand.

Rawdon shook it.

Alex would need to rely on his small company of men, whether the talks with the Cherokees proved successful or not. In the case of the former, for wisdom and restraint. In the case of the latter, to battle his long-held enemy with honor.

The face from his nightmares floated before Alex's memory. There was little doubt that Split Ear would be coming to the fort. What would Alex do if the turn of events not only allowed but sanctioned vengeance on his enemy?

～

*E*lspeth spent many hours with her father's Bible and kneeling in prayer in her loft retreat following his enjoinder to attend to her own heart. It had come to what she feared...a willingness to give up Alex. She must accept that he might never return to her. And pray that he would find peace even if his life never included her.

As April turned to May, peace of her own began to inch back the ache of pain and longing as it had when she had first come to terms with her return to this land. Much as the fingers of sunlight lingered longer and longer every day.

Her mind kept circling around to a single Scripture. *They that wait upon the Lord shall renew their strength.* And indeed, as she waited, strength trickled into her inner reservoir, slowly filling the void in her heart.

The weeds in the vegetable patch offered a likely place to vent her energy while Ulisi oversaw the planting of beans in the cornfield in the fashion of their people. The beans would replenish the soil, while the cornstalks provided support for the trailing vines. Later, they would add squash, which would help prevent weeds and hold moisture in the earth.

On an especially beautiful afternoon, her father had taken his horse to be reshod in New Bordeaux, leaving the women at work in the garden and Inoli clearing brush near the road. Elspeth had taken a moment to wipe her brow and tilt her face beneath her straw hat up to the sun when Inoli's cry made her eyes flash open. They had trusted him to take his musket, but had someone startled him? Taken him unawares?

She ran down the driveway, Ulisi and the girls following. Elspeth stopped halfway to the road, for a group of warriors encircled Inoli—a dozen, at least. And not on foot as had been their prior custom, but on horses.

Inoli stood in the arms of a young girl Elspeth had never seen before, a spotted pony switching its tail behind her. She wore the traditional Cherokee buckskin dress, and her dark braids gleamed with bear grease. Her smile flashed so white as she stepped back from Inoli that it momentarily stunned Elspeth. Who was this?

And who was the man who rode at the front of the party with feathers in his long gray hair and an excess of beads and embroidery decorating his clothing? Undoubtedly, a chief.

Before she could bow or acknowledge the new arrivals in any way, several braves fanned their horses out before Inoli, the girl, and the chief. Split Ear and Five Kills rode at their front, gorgets shining and weapons bristling.

Elspeth's knees went weak. This would be the first time she had faced them without Alex or her father...and the first time she had done so knowing what she did about Split Ear.

His tomahawk was the one that had whispered through the canes like the grim reaper's. His eyes masked in black paint had searched for their movements, for grim trophies of war. His hand had dealt death to Ethan Morris and unspeakable pain to Alex. She had almost died herself, and now she stood before him, unarmed and alone save a passel of Cherokee girls who would go to his side the moment he called. Even now, he watched Elspeth as if waiting for her to run.

Ulisi, who had drawn up next to Elspeth while the girls waited to the side, watched her too. She would disdain any display of fear. But Elspeth had to rely on her.

"Ulisi, will ye see what they want?"

Lips in a firm line, the old grandmother shuffled forward.

The braves nodded to her in respect. At first, Elspeth's addled brain failed to follow their rapid speech. Then she grasped that the delegation was bound for Fort Charlotte to fulfill their promise of the autumn prior. They would hear what the white chief had to say. Learn what he had to offer.

When Split Ear stopped speaking, Elspeth inched forward and forced her question out, though she could only direct it to Ulisi. "*A-ge-yu-tsa?*" Surely, if they had a girl with them, they bore no intentions of war.

Split Ear answered her in simple Cherokee, enthroned atop his stallion. "My niece. Sister to Inoli. She will help with the words of the white men."

"But how...?" Elspeth stepped closer to her trio of students, drawing comfort from their familiarity.

Ulisi jerked her head at the young woman who still watched Elspeth intently, almost curiously, her arm around Inoli. Indeed, they could be kin, with their almond eyes and the same skin tone, a bit lighter than that of the others. "Awenesa learn English from the white man of God before your father. When he came to Dukas'i. You call...Toxaway."

Toxaway. Yes, the small village most of them hailed from. She must be a skilled translator, indeed, if they would choose her over a scout—though, of course, she must miss her brother and had perhaps been chosen so she could visit him. Indeed, she must crave the time to catch up with him even now.

Elspeth stepped forward. Anxiety might still shorten her breathing, but she ken what she had to do. These people had traveled far. Her father would wish her to offer them proper hospitality. "Ye must be hot, thirsty. Would ye come to the house for refreshment?"

Five Kills edged his stallion to one side, his dark brows a slash above his eyes. "*Tla-no.* We will take the boy with us to the fort. We go now." Even as he spoke, his mount danced as though to illustrate his impatience.

Elspeth's hand fluttered to her chest, but her protest lodged just above it. To argue with almost a dozen armed braves 'twould be foolhardy, indeed. When her father returned, he could gather intelligence about what was happening at the fort. "May I say goodbye?" It was the most she could ask, when her real question was whether they would bring him back.

Split Ear gave an almost imperceptible nod.

The girl named Awenesa came forward several steps, then allowed Inoli to run past the horses and into Elspeth's waiting arms. As Elspeth squatted with the small but strong body clasped tight against her, her chest constricted. What did all this mean? Would she even see him again?

She drew back to cup his face. "Always remember what I told ye about sacrifice, Inoli. About how Jesus loves you...and so do we." She could barely discern his solemn nod past the film of her tears.

When Inoli returned to her, Awenesa smiled. The smallest hint of a smile, but just the same, the effect again stole Elspeth's breath. How approachable she was when she smiled. Like a friend one might go berry-picking with and tell secrets to.

But then the girl turned away, guiding Inoli to her horse, where she helped him up before her. Reminding Elspeth that Inoli had a sister. Elspeth did not.

CHAPTER 21

Somewhere up on the parapet, a shrill fiddle note split the dusk. Sparks danced from the big bonfire in the center of the fort's yard to the purpling sky. The flames illuminated the faces of the men gathered around, telling stories and puffing sweet-smelling pipe smoke. Many more lingered near the rum barrels.

From the log where he shared a pipe with Chief Running Bear's party, Major Mayson caught Alex's eye as he stood in the shadows. He rose and sauntered over.

"How fare you, Captain?"

Alex searched his mind for a truthful answer that would not lodge at his lips. "Is there anything ye need, sir?"

Mayson gave him a wry smile. "That was not what I asked, but methinks you have answered, just the same. All I require is that your men keep a vigilant eye and the food and rum supplied."

"As to the last..." He slipped his hands behind his back. "Must there be quite so much of it?"

His commander frowned slightly. "You know how this works, Morris."

What Alex needed to say weighed more heavily than his favor with the major. "If everyone imbibes at this pace, no one will be fit for anything until tomorrow afternoon. And I canna see that much was accomplished today, judgin' by the little that Indian maiden said."

That the delegation included a woman had taken everyone by surprise. The warriors kept the girl surrounded except when they sat at the council fire. There even the chief seemed to defer the more complex communication to her. When she had first spoken, her voice had been so soft and her English so clear that Alex had stopped what he was doing to listen.

Thankfully, Mayson laughed. "Of course, we must start with posturing. The real talks will begin tomorrow. Naturally, the process will take several days."

Alex cut his superior a sideways glance. "Sir, did ye find it of any alarm when they asked the numbers and placements of our troops?"

"Not especially. They were forthcoming enough with theirs. And they said the same as they told Drayton last fall."

"Aye." Alex suppressed a shudder. "Around two thousand warriors combined from Lower, Middle, and Overhill towns."

"'Tis a formidable force, one we would rather have at our backs than shooting at us." Mayson puffed on his pipe, studying him.

Alex worked his jaw, nudging it from one side to the other with a knuckle. "I grasp the reasoning, sir, but I still dinna trust them."

"Understandable. I am grateful you can bear with us through this. It can't be easy for you, placing duty ahead of your personal feelings."

"Duty always wins out, sir."

Mayson thumped his arm. "And that is why you are one of my most trusted captains. Listen, if you need to get away for a day or two, why not ride a circuit around the fort? Make certain our friends are all inside, not without. You see?" He winked. "I never fully trust either."

Alex gave a soft laugh. "And that is what makes ye a wily commander. Aye, sir. I will think on it."

He moved away as Mayson returned to the bonfire. Perhaps a ride about would ease his strained nerves. Surrounded by those he had long looked to battle, he couldn't relax his guard a moment. How many times had he already envisioned what would happen if the Cherokees inside the fort decided to turn on them?

Passing the officers' quarters on his way to the barracks, a flash of deerskin tunic caught his eye. The translator they called Awenesa came onto the porch and dipped a kettle into the rain barrel. He and the other officers had given up their lodgings for her party. In fact, she likely slept upon his very cot. Curiosity stirred, but what would he say to her? Even if she *could* speak near-perfect English.

Another figure appeared on the porch—a smaller one. Alex had seen Inoli when the party arrived, but he had been beside Split Ear. Thankfully, the boy's guardian had sat near the chief during the negotiations, of which Alex had no part. But why had they brought Inoli to the fort with them?

"Cap-tain!" Inoli waved both arms and bounded off the porch, bypassing the steps entirely. He loped over with a grin and pointed to his calf. "Leg is good. See?"

"I see." Alex patted the child's shoulder. "Also good here." He indicated his torso. "Ah, I have something for you." He felt in his waistcoat pocket while Inoli's eyes went wide.

Awenesa approached, her forehead furrowed. She asked a question in Cherokee, and Inoli answered in kind.

He gestured toward Alex. "*O-gi-na-li-i.*" *Friend*. "Cap-tain. Miss El. *Di-do-le-qua-s-di*...school. Miss El all the time say, 'Cap-tain, Cap-tain, Cap-tain!'" The way he clasped his hands under his chin and repeated the title with lilting emphasis put a decidedly romantic focus on his meaning.

Alex flushed and bowed slightly to the girl. "Alex Morris. And ye be...?" Although he had already heard her name, of course.

"Awenesa." She placed her arm around Inoli's shoulders. "My brother."

Alex took a small step back. "Yer brother?"

"Yes."

"May I ask...where did you learn such good English?"

"The missionary at the school, the first one there...he came to Toxaway, our village."

Toxaway? So that was where Split Ear was from. Alex cocked his head. "He must have spent much time there. Yer accent is so slight..."

"Yes." Awenesa's dark eyelashes fluttered. "Come, Inoli. We stay inside."

Did Split Ear wish to hide them away? Because of the rough men about, or was there more to it? Something made Alex reluctant for her to go. He angled slightly into her path before she could turn the boy away. "How do ye think the talks are going?"

She met his gaze with her mouth firm. "Too much rum."

"That we agree on. But otherwise?"

"Your chief, he should have brought powder or guns."

"I see." Alex rubbed his jaw. Again, she made to leave. "Wait. I was just givin' this to Inoli." He knelt and uncurled the fingers of his other hand.

The boy's mouth dropped open as he spied the bear claw, secured on a strand of rawhide, resting on Alex's palm. "Is it...?"

"Aye." Alex couldn't stop the grin that wanted to break out. Such was a proud moment for any boy, no matter his background. "The one we killed."

"*You* killed."

"Well, I never would have come upon him had ye—"

An explosion of Cherokee syllables halted Alex in mid-sentence. His back tingling, slowly, he rose. He already ken what he would see as he turned around—Split Ear, striding toward him with his hand gripping his tomahawk handle. Alex's throat went dry, and cold washed him from tip to toe, but he wrestled his expression into the stony blankness so often worn by his foes.

"*E-du-tsi!*"

After Inoli's first word, *uncle*, Alex couldn't follow anything he said.

The man who had shattered Alex's youth approached him now, stopping only when they stood nearly toe-to-toe, locked in a stare-down that only a child could hope to break. Did Split Ear remember Alex? Aye, at least from the mission, but then, they hadn't been this close. Could the man see his scars, the evidence of the brutal attack with his own weapon? Likely not. The shadows lay too thick.

Split Ear's ire must stem entirely from Alex's proximity to his kin. His fingers twitched for his dragoon pistol, but he must not reach for it.

Love your enemies. Forgive, and ye shall be forgiven.

What an inconvenient time for him to think of those particular words.

A small finger wiggled into his palm, and Inoli, still talking, drew the bear claw necklace away and held it up to show his uncle.

A gasp came from Awenesa. "You killed bear? To save my brother?"

"Aye." Alex eased the word out, then slowly raised his hand in a spread-fingered gesture of peace, edging it toward his collar. He ken not whether he would ever face this man again— as enemy or ally. The time for battle might yet come. However he might feel about that, it was not today. Alex tugged a rawhide string bearing a claw of his own from beneath his stock and held it out.

Split Ear stared at it a moment, then dropped his hand and stepped back. He gave the briefest of nods. "Bear Killer."

When Alex only blinked at him, Awenesa edged forward. "He honors you with a Cherokee name."

Who would have ever thought? Alex managed a small dip of his chin in response. His gaze, despite his best efforts, strayed to the cloven member on the side of the man's head. If only the warrior ken it was Alex's brother who had given *his* name. What would happen if he revealed such a thing?

Awenesa touched Alex's arm so lightly he almost missed it. "Thank you, Captain." Then she whisked Inoli away, their uncle following.

But for a moment, the Cherokee man looked back.

~

*A*fter the encounter with Split Ear, Alex lay awake for hours. The snoring and rustling of the men crammed into the barracks did not help. Indeed, a pine bough beneath the stars would have offered more rest. Before dawn, he informed Lieutenant Rawdon of his departure, gathered his gear, and left the fort to saddle Charlie.

'Twas not likely that trouble would stir south toward the settled lands of New Bordeaux, so he crossed the river and conducted a foray between the forks of the Broad and Savannah. Returning to South Carolina, he made his way down from Corner Tree. As the shadows lengthened, still he was not ready to return to the fort. He neared the mission. He could overnight there, but how would Elspeth respond to a visit? Doubtless, she would be eager for news of Inoli, but after that?

Her father must have told her of his softening toward God, but he couldn't claim the same toward his lifelong enemies.

Would he have been able to show the same restraint had the young people not been present? Had they not been sharing the fort to negotiate as potential allies? And if he could not, how much had he really changed? Did he even want to change?

Another possibility had him turning Charlie away from Russell's Creek. For if Elspeth rejected him now, he would not be able to go back. And never seeing her again was more than he could accept. Instead, he followed the game trail to the ridge where he and Inoli had faced the bear. The bones he had left after collecting the meat, fat, and claws gleamed in the evening light.

Alex made camp beneath the rock overhang, finding prayers and peace came much more readily as the soft forest sounds lulled him to sleep.

'Twas still dark when another sound jolted him into awareness—footsteps on the ridge above. And not especially subtle ones, so not an Indian. Alex jerked back under the overhang next to his rifle in case the newcomer should venture farther down the trail. From there, he ascertained that Charlie remained where he'd been picketed below, in a small glen next to the creek, mostly surrounded by mountain laurel blooming in white and pink. The steps stopped, and Alex waited.

"Si-yu."

Alex still had not heard a second person approach when an Englishman gave the greeting in Cherokee. A voice so cultured, so familiar, that he had no choice but to verify the man's identity with his own eyes. Alex inched forward, then rolled to his knees and began to ease around the edge of the boulder.

"The soldiers at the fort give only spirit water and empty promises." The stilted reply came from a brave who stood with his back to Alex.

And facing downhill toward Alex in partial profile...Roger Bailey.

"The great king over the water keeps his promises. By now,

the powder and lead from John Stuart in Florida will have traveled up the Peachtree Trail to your villages."

Loyalist wrangling came to light again at last. The rampant rumors of Stuart and Cameron and their dealings gave birth to a plan embodied. Alex forced his breathing to remain steady as he peeked around the boulder. Bailey sported a stained hunting shirt and breeks that appeared to have seen a considerable amount of wear. He carried a rifle. Did he even ken how to use it? Why had the man not remained in Charlestown?

"The Delawares, the Shawnees, the Iroquois all would pass the red stick of war. But we must know the English not go back on what they say." The brave shifted, and Alex held his breath. Five Kills...who apparently ken much more English than he ever would have let on.

"We won't go back. All is arranged. The attack will take place just after the ranger escort the fort will send with you turns back at the boundary of your land. It will look as though the Patriots have set upon you." Bailey paused as if to make certain Five Kills understood. "I give my word that no Cherokee will be killed or mortally wounded, and those who fake the attack will quickly withdraw. Your warriors must not pursue. But the incident will give all the reason you need to take up the red stick of war. To fall on the farms and forts along the frontier. When you do so, the great white king will send soldiers to your aid."

Was Alex hearing this correctly, or had he fallen into some sort of fevered dream? He would know as soon as he got Five Kills in his sights. Five Kills, for obvious reasons. By the time Roger fumbled with his new rifle, Alex could discharge his own and also draw his pistol if necessary. But all he might needs do was call an order to surrender. Five Kills might flee, and Roger might panic.

He moved into a crouch behind the rock and was just bringing up his rifle when Charlie gave a snort. The conspirators jerked their heads toward the ravine. Before he could say Jack Robinson, they sprinted different directions.

Alex whispered under his breath and lowered his rifle. So far, all they ken was that someone or some beast approached. Had he called out, they would also ken they had been overheard. He could only hope both men fled the area so that he could make his way to Charlie, mount up, and ride to Fort Charlotte in time.

CHAPTER 22

hree days after Split Ear and his niece had taken Inoli to the fort, Elspeth and Ulisi sat on the porch with the girls. They took turns at the butter churn and a game of butterbean to relieve the monotony. Kamama kept darting down the steps to chase any butterfly that entered the yard, certain the insects came to visit her, their namesake. 'Twas all Elspeth could do to keep the girl from catching one.

The rolling of wagon wheels came as a complete surprise— any time of day, but especially this early in the morning. Why, they had but broken their fast. The occupants of the wagon proved even more surprising. An older Cherokee man drove the team of two horses with another riding along beside. On the seat of the vehicle, Awenesa and Inoli swayed and bumped along.

The girls abandoned their butter-making, butterflies, and butterbeans and ran to investigate with questions shouted as to why the brother and sister were riding in a wagon.

"We come for you!" Inoli rose in the front of the wagon. "We ride long way home."

Elspeth's heart bottomed out. "But ye *are* home." She came to stand on the steps.

One of the unfamiliar warriors dismounted and approached the wagon as soon as it stopped. He swung Inoli down, then reached for Awenesa.

Inoli ran over and stopped just in front of Elspeth. "All our people leave."

"Leave the fort?" Clutching her hand at her chest, Elspeth barely noticed Ulisi behind her.

"*V-v.* Yes."

"Why? Did the talks not go well?"

"Talks good. Talks good." The boy bobbed his head emphatically, but he put Elspeth in mind of one of the string puppets she had once seen in a traveling show.

Awenesa addressed Ulisi in rapid Cherokee, her tone low and urgent. Ulisi turned and went into the house. Awenesa waved a hand, shooing the girls along behind her. "*U-tli-s-da.*"

Elspeth drew herself up. If this Indian princess thought she could roll up here and give orders without the courtesy of an explanation, she had another think coming. Did she not ken Elspeth grasped enough Cherokee to understand her? "Why are ye telling Ulisi to pack and the girls to hurry? I dinna understand. If the talks at the fort went well, why are ye leavin'? Where are ye takin' them?"

Dark brown eyes fixed on her, not bereft of compassion. "Talks done. Children learn much here but must go home now." She nodded. "Thank you." 'Twas not so much the musical lilt of her voice, or the English rendered without the nasal quality, but the slight, gentle smile she bestowed on Elspeth that completely stole her breath...as before.

Someone may as well have thwacked Elspeth with the broom. "Do I ken ye? Have we met?"

"Not possible." Awenesa shook her head, her braids sliding

over her shoulders. In the sunlight, Elspeth could almost imagine reddish tones within the black. "Please. Must hurry."

A dozen thoughts buzzed like so many bees in Elspeth's mind. "Why must ye hurry? Why must ye take them at all?" What would she do without these children? They were her whole purpose in life. "Ye canna take them."

"We ride ahead of others. Wagon take longer."

"Nay. Ye must not rush them. The children need time." *She* needed time. Long enough to think of a reason to talk them out of this—or at least until her father returned home. "Have ye provisions for yer journey? We have corn cakes, bean bread..." When Awenesa mounted the steps, peering through the open doorway into the darkened interior, Elspeth followed.

The Indian girl made a dismissing motion. "No corn cakes. No bean bread." She called again into the house, "U-tli-s-da."

Elspeth wrung her hands. "Will ye bring them back?"

Before Awenesa could answer, Galilani dashed from the house and waved a rolled bundle at Awenesa. Sight of it brought a sound half cry and half sob from Elspeth. So suddenly, she couldn't just—

Galilani shoved her belongings at the older Indian girl and threw her arms around Elspeth's waist.

Elspeth pressed her sweet little head close. "Tell her ye canna go, Galilani. That ye dinna want to go."

"Must go, Miss El."

Kamama and Ayita displaced her, giving their hugs in turn. When first they had come, they had never done so, but they had become quite fond of the English custom. As Elspeth had of them. Could her poor heart take much more?

Nay, for when Inoli stepped onto the porch, she broke down entirely in a very un-Cherokee crumple of sobs, clutching the boy as if she would never let him go. What would she do without his antics to keep her days interesting? With just herself and Da in the big house...doing what?

Inoli tugged her sleeve. "Tell Rev-rend goodbye. Tell Captain goodbye."

She used the sleeve he released to swipe her face. "Ye did not tell him yerself?" A sinkhole of panic drained her final reserves. Had Alex left the fort without her even being aware?

"*Ga-lu-tsv.*" *Come.* Awenesa turned Inoli with a hand on his shoulder.

Galilani bounded out of the house. Elspeth hadn't even seen her go back in. She carried Leana's doll with the stuffed cloth body and painted face. With a solemn nod, she offered it to Elspeth.

But it was the deep breath Awenesa sucked in that drew every eye in the yard.

~

Tension sang through Alex's body from the moment Mayson told him that Awenesa, Inoli, and two braves had already departed with a wagon. He had arrived at the fort in time for the major to double the escort preparing to ride out with the Cherokee delegation and include instructions for half of that number to comb the forests ahead at the potential site of ambush.

But would Alex be in time to prevent the wagon with the children from the mission from setting out ahead of the delegation? He had selected two trustworthy privates to accompany him for the task. They rode out as the sun was just topping the trees.

Elspeth would be beside herself at the removal of the children. That he fully expected. What he did not expect was to meet the wagon in her driveway with her stumbling along not far behind, clutching...her sister's doll? A shaft of worry pierced him. Had the lass gone daft?

"Halt!" He gave the command with pistol in hand as he drew up on Charlie's reins.

The driver made a move for the rifle behind his seat but thought better of it when the privates flanked Alex, pistols at the ready.

"Cap-tain!" Inoli flashed a grin, undisturbed by the proximity of loaded weapons.

"Si-yu, Inoli." Lightly holding the reins, Alex raised his other hand in a gesture of peace, then slowly lowered his weapon as both Cherokee men remained stoic. His rangers followed his example. He directed his next words to Awenesa. "I'm afraid I must ask ye to return to the mission. We have reason to believe trouble lies ahead."

"Trouble?" She frowned and darted a quick, almost panicked glance at Elspeth.

Elspeth had stopped behind the wagon, her tear-streaked face slack with apparent shock at the sudden appearance of Alex and two other rangers.

"An ambush." Alex switched his gaze between the two men. "Did ye ken of this?"

Awenesa drew in a quick breath. In response to the furrowed brows of her escorts, she spoke a sentence or two in their language. They stiffened, and their countenances darkened even further.

"*Tla-no.*" The mounted brave shook his head with a slow, angry movement.

"What of Split Ear?" Alex cocked his head.

Awenesa's spine stiffened. "E-du-tsi would never send us into danger."

"And yet I heard Five Kills with me own ears this very dawn, plottin' with a Loyalist." He turned his gaze on Elspeth, who had inched forward during their exchange. "Roger Bailey."

She covered her mouth and stared at him with round eyes.

"He isna here?"

"Nay." She lowered her hand and responded in an indignant tone. "Of course he isna here."

Alex had half expected the man to take shelter behind Elspeth's petticoat...and attempt to continue his façade as a peacemaker. "He'll be with the others settin' the trap, then."

"What kind of trap?" Elspeth asked.

"The one that starts a war between the Patriots and the Cherokees. Our commander has sent men ahead of the delegation to divert it, but until the road is clear, we would not put the children in danger."

"Nay, indeed not. Ye must all return. At least fer now." As she cradled the doll in one arm, Elspeth's tone and expression fairly pleaded with Awenesa.

The Indian girl would not look at her, though she gave a slight nod. Elspeth must blame her for taking the children. What words had passed between them before he arrived?

Her shoulders sagging, Awenesa released a sigh. She directed a stream of Cherokee to her driver.

Alex and the privates cleared out of the way so the wagon could turn around in the intersection. As they did, he dismounted and led Charlie to where Elspeth waited. Before his inquiry about her state of mind could leave his lips, she tossed her free arm about his neck. "Ach, lass," he said as she stood unmoving, clinging like a vine. "I missed ye too."

At his attempted lightheartedness, she stepped back, wiping her eyes. "I did miss ye, Alex. Verra much."

His mind darted in several directions. Where to begin? "We have much to speak of."

"Aye, but first, I must thank ye, for God surely sent ye just in time, as he did that day to Inoli."

"I was only doin' me duty, lass." Though he hated to sour his excuse for returning in good graces, he could not allow her false hope. "And I fear ye will gain only a few hours more with them, at most."

"Nay, Alex. Ye dinna understand." Almost reverently, she cupped the head of the doll she held. "Galilani brought me this to comfort me as they were leavin', but when Awenesa saw it, she ken it. She *ken*, Alex, though she hurried away before I could make her admit it."

Awareness sent tingles over his scalp. "What are ye sayin'?" He grasped her forearm.

"I'm sayin' that ye didna just bring back the children. Ye brought back me sister."

The wagon rumbled past them, heading up the driveway. Alex tore his gaze from the woman in front of him to the tawny girl on the seat. "Nay." His fingers tightened on Elspeth's sleeve. "It canna be. It would make sense of her grasp of English, but what of her skin color? Yer sister was fair, if dark-haired."

"Would she be so fair if she spent all her time outside? She is lighter than the others."

"She is Split Ear's niece, Elspeth. Inoli's sister."

A flame burned behind her eyes. "His *adopted* sister, maybe. Who is to say Split Ear's family dinna take her in?"

"It's crazy." He gave her arm a little shake. "Why would he bring her here, of all places?"

Elspeth pulled away and shrugged. "Perhaps he thought enough time had passed. Became overconfident. Besides, he had no way to ken the family she was taken from ran this mission."

That much could be true, but... "Lass, if ye be wrong, or even if ye be right and she leaves ye..."

"What?" She squared her slender shoulders.

Alex shot a glance at his two privates, waiting a respectful distance away but still mounted. They cast him veiled glances. He lowered his voice. "I dinna want to see yer heart broken again."

"Ye mean the way *ye* broke it?" She arched a brow in challenge.

He bristled. "I seem to recall bein' told to go, no' the other way around."

"And ye ken why well enough. Yer heart was so full of anger, ye had no answer when I spoke of how I felt about ye." She started to walk away, but he took hold of both her shoulders this time, forcing her to face him.

"I do have an answer."

At the same moment, taking the opportunity that had opened when Elspeth turned, one of his men spoke up. "Captain, if we hurry, we may yet intercept the advance column."

Alex let out a soft huff of breath. "Aye, Private. I will be right there." Obviously, his men wanted in on the action, and he had no call to hold them here while this private family drama unfolded—or, however much it might concern him, to stay himself. "Listen..." His fingers flexed gently on Elspeth's arms now, more of a caress. "I have to go. You will tell Awenesa— whoever she is—to wait here until someone comes for them. I dinna ken how long. I will return when I can. Then we will talk. Verra well?"

Her lower lip caught between her teeth, she nodded. Searching his eyes. For sincerity?

"In the meantime, do nothing to make her feel trapped. She must not leave until it is safe."

"I understand." Elspeth wrapped her arms around his neck.

His chest constricted, and his breath seemed to drain out of him. But in awareness of the privates reining their dancing horses in a circle nearby, Alex merely pressed a kiss on the top of her head. Her hair smelt of a patch of lavender, warmed by the sun. He whispered, "Whatever happens, lass, I willna leave ye again. Not in the same way."

The wonder in her gaze as she pulled back gave his heart wings. But Alex's gut swirled with misgivings as Elspeth turned and hurried back to the house.

CHAPTER 23

"*L*eana?" Elspeth spoke the name low as she approached the creek bank where Awenesa crouched, splashing her face with cool water. The shoulders that sloped at just the angle Elspeth remembered drew back. But whether it was in recognition of the name or defensiveness at being followed after she'd abruptly left dinner, 'twas hard to say. Elspeth took a step forward. "That is yer name, is it not?"

Slowly, Awenesa straightened. Graceful, like a shoot unfurling from a stem. And slowly, she turned to face Elspeth, her chin held high. "I am Awenesa, daughter of Ghigau and Chenowee of the One People."

Elspeth clenched her trembling hands so she would not reach out to the girl before her. "Maybe ye are now, but before... before, I believe ye were Leana Lawrence, daughter of Duncan and Bridget Lawrence." *Believe.* That word crept into her sentence as doubt lowered her guard. The stoicism of the girl before her shook her confidence.

"I do not know these names. I do not know you."

"But if Da were here, he would ken *you*." When Awenesa moved as if to go around her, Elspeth cut her off. "We didna used to live here, ye ken. Ye wouldna remember this place. How old are ye?"

The dark brows lowered. "I will soon be twenty-one summers."

"Aye." Elspeth nodded eagerly. "Ye were four when ye were taken. Taken by the people ye now call yer family." Her throat closed up on the last.

Awenesa's face hardened. "You speak what you do not know. Ghigau is Beloved Woman who warned your people before the attack many moons ago. She was friend to your people. Married to Chenowee, son of white trader and Cherokee wife. This is why Inoli come here."

Elspeth swallowed the lump. "So...ye have...mixed blood?" Could she be wrong? In her enthusiasm—her desperation?—to claim what was lost, could she have stumbled into error? As she had with Alex?

Awenesa gave a brief nod.

"And ye ken of the attack at Long Canes Creek?"

Awenesa's lips firmed. "Ghigau is a legend among our people. Though not beloved of some."

Due to her warning the settlers. "A legend, ye say? Is she not...?"

A flicker passed behind Awenesa's eyes. "She did not survive the birth of her last child."

"And yer father?" Why was he never in the parties that visited the mission? Elspeth scrambled to understand, to fit the pieces together. Surely, she would find the hole.

"He also is dead. A fight with Creek warriors two winters ago."

"I am sorry." Elspeth flexed her fingers. "But ye have a family still...Da and me. Will ye no' stay until he comes back? If ye dinna recognize me, I am sure ye will ken him. As ye did the doll that once belonged to ye."

Awenesa's gaze diffused, skimming the green woods in an unfocused manner. Soft rustlings like secrets stirred the trees around them. "I did not like the doll."

Elspeth's heart surged, for why would Awenesa be repulsed by a toy that held no meaning for her? "Ye had it the day ye were taken."

Awenesa refocused on her with startling intensity. "I know nothing of the girl you seek."

Elspeth could no longer restrain her hand, which shot out and encircled her companion's slender arm. "Split Ear is not the man ye think. He caused great harm to the one I love, the captain who brought ye here." The temptation to reveal all waged a fierce battle with the longing to pull her long-lost sister into her arms. Either could frighten Awenesa away, which Alex had so strongly warned against.

The fire in the other girl's eyes as she shook off Elspeth's hand quelled further notions of reconciliation. "Split Ear is my father now. He will come for me."

With a toss of her proud head, Awenesa left Elspeth standing by the creek.

~

*A*lex's small company surrounded the contingent of prisoners they escorted into the fort with the rest of the rangers bringing up their rear. Exploring ahead of the delegation, they had first encountered half a dozen horses picketed by a stream near the border of Cherokee land. Securing their own mounts, they had fanned out on foot and crept through the woods until Lieutenant Rawdon signaled a sighting. They had taken the Loyalists from behind, crouched in a rocky area that overlooked the road—clad in the same uniforms that they themselves wore.

One of the faces of those captured sank Alex's heart. Finn's hazel eyes had grown wide upon sight of Alex, even as he lifted his hands in surrender.

"Why, Finn?" Alex had asked the question as his cousin's wrists were bound with rope.

Finn's answer echoed in his ears the whole way back to the fort. "Duty, Alex. Same as ye."

How could two men of the same family interpret duty in such opposite ways? And what made it worse was that several of those captured had been among Finn's and his own companies when they had enlisted as the Regiment of Horse.

What the encounter lacked in excitement the capture made up for in pride—at least for those of Alex's new company who did not share his heavy heart. The soldiers at the fort cheered their entry. And Alex and his men were able to present the Loyalists to the members of the provincial congress who remained at the fort following the Cherokees' sudden departure.

After doing so, Alex saluted Major Mayson and Major Williamson as a balmy wind off the river rippled the colony's new standard on the flagpole mid-parade ground. Colonel Christopher Gadsen had presented the design of the coiled rattlesnake on a field of yellow bearing the words *Don't Tread on Me* to congress earlier that year.

"According to the number of horses picketed nearby, we were able to bring in all the Loyalists who laid the ambush." Alex glanced at his second-in-command. "Lieutenant Rawdon got the drop on them."

Rawdon stepped forward. "With no shots fired, sir."

"Good work, Captain Morris. Lieutenant Rawdon." Mayson nodded at them each in turn. "We owe much to your vigilance this day."

Alex dipped his chin. "Thankee, sir." He would not mention that he had brought in his own kin.

"And the Cherokees?"

"The Cherokees have safely passed into their own lands."

"We will never know how many of them were party to this plan, I suppose." Williamson's mouth drew into a flat line.

Alex raised his head. "Nay, sir, although I dinna believe the brave known as Split Ear had knowledge of it." Awenesa must have stated accurately that her uncle would never put them in danger. Five Kills, a younger, more volatile brave, must have acted without his knowledge. "As soon as he learned of the ambush, he set off for the mission to retrieve the children we had secured there. They, too, should be on their way north by now."

And following that departure, what state would Alex find Elspeth in? He would check on her as soon as he was granted leave.

"And these sorry fellows..." Williamson turned his attention to the huddle of prisoners under the rifle barrels of Alex's men. "Whom do we have here? And in our very own colors."

"Ye will spy some familiar faces among the lot, sir, includin' those who brought forth this foul plan after capture of their ringleaders this past winter. Roger Bailey and Edward Nash, to name a couple." As Alex spoke their names, the men in question looked up.

Bailey's blond locks streamed loose of his usual neat queue, and dirt smeared his square jaw, but his eyes blazed like emeralds. "May the devil take you, Alex Morris."

"'Twould seem he already has *ye*, Bailey."

Using the end of his walking stick, Williamson lifted a braided cord from Bailey's jacket. "Where did you obtain these uniforms?"

"You don't recognize them?" Bailey grinned. "Your captain does."

"What say you?" Patience clearly running thin, Williamson cocked his head.

Bailey maintained his smug demeanor. "Finn Morris." He tilted his chin toward Finn's bowed auburn head. "Cousin of Captain Morris. And some of their former men. The extra uniforms belonged to others who defected to our cause in November."

Nash snickered. "Easy enough to hide them on my property."

Mayson moved closer to Finn. "*I* remember you. And I'm sorry for Captain Morris, but you will face charges as a traitor, Finn, you and your men. Your cousin won't be able to save you from whatever verdict congress imparts."

Finn fixed Alex with a narrowed stare. "I wouldna ask for his help. Nor expect it. For he kens nothing of loyalty."

The barb pierced Alex at his weakest point. He swallowed and hardened his jaw.

But his major straightened, lifted his head, and swiveled to regard Alex. "I would not say so. In fact, I would say the opposite. Captain Morris demonstrates a keen aptitude for determining where his deepest loyalties should lie."

"Thankee, sir." Did Major Mayson have any idea how much his words meant? "I can forgive me cousin. He has always been but a follower." Releasing those bonds of the past once and for all, Alex turned to Bailey. "But whatever possessed ye to risk everything ye had to return to these parts, Bailey, when ye could have waited out this conflict safely in Charlestown?"

"Rest on my laurels on the coast while my farm, my home, and my land are overrun with rebels?" Bailey scoffed. "Do you think this is all of us?" His bonds cut short his gesture toward his compatriots. "Hardly. You may have avoided this battle, but soon, the war will be upon you."

"What do you mean?" Williamson stepped closer to him,

eyes narrowed. "You speak of the powder and shot Captain Morris heard you tell that brave, Five Kills, about."

"I speak of the key ringleader, as you would call him, who got away from you. And who is even now raising a troop of rangers in British East Florida, with the sanction of the governor of that territory. Do not think for a moment you have seen the last of him."

Thomas Brown. *An instrument to wipe the Patriot scourge from her soil.* A chill unfurled along Alex's spine.

Williamson's mouth turned down, and he snapped his hand toward the fort's jail. "Take these men away. We will bring them with us to Ninety Six when we are prepared to depart."

Alex turned rather than meet the eyes of his cousin. He would prefer to remember Finn from better times.

Even as a ranger led him away by the arm, Nash started to laugh, the sound more than a bit unhinged. "The Cherokees are coming to the backcountry. The British to the coast. And locking us up won't stop them."

~

*E*lspeth had received a message from Alex that the extended stay of the commissioners as they settled business after the attempted ambush required his attendance. At last, on a bright day in early June, he showed up at their door. 'Twas a week after Split Ear and his men took away the girl Elspeth still thought to be her sister and the children she had grown to love, leaving the mission silent and empty.

After Alex apprised her and her father of all that had transpired at the fort, she asked him to go for a ride. But she had learned her lesson about unpleasant surprises. Thus, she revealed their destination before they mounted up.

"I want to take ye to the place where yer brother and most of the others killed at Long Canes are buried."

His mouth opened, then he asked, "At the creek?"

"Nay, not there. Several miles east of the creek. Would ye like to go?" When he'd merely blinked at her, she added, "'Tis a peaceful spot. Not fearsome like the other. I thought ye could say a proper goodbye. With how things ended with Finn and Leana, we dinna always get that option."

Finally, he nodded.

They followed a bridle path southeast of Fort Charlotte. She stopped in a meadow to collect long stems of lavender skullcap and golden ragwort. At the clearing in the woods where the gravesites lay, she dismounted. Alex followed suit, and Elspeth handed him the flowers, then reached for Charlie's reins. "I will wait here for ye."

He went forward and knelt at the low mound of earth, placing the flowers by the rough cross erected at the head. Birds sang softly from the trees, and shafts of sunlight pierced the branches.

Elspeth watched from a distance and prayed.

After a while, Alex's shoulders drooped, then began to shake. Still, she held herself back. She ken now, some things had to remain between a man and God.

When he finally rose and returned to her, his face damp from tears, she allowed the horses to foray in the underbrush and raised her arms to his neck.

"Thankee." The word was muffled in her hair.

Elspeth stroked his back and held him as long as he stood there. But the peace that filled her came from above, not from the man in her arms. How strange, how wonderful to find him there when she had at last surrendered him.

When he moved back to wipe his face, she reached for her mount's reins. "Shall we go? That meadow would be a good place for the cider and biscuits I packed."

Alex nodded. They walked, though, rather than rode. He

cut her a sideways glance. "Ye are calmer than I reckoned ye would be."

"After the children left, ye mean? Aye. The quiet has given me much time for reflection."

"What will ye do now?"

"Whatever the Lord shows me. I'm still waiting." She glanced at him with a smile.

He did not return the gesture. Something was on his mind. "Regarding yer sister...ye are resolved to leave well enough alone?"

Her shoulders rose with a sigh. "I dinna see as I have a choice in the matter. We take the removal of the children to mean the Cherokees anticipate the coming conflict."

"Aye. We took it the same way." Alex doffed his hat and swiped his forehead with the back of his shirtsleeve. "But if ye had another chance to inquire of Leana, would ye?"

She stopped walking and turned to face him. "Why would ye ask me that, Alex? When I've just found me peace in the matter?"

They stood at the opening of the meadow. Alex released Charlie and gave his rump a little pat. He trotted over to a patch of green grasses and started crunching. Elspeth allowed her father's horse to follow him.

"Tell me why," she repeated.

Alex replaced his cocked hat. "Because I dinna want any regrets to come between us."

"Between us? What do ye mean?"

He reached out and ran a hand down her arm, then stepped back and scrubbed his eyes. A heavy sigh caved his chest. "I have an opportunity to go into Cherokee Territory, Elspeth. 'Tis not widely put aboot, but Major Williamson is organizin' a mission to recover property taken in recent raids against the colonists. At least, that is the supposed purpose. James McCall will lead it."

"James McCall, husband to Elizabeth Calhoun, who was selected one of the captains of militia at Long Canes?" She had been present that day, though it now seemed long ago.

"Aye. The same. He was with us in the fight at Williamson's Fort."

"But ye believe there is more to this mission? An attack, ye think?"

He shrugged. "If I had to hazard a guess, 'twould be that it has somethin' to do with Alexander Cameron. The Council of Safety wearies of the rumors of his insurrection."

Her breathing had become shallow, her heartbeat fast. "But ye have aught to do with James McCall."

"I could if I wanted. They might send a detachment of rangers at my request."

"Because of yer experience. Yer success with Roger's capture."

"Aye."

She lifted her chin, sensing an out to the dilemma he put before her. "How do ye ken the journey would even take ye to Toxaway?"

"The route is to the Lower Towns in that area. It is not inconceivable I would see Awenesa. In fact, it is very possible. Should ye wish it." His stare did not waver until she could take it no more, and with a groan and a slap of both hands against her petticoat, she broke away from its magnetic power.

She turned in a circle, the brightness of the meadow suddenly blinding her. She covered her eyes. "And yet the goin' would put ye in danger." Even if the stated mission of bargaining for returned property was the true and only goal, in this time of high tension, things could go wrong. The Patriots could be attacked. Captured. Killed. "So to gain another chance to learn of the sister I love, I must risk the man I love." Her eyes were still closed when his arms came around her.

His breath fanned her cheek as she dropped her hands.

"Remember the promise about yer sister I made, Elspeth? I wouldna break it now."

"And if I release ye?" Despite her words to the contrary, she eased her arms around his neck. "Could I have ye then, free and clear? Is it selfish that I would still want that?"

He tilted his head to one side. "Why selfish?"

"For a long time, I pushed ye too hard, Alex. I needed ye too much. I see now I must draw me strength from God. But the way I ha' felt about ye these many years..." She drew a trembling breath, then let it out slowly. "It doesna go away overnight."

His lips flashed up in a smile, then relaxed just as quickly. "'Tis glad I am to hear it."

Her heart leapt. But she cautioned herself. "And what of *yer* heart?"

His dark lashes veiled his eyes. "Methinks the promise must stand, because only in the keepin' of it can I prove me heart is true—and rid of the darkness that kept us apart for so long."

Her chest inflated against his. "It is as me father says? Ye have begun to walk with God?"

"Begun, aye. Thanks in part to yer mother's Bible. Would ye like it back, lass?"

"I would like nothing better than for ye to keep it. As I ken she would." She smiled and smoothed the hair in his queue.

"Ye do me a great honor. But I've a long path ahead. And me faith has yet to be put to the test. Elspeth..." A frown danced about his forehead. "I fear every day sinkin' back into the murk. When the Cherokees were at the fort..." His fingers tightened on her waist.

"Nay. When ye gave yer life to Christ, Alex, ye became a new creature. The old was made new. Dinna attend to the lies Old Scratch would put in yer head."

"I want to believe that I can do me duty in the power of God's Spirit, as yer father said—not from hate of me enemy."

"A much stronger place, I believe ye will find. But if it is a test ye are seeking..." She reached up and tipped his hat off his head. It fell among the wildflowers, and she cupped his face. "Then go. With me blessin' and in the strength of God."

"Aye. And I will do me best to find yer sister."

Did she imagine it, or did he dip his head toward hers, then suddenly straighten? Before he could step back, Elspeth locked her fingers behind his neck and fixed him with a fierce stare.

"Is there somethin' ye would ask me, Alex Morris?"

"Nay." He cleared his throat. "But there is somethin' I should tell ye."

"And what is that?"

"I should answer the many times ye have honored me by speakin' of yer own feelings with the knowledge that...that I love ye, Elspeth Lawrence. As never I thought meself capable of lovin'."

Joy. It blazed through her, consuming her from her feet to her head in a solid tongue of flame as she laid the side of her face against his. She slid her fingers into his hair. Their noses aligned. Their breath mingled. She could barely resist turning her head, ever so slightly. Not until first...

"There *is* something ye should ask me."

"I...I would like nothin' better than to kiss ye, but I daren't—"

"Please." She let her lips whisper over his. "*Please.*"

His mouth melded to hers with all the passion and belonging she had imagined. The wholeness she found within allowed her to receive it as an equal rather than from a place of desperation. But that did not mean she was not desperate to return his caresses. To offer a taste of what he must come back for.

He groaned as he drew apart for air.

"Now that," she whispered, "should have been my first kiss."

"I vow, ye willna have any from another."

As he kissed her again, Alex twined his fingers in her hair. Cupped her cheek. Braced the tip of her chin. And his kisses grew so gentle, so achingly tender, that she was left in no uncertainty of his feelings for her. He would return. And he would make her his wife.

It had to be.

CHAPTER 24

*T*he wide Keowee River flowed between McCall's camp and the village of Toxaway. Alex did not mind the separation. In fact, it greatly lessened his anxiety that the leader of their expedition chose to bivouac his men apart from the Cherokee towns they visited. Captain McCall and his interpreter went into the villages to negotiate each day, sometimes not until the evening when their hosts felt more hospitable. Sometimes they returned before the next day, sometimes not. But Alex had to find a way into this particular village before his group moved on to the next one bearing their trophies of goodwill—property taken during frontier raids.

Alex snorted at the sham and ducked into the river, splashing water over his head. Allowing it to drip over his bare torso. Guards along the bank made any aggression on the part of the Cherokees improbable, so they could take turns washing the sweat and dirt of the trail from their bodies.

Thus far, the true purpose of their mission—learning the location and the subsequent capture of Alexander Cameron—remained unrealized. The chiefs of the small towns they had visited vowed they had no word of him. Unlikely, but not surprising they would say so.

Their expedition had crossed at Cherokee Ford on the twentieth of June. Alex had selected five of his own men but explained to Lieutenant Rawdon that he needed him most at Fort Charlotte. In truth...should Alex not return. And if he did, there would be other missions.

Before leaving, Alex had tied Inoli's feather to the leather thong that bound his hair. It might symbolize bravery to the Indians, but to Alex, it symbolized his new commitment to let honor guide his decisions.

Upon reaching the entrance of Cherokee lands at Cane Creek, McCall had broken the seal on his orders from Major Williamson. None among the more than thirty soldiers present had protested the directive that they should attempt to return Cameron to South Carolina. McCall had hopes of locating or at least catching word of the superintendent at one of the larger towns.

Alex sucked in a breath and immersed himself. He could swim the river after full dark, creep among the trees, and spy out the negotiations in progress. If God was with him—

Nay, he ken now that God was with him. Had guided him these many years to a place of—if not yet forgiveness—understanding. That these were people, not monsters. Their anger at the loss of their freedoms ranked no lower than his. Was he not joined to the Patriot cause, fighting for the same reasons as they? Whatever side they took, like the whites who remained divided, they took it for the best chance of preserving that freedom. Their way of life.

God would get him to the rest. This new man Elspeth spoke of...well, he hated to disappoint her. Rather than an instantaneous transformation, his refashioning more resembled the making of a new wineskin to replace the old as described in the Good Book. The stitching together took some time. The stretching took even more. Hopefully, she could be patient. For she was the other clear evidence that God had been with him.

He came up and drew a deep breath. The proper way to put it would be *if God was willing.* If that be the case, he might also glimpse Awenesa in the village. And obtain even more favor by finding a way to speak to her.

Alex wiped the liquid from his eyes.

A figure stood on the far bank. The boy wore only a breech-clout, his brown skin gleaming above and below. His arm waving. Alex scrubbed his eyes again and strained to focus in the dimming light. Was he seeing things?

"Cap-tain!" The call came as quietly as the high-pitched voice of an excited boy could make it.

"Inoli!" Amazement rushed through him more swiftly than the current. And...happiness? He was happy to see Split Ear's nephew? Aye. Even now, the bear claw dangled at the child's neck, just as its twin did at his. The experience had joined them in some strange way.

"Come." Inoli gestured broadly toward the village behind him.

"Now?" He looked down at himself. He wore only his breeks, and his weapons all lay on the bank. He held up a hand. "One minute." He could swim back swiftly and hope to make the river crossing without dampening his powder.

"Tla-no. Now." The boy's movements became even more emphatic. "Sister says come."

Awenesa wanted to speak with him? What if she only had a moment to spare undetected? He must not squander it fumbling with brass buttons and boots. As for his weapons, maybe it was meant that he go without them. Ach. He *was* changing. The old Alex never would have considered such a thing. "God, I'm trusting ye with this one." He muttered the odd little prayer before launching himself across the river, swimming with quiet, even strokes.

On the other side, Inoli did not spare hugs, greetings, or even glances along the riverbank. He set off into the woods, and not on a trail. In the failing light, Alex dodged greenbriers and poison ivy and prayed he also dodged anything with fangs. He did his best to set his feet—tender on the bottoms after months in stockings and boots—in the bare dirt, among decomposed leaves, or on soft patches of wood sorrel. At least the braves wore moccasins on the floor of the summer forest. Inoli, however, did not. And he seemed to ken just where to step.

At last, they came to a glade where an abundance of lush ferns spread a carpet of green along a trickle of a stream.

Awenesa rose from the downed, moss-covered tree where she had been sitting. Her dark hair was unbraided and flowed down the back of her deerskin tunic. "Captain." She spoke his title calmly. His state of partial dress did not seem to faze her, but then, it wouldn't. What did attract her attention was the feather in his hair, which she undoubtedly recognized.

"Inoli says ye want to speak with me." He indicated the child who hung a few steps back, as if he ken this conversation was not one he would take part in. He gave Inoli a warm smile to show his gratitude, which was returned.

She offered a slight nod. "I knew you would be with the soldiers. And I saw you watch from the riverbank. You are here because of her, are you not?"

"Elspeth?" He swallowed down his surprise at her direct approach. "Aye. She wants her sister to come home."

Awenesa lifted her chin a fraction. "Her sister is dead. She must accept this."

Alex lowered his brows. "Ye ken that for certain? How?"

"I have heard her story. The story of the captive, Leana Lawrence."

Did he imagine it, or did her voice quaver with the saying of the name? He stepped closer. "And ye bring me here to tell it?"

"I bring you here so you do not enter our town and be found there."

He cocked his head. "And why would ye care if I was?"

"Such action could start a war." She made an abrupt slicing gesture at her side.

"Nay." He considered her a moment, the rapid rise of her chest, her gaze now averted. "I dinna believe that is why. She is right, is she no'? Ye *are* Leana Lawrence." Until that moment, he hadn't fully believed himself it could be possible. It was so hard to identify any resemblance past the differences in dress and demeanor.

Her eyes snapped back to him. "You must tell her the girl is gone. For she is."

Slowly, he shook his head. "Lyin' to Elspeth is something I could never do."

"You are the man she loves. You can comfort her."

"I willna comfort her with lies."

"A lie would be softer than truth." The sentence seemed snatched out on a breath without her consent, for her eyes widened, then she turned away.

Compassion flooded Alex, and he ventured a feather-light touch on Awenesa's—Leana's—arm. He gentled his voice as well. "Do ye remember me, lass? I used to play with ye and yer sister."

She shook her head, still angled away. "I remember none of that. But I did hear of a girl who was taken from the creek where many of your people died."

"Split Ear? Did he tell ye?" She must have asked the questions after leaving the mission, which had led to her learning the truth and initiating this meeting.

She gave no acknowledgement he had spoken, merely continuing her story. "She was taken to replace a child of the same age who had died of fever. She was young enough to join the people as one of them. Tell your woman, the girl was loved."

Alex's heart squeezed. "I will." She would not be telling him this if she did not care about Elspeth.

"She had a brother she loved." Awenesa shot a quick glance at Inoli, still standing in the deepening shadows. "A kind grandmother. Her uncle, who took her into his lodge and brought her meat after her father died, was a hard warrior but good to her in time."

"I am glad to hear that, but did she not long to return to her own kin?"

She faced him, her eyes pools of darkness as the light faded. "Her whiteness was washed away. You see? She *was* with her own kind. She would know nothing else."

"Her sister and father never gave up hope of her return. If ye think they will now—"

"They must. You must make them understand." Suddenly fierce, she grabbed his arm and squeezed it. The snap of a twig had her head swiveling to one side. "I must go. Take this. For her. For her care of Inoli." She pressed a cool strand of beads onto his palm, then darted away before he could catch hold of her.

"Leana, wait." But she was already bounding away into the shadows.

Poised to follow, Inoli looked back over his shoulder. "Goodbye, Cap-tain."

~

*a*lex lay on a pine bough with a blanket rolled under his head, fingering the beads Leana had given him. His stomach roiled with unease. How would Elspeth react to him returning with only a necklace to show for his efforts? He should have done more to make Leana listen. But his attempt to follow the siblings had proved unsuccessful, and he'd been forced to trace a small stream back to the river and return to camp. Captain McCall was already there by the time he arrived. And the next morning, they had left for the larger village of Seneca.

The town occupied both banks of the Keowee near the mouth of Coneross Creek. On the east side, the smoke of cooking fires rose from a great number of houses, while the west side supported the lodges of the chief and other important headmen and the council house. It was there that Alex supposed McCall to be even now, smoking, drinking, talking. Thus far, they had been received with diplomacy. The men in their camp ate and then drowsed, campfires burned low, and soon, snores permeated the night.

Still, Alex remained awake. McCall had not been apprised of his personal mission. He should have entrusted the commander with knowledge of Leana Lawrence. Should not have let them leave without her. She was property that had been taken, was she not? He would confide in the expedition's leader in the morning and ask that they return to Toxaway and treat for the girl.

Against her will, though? Aye. She must only be afraid. Any obligation she might feel toward her captors would fade with time and with the telling of the story from the Lawrences. She would realize all they had suffered. Eventually, she would become Leana Lawrence again.

His eyelids grew heavy. Elspeth beckoned him to join her in his dreams.

Alex, come see...

Only now, she was a woman, calling him home. Dare he imagine he might soon lie in her arms? How long would it take to get there? How many more villages first?

In his mind, he was traveling, but not riding. Walking.

Wagon wheels were turning and turning. A little girl dropped her doll. He ran to help.

Thankee, Alex...

But he hadn't helped. Not really. For the girl was still lost. He had to bring her home.

Something crackled, then whistled nearby.

Alex, what are ye doin'?

He sat up at the sound of a thud and an indrawn breath. His man who had been sleeping not ten yards away clutched something long protruding from his chest.

A dark figure came straight at Alex. Moonlight flashed on a blade. They were under attack!

He fumbled for the pistol he had left lying near his head. It was stuck in his belt!

His attacker drove a knife toward his chest.

Alex rolled. The blow intended for his heart entered his left arm. Deep, slicing pain drew a cry.

Screams and whoops and grunts now sounded all around him. But he had hold of his pistol, and he jerked it toward the brave before he could regain his footing. A flash in the pan, and the man fell backward.

The moonlight illuminated a painted face twisted in pain. Five Kills?

Alex had no time to tell whether he was dead or wounded, for another assailant whooped and ran toward him. Something heavy whooshed from his hand. Alex ducked, and a tomahawk planted in the tree behind him. No time to locate his other guns in the dark. He whisked his sgian-dubh from his boot and crouched.

The brave had drawn his knife as well. Its longer blade meant Alex needed to stay out of range and, if possible, disarm him. He went for the back of the man's hand, but his opponent used the war club clutched in his left to block. As stone or bone protrusions from the weapon crashed into Alex's forearm, he grunted. Brought his knife up to stab at the brave's extended arm. A hiss indicated he'd drawn blood.

What followed next became a blur of feinting, circling, lunging, and blocking. Until his opponent backed him near the tree and Alex's boot caught on a root. He went down, his sgian-dubh skittering from his grasp. In a second, the brave was over him, long knife raised. Alex brought up his knee. The war hammer came down on his shin. Pain radiated along the bone, but the weapon spun free. He grabbed the hand that held the knife before it could find his abdomen.

"No!" The cry that came from nearby momentarily froze both Alex and his attacker. A woman?

Alex twisted the hand of his attacker backward until the knife fell to the forest floor. Then he grabbed the weapon as he hooked the man's leg with his own. And he was on top.

"Alex. Stop!" A shape materialized from behind the tree. Leana.

And Alex realized who he was fighting. He finally had his brother's killer under the knife.

CHAPTER 25

$\mathcal{E}$lspeth moved slowly down the row, filling her basket with beans. Her father had taken the hot part of the day to work on some correspondence, but she had been restless. Like a lone dried pea in a gourd, rattling around.

After wiping the perspiration from her brow, she secured the ribbon of her hat beneath her mob cap. The corn was still not tall enough to fully shade her from the noonday late-June sun in the cloudless blue sky. Nay, it was July now. Yesterday, Monday, was the first. Over a month now since the children had been gone and almost two weeks since Alex had departed.

Her heart hurt as she stopped to select two ripe yellow squash to add to her bounty of beans for tonight's supper. She recalled which girl had planted each row of the plants, now in glorious vine. Wouldn't they be proud to see how well this year's garden had turned out?

Elspeth stared into her basket through a sudden sheen of tears. Why had she picked so much? 'Twas only Da and her. One would think she would be used to it by now. Well, she might as well keep going at this pace and string some up to dry.

She blamed her lack of sleep. The past week had found her

wakeful in the hours of the owl—ever since that one night she had felt the strongest need she had ever experienced to pray. She had not been able to fall asleep that night. When she had spoken to Da of it the next day, he said the Good Lord often made him aware he should intercede at a key time.

Intercede? Her mind had immediately skittered hither and yon. Was Alex in danger? Had he gotten into trouble while seeking out her sister? The lack of information made her imagination run wild.

Fear stabbed her heart even now, but she pushed it back.

Second Timothy 1:7. For God hath not given us the spirit of fear; but of power, and of love, and of a sound mind.

She had just settled into that sound mind when horse hooves pounding the driveway kicked her pulse back up again. She swayed, torn between running from bad news and running toward good news. But it could be Alex himself, could it not? She dropped the basket and darted down the row for the cabin.

The rider dismounting at their hitching post wore a blue uniform, white breeks, and a black cocked hat. Her hand fluttered to her mouth. Then dropped abruptly.

Lieutenant Rawdon met her gaze. "Miss Lawrence. Good afternoon."

She went straight to it. He would forgive her. "Have ye news of Alex?"

"No, I am afraid not. But I do have news. Where is your—?"

The door banged open. "I am here." Da stumped over to the edge of the porch. "What brings ye to us in such haste, man?" His frown said he ken it couldn't be good, no matter what the lieutenant called the afternoon.

"I would suggest you pack quickly and accompany me back to the fort. We have received word of two attacks in the settlements."

"Attacks?" Elspeth croaked.

Rawdon nodded. "Cherokees. The first on the family of

Anthony Hampton near the line. Tyger River. He, his wife, his eldest son, and an infant grandson were all killed and the cabin left in flames. The second, nearby in Long Canes."

Elspeth gasped, and Da pressed forward. "Who?" Only two days ago, he had preached at Boonesborough.

"Aaron Smith. His boy, John, had two fingers shot off but managed to flee on a horse to Major Williamson at White Hall. 'Tis how we know it was Cherokees. Even now, the regiment of Ninety Six is being called out. Folks are leaving the area or fortin' up. And you couldn't be safer than at Fort Charlotte."

Da turned without another word and hurried back into the house.

Elspeth's feet had grown roots. "What does this signify?"

"If you mean what has provoked them, there is speculation it could have to do with McCall's mission. But I would not wait around to inquire of the next war party that comes through."

She swayed slightly.

Lieutenant Rawdon stepped close and supported her elbow, his forehead furrowing.

Her eyes sought his. "That means something went wrong. But where are they?" Captured? Dead? A moan tore from her throat.

"Elspeth!" From inside the house, Da called.

For God has not given...for God has not... How did it go? She was caught in a river current, swirling toward rapids.

Rawdon squeezed her arm. "You must not think the worst, Miss Lawrence. Ready yourself and let us depart. Alex would want that, wouldn't he? 'Tis why I came."

"Aye." She fixed on his broad, flushed face, so earnest and kind. "Ye are a good man."

His lips twitched in a smile. "I am not above collecting a favor when he turns up at the fort, for that is where he will go first, is it not? And find you there waiting for him."

~

*W*ait she did. All through that day and the next, as reports of destruction trickled in with various civilians. Small parties of Cherokees fell upon single families, murdering the weak and elderly, taking a handful of prisoners. Opening fences to allow cattle and hogs to trample and consume the wheat standing ripe in the fields. Burning cabins and outbuildings. It was 1760 revisited. This time she was safe, but Alex remained at risk.

Her father rose to the occasion, greeting the traumatized settlers at the gate and huddling with them in prayer. Now was not the time for sermonizing, but he gathered those in need of spiritual succor beneath the proud golden banner in the parade ground and read from God's Word.

Elspeth endeavored to assist. She handed out bread and cider and held crying bairns. Would she ever hold her own? Alex's children? The terrible pain of longing swept through her until all she could do was pace and pray. A word here, a sentence there. But God answered with calming relief and redirected her focus outward again and again.

At twilight, a cry rose from the sentry. "Open the gate!"

She straightened from making a pallet for a child on the porch of the barracks. Where would they put these new arrivals?

But 'twas no frontier family that straggled in. Two men in blue sagged atop horses whose heads hung low.

Someone on the parapet gave a shout of recognition. "Captain Morris!"

Elspeth's own cry got stuck in her throat. She almost tripped off the porch as she ran toward the new arrivals.

Alex's head came up, and he immediately stopped Charlie and swung down.

She threw herself into his arms. The force of her embrace

had him stumbling back into the stallion with a grunt, as though his leg gave way.

"Are ye hurt?" She released him and examined his uniform for tears or stains. Though dirty, it appeared sound enough.

"Nay. For all I can feel seein' ye is joy." He drew her close again, but so gingerly she stopped him with a hand to his jaw and peered at him through narrowed eyes.

"Ye *are* hurt."

"Nothing a week or two won't fix. Now, do I get to kiss ye, or no?"

"Aye." She pulled his mouth down to hers and showed him without words the force of love and longing she'd been holding inside.

An outburst of clapping and cheering from the men on the wall and some bystanders reminded her that not only were they not alone, but her father could also be watching. She drew back, flushing, yet not ready to release the man she loved. She cupped his face. "Ye came back to me. Praise the Lord."

"Aye, for it was His doin'."

"But where are your men? The rest of the expedition?"

"This is all I was able to make it out with." He nodded his head toward the private easing out of his saddle at a nearby hitching post. She could practically hear his bones creaking.

Elspeth sucked in an unsteady breath. "What do ye mean?"

"We were set upon in the dark of night the twenty-sixth. Outside Seneca town. There must have been two hundred braves."

Elspeth's heart skipped a beat. "Wednesday, a week ago?"

"Aye."

A shiver worked its way down her spine. The very night she had been impressed to pray.

"Have no others made it back yet?" He glanced around. Lieutenant Rawdon was striding toward them.

"Nay. Ye are the first."

Alex's jaw hardened. "I pray there will be more." He dropped his arm and turned her to include Rawdon in their conversation. Several privates ran forward to attend to the horses as the lieutenant joined them. "An attack at Seneca, Rawdon. We had no time to organize a defense, but the men gave a good account of themselves. Though I suspect Captain McCall and his interpreter were taken captive in the town."

"Alex." The lieutenant clasped Alex's free arm in an extension of a handshake, eliciting another wince. "Come to the officers' quarters. Tell us everything."

"Yes, let's." Elspeth clung to Alex's waist like a bur to a saddle. Under no circumstances would they be getting rid of her. Her first order of business would be to shuck off the captain's coat and examine him for wounds. But as they followed Rawdon across the yard, she whispered the question she couldn't contain. "What of me sister?"

He sighed. "That, lass, is a story for tomorrow."

~

"You ou don't know how it pains me to ask this of you, miss, but I fear I must."

The sun hadn't even topped the walls of Fort Charlotte the next morning. And yet already Lieutenant Rawdon blocked her way down the steps of the barracks, and to Alex, who presumably still lay where he had fallen last night on his cot in the officers' quarters. The twisting of the lieutenant's round face in remorse might mollify a child or a woman of less determination than she. But Elspeth was about to shove him to one side when he outmaneuvered her and continued his plea.

"'Tis that we are running terribly low on food stores, you see. And I couldn't help but notice a couple days ago that your garden was bounteous. Might we form an escort for you and bring back some supplies? Captain Morris would come along, of course," he hastened to add. "Along with myself and Private Dandridge. The man who—"

"Yes, I ken who he is." She had suffered his presence late into the night, along with the lieutenant's, as Rawdon faithfully set down every word they spoke in preparing a missive to Major Williamson. Clearly, this man had no sweetheart. If he did, he would harbor more sympathy for a woman starved not only of the presence of the one she loved but even of knowledge of his well-being. Yet all around her, the civilians in the fort were stirring. What would they put in their bellies this day? Tomorrow? Elspeth sighed. "Verra well. We can use the baskets at the house. Have someone saddle me father's horse."

"He will be going too." Rawdon spoke as she eased past him.

She whisked back around. "Whatever for?"

"Another man along would offer added security." His reply came a moment too soon to satisfy. "And...we might have need of him about the place."

Elspeth cocked her head. "If it is that dangerous, perhaps ye should send a whole company."

"No." Rawdon waved his beefy hand and gave a little chuckle. "The five of us will do."

She raised her chin a notch. "Then I will ride with Alex." She turned toward the officer's quarters.

"Of course you will."

She did not turn around again at the smirk in his voice. As she suspected. No sweetheart.

Elspeth cared not what her father and the other soldiers thought of her hugging Alex's waist as they set forth on Charlie. Questions sped through her mind. When could they finally be alone? They had so much to discuss. For how long was he home? Would he continue to oversee the company at the fort, or would they be sent out to fight now that war had broken out with the Cherokees? She couldn't bear to think of that. Not yet.

As they turned in their driveway, she raised her chin to his ear and murmured. "Maybe after we finish here, we might have some time alone?"

With a soft growl of frustration, he swiveled his head toward her. "I would love nothin' better, lass, but I dinna ken if it will be possible."

Her heart sank. "Surely, we can find some corner of the fort for a quiet talk. Or perhaps they can give us a few minutes in the cabin before we return. There is so much yer report last night didna tell that I would needs learn."

"Such as the part about yer sister?" Alex eased Charlie up to their hitching post.

"Aye." She answered whisper-soft before he helped her down, then dismounted behind her.

"Right. Well, that is why I brought ye here. Not for the veggies. Although Rawdon and Dandridge will pick aplenty." He chuckled deep in his throat.

"So ye can tell me?" How clever he was, buying this time to relate sensitive information to her and Da without the discomfort of listening ears.

"So *she* can tell ye." Alex nodded his head toward the cabin.

Elspeth froze in place, all the courses of time seeming to stop in that one instant. For there in the open doorway stood her sister.

~

*A*lex reclined back against the table, his booted legs sprawled out as Leana finished the tale she had told him in the forest glen, though she gave more details to her father and sister.

Ah, but his leg pained him...even worse than the gash in his arm which Elspeth had tended with her salves and linen strips. The place where Split Ear's war club had contacted his shin resembled the eye of a tornado. He would not be surprised if the bone was fractured. The pipe he puffed helped soothe the ragged edges a bit. Although what he would not give to stretch his leg out upon Reverend Lawrence's bed just yon. But he would not miss this exchange for the world. Not a word or a look.

So far, words and looks were all that had passed between the Lawrences. Leana held herself aloof. Her guarded glances and fluttering hands warned that she might flee if pressured. Elspeth and her father had kept their questions to a minimum and gentle when posed.

Again, in stilted but proper English, Leana told her story in third person. Alex could see that wounded Elspeth a bit, but the reverend...well, his gaze hadn't wavered from his dark-haired child since the moment he first beheld her. The power of God must be strong within him indeed for him to restrain himself from swooping her into his arms.

Leana had come to the place in the tale when she stepped from behind the tree. "I could not let Uncle harm the captain. He must come back to you since I would not. But at my cry..." She paused as if searching for words.

Alex removed his pipe from his mouth. "I gained the advantage. And when I saw her, I ken who I held under me knife. The man I had long intended to kill."

Elspeth gasped, her eyes widening.

Reverend Lawrence straightened. "And did ye?"

A smile stole control of his lips. "Nay. How could I do so before yer daughter? Take the one who cared for her and Inoli away from them, same as had been done to me? What's more...I didna want to."

"Ye didna?" If Elspeth leaned any farther forward on the

bench in her attempt to assess Alex's expression, she would fall off.

"I ken it is surprisin'." He patted her knee. "I'm still attemptin' to understand it meself. But in that moment, I saw a man as lost as I had been. I couldna dispatch him to meet his Maker."

Elspeth made a small sound and covered her mouth, blinking rapidly.

He chuckled softly and shook his head. "All those Scriptures in yer mother's Bible have the most inconvenient way of surfacin' in me mind. Like a voice, always talkin' there." He tapped his temple.

She grabbed onto his hand and squeezed. "Oh, Alex. That be the Holy Spirit, guiding ye. But what did ye do?"

He took a deep breath. "I dropped the knife and with the man still pinned to the ground, I told him who I was. And who Ethan was. And I said that I would not kill him."

Leana folded her hands in her lap. "I told Uncle we owed Alex a life. Not only for his brother, but for mine."

"The bear," Elspeth breathed.

Reverend Lawrence looked between Alex and Leana. "Then what happened?"

Alex grunted a chuckle. "Well, when I let him up, he didna kill me. Although I didna give him back his weapon either." He pulled aside his coat to show them the long knife tucked in his belt.

Leana dipped her chin. "We help him get away from the battle. To his horse. That is where Uncle told me to go with him. He said war had come, and no one would be safe in the Cherokee towns. He said I would be better off with the people of my birth." Though resignation laced her tone, she did not raise her gaze from her lap.

Elspeth dropped Alex's hand and extended hers to Leana.

He held his breath as the younger Lawrence girl, still a

Cherokee in all but name, stared at it. He would never tell Elspeth how Leana had fought her uncle, how he'd needed to pull her atop his horse as Split Ear shoved, then smacked Charlie's rump to send them away.

And now, so much rode on that one gesture. Would she reject them, even as she lived among them for who ken how long, or would she embrace those she did not even remember? Of all people, he had sympathy for that.

At last, Leana's fingers came out. Just part of the way. But it was enough for Elspeth. She reached the remainder of the distance, took Leana's hand, and squeezed. Tears overflowed from her eyes and ran down her cheeks.

"*I-gi-do*. Sister. Thank ye for comin' home to us."

Leana nodded, and her lower lip trembled.

Reverend Lawrence sat forward. "I have to ask, lass, do ye remember me at all?"

She blinked at him a moment. Then she whispered, "I remember your voice."

The older man stifled a moan and went down on one knee before her. "Me sweet Leana, I never stopped lovin' ye. Welcome home."

When she took his hand, Alex could have sunk into a puddle on the floor. Much work lay ahead, much understanding, much forgiveness, but the Lawrence family was reunited.

Almost. Bridget Lawrence would never see her younger child again this side of heaven. But might Alex hope to join their small circle?

EPILOGUE

*A*lex held Elspeth's hand as they strolled away from the fort. The evening sun wove ribbons of gold through her unbound hair, and the breeze off the river teased it into shimmering strands about her rosy face. Never was a sight so bonny. He attempted to put words to his emotions. Such light and joy often struck him dumb of late. And sometimes, breathless too. "Dinna get me wrong, I am sorry for the reason the settlers have forted up, and I dinna enjoy the crowds and inconveniences. But I have to admit, I have been glad to have ye here."

Breathless he became when they reached the edge of the cornfield and she whisked him around the corner. And breathless he made her out of sight of prying eyes. The ground had been cleared for almost a mile around the fort, but they had found this one place where the stalks were tall enough to give them a moment of privacy. They had to make those moments last. Especially this one, with the solemn knowledge that tottered like a loose boulder over Alex.

For now, he stroked her back and her hair and rained kisses

over her upturned face. Then he claimed her lips until they were rosier than her cheeks.

When she muffled a sob, Alex stopped. Pulled back and frowned. "Did I hurt ye, lass?"

"Nay. But I ken why ye kiss me like that."

"How is that?"

"As though it may be the last time."

"Dinna say such things. Ever." He swiped a tear from the corner of her eye with his knuckle. "What makes ye speak so?"

"I hear the talk around the fort, even though I ken ye hope I don't. I ken that even the Loyalists are joining Williamson's new militia. And with McCall's men who survived the attack stragglin' back in and McCall held captive, I ken the rangers at Fort Charlotte expect orders any day to ride to Williamson's camp. And from there, to invade the Cherokee Nation."

Alex's shoulders sagged. "I canna deny any of that. The time is ripe for an invasion."

Not only in reprisal for the attacks at Seneca and along the frontier, but because reports coming through command at Ninety Six stated that William Moultrie had successfully defended a British naval attack on Fort Sullivan outside Charlestown. England had pulled her fleet back into the Atlantic. With that threat removed, the Patriots could concentrate on defeating the Cherokees.

Elspeth moaned. "How soon?"

"Probably a matter of days. A week?" He sighed. "The good news is, the overtures of the Council of Safety to the Creeks seem to have paid off. It is said they willna join the fight on the side of the Cherokees."

"That is supposed to comfort me?" Elspeth's question bordered on a wail.

"Nay. What is supposed to comfort ye is that I have me head on straight now. I canna explain it, but everything is clearer. I used to think the anger inside gave me power, but I can see now that reason is a far better master than emotion."

"Well..." She slid her fingers up into his hair, playing with the tip of his ear. A sly smile teased the corners of her mouth upward. "Most of the time."

Ah, how he would like to explore that further. He allowed himself another brief taste of her soft, clinging lips before pulling back. "Speakin' of a clear head, which I definitely dinna have when ye do that..."

She chuckled. "Oh, aye?"

He focused. "There is somethin' else I've been meanin' to tell ye, though I didna want to say it in front of yer sister that day. Or anyone else since."

Uncomfortable with the notion of so many soldiers and curious "English" at the fort, Leana had chosen to remain at the homestead. Elspeth had protested at first, most certainly out of fear that the girl would take the opportunity to flee. Alex secretly shared her concern. But Leana had promised she would not. She said the time alone would be needful for her transition. That she would keep the house and garden for them, as she was in no danger of war parties.

And indeed, when Alex had taken Elspeth for another visit a few days later, Leana had greeted them with a shy smile. It had warmed his heart to observe their equally shy but increasingly warm interactions. Leana had made her new nest in the loft, under the watchful eyes of her old doll.

"Well, what is it?" Elspeth stepped back, and his arms fell loose.

He took a deep breath. Speaking of matters of the heart he found hard enough. Matters of the soul roundly resisted utterance. "Because of what ye said to me that day at the creek..."

"Aye?"

"About forgiveness." He shifted his weight.

"Aye." Not even a hint of impatience marked her third prompting. Her blue eyes fixed on him, unblinking.

"I was able to let Split Ear go because I forgave him. And that was harder than no' killin' him."

She pressed her lips tight, but a small laugh escaped her nonetheless. "I'm sorry. 'Twas yer earnest expression that got me. I'm very happy to hear that, indeed." Elspeth stroked his arm.

He shot her a wry look, reaching up to rub his jaw. But his shoulders relaxed some. Somehow, she had known he needed her to lighten the moment. "There's more. When we got to the horses, I thanked Split Ear for his help and told him I forgave him for takin' the life of me brother."

Elspeth was perfectly somber now. "Oh, Alex."

He rushed on before he lost steam. "He looked at me and asked why I would spare the man who killed his brother."

She gasped. "What did ye answer?"

"Time was short, the sounds of the battle near, so I couldna say much. There was only a moment. I told him to ask Inoli about sacrifice." Alex allowed a grin to break forth. "A life for a life. Because did he not learn about that while he was at the mission?"

"And from you. Aye." She was back in his arms, pressing her cheek to his waistcoat and wrapping her own arms around his back. "I am so proud of ye, Alex."

"Proud enough to call me yer husband?" The grin remained as he spoke the words, for while they might seem sudden to Elspeth, he had already presented them for consideration to her father...who had heartily bestowed his blessing.

She whisked her head back from his chest and stared at him with her pert lips agape. "Do ye mean it? What, now?"

"I do. Because if ye are mine to come back to, I will be certain to return."

"Then by all means, let us ask me father if he can perform a weddin'. Although this will likely be the shortest betrothal in the history of the colony."

"Elspeth..." Alex smoothed her hair back from her face, causing her to sober. "As much as I ache to make ye mine this very night, I need to be honest with ye."

Her throat bobbed. "Go on."

"I dinna ken how long I will be gone, how long this war will last. We might not can be together like normal married folk for a long time. Nor do I ken where home will be when I return. Here, in the Ceded Lands, or somewhere else. Or even if we will be America or still belong to England. We may not have two pence to rub together. The truth is, I have never had a real home, so I canna even imagine what that will look like. But with ye by my side..."

She pressed her fingertip to his lips. "Wherever we are together is home. Aye, Alex. The answer is aye. I have already waited a lifetime to be yer bride."

So much for his proposal startling her. He laughed and planted a kiss on the tip of her nose. "My verra deeply cherished bride."

Did you enjoy this book? We hope so!
Would you take a quick minute to leave a review where you purchased the book?
It doesn't have to be long. Just a sentence or two telling what you liked about the story!

Receive a FREE ebook and get updates when new Wild Heart books release: https://wildheartbooks.org/newsletter

AUTHOR'S NOTE AND ACKNOWLEDGMENTS

On June 24, 1776, William Drayton gave the orders to decimate the Cherokee towns. Major Andrew Williamson's South Carolina militia joined Patriot troops from Georgia, North Carolina, and Virginia in retaliatory expeditions. Williamson's three hundred and thirty men faced twelve hundred Cherokees and Loyalists who laid in ambush at Seneca, but the timely arrival of Andrew Pickens and company turned the tide of the battle. From there, the Patriots went on to destroy most of the Lower Towns.

Captain James McCall was held for several weeks in an Overhill village, where he witnessed the death by torture of other captives, possibly including one or two of his men. Through an old woman in camp, McCall repeatedly tried to contact Alexander Cameron, who never replied. Speculation that Major Williamson had tipped off his former friend concerning McCall's mission swelled in 1780 when Williamson returned his loyalties to the crown. McCall was finally able to escape with the help of the old woman. He rode bareback all the way to Virginia.

By autumn of 1776, the Cherokees had been put to flight. But the war with Britain was just beginning.

The Lawrences' mission was a fictional creation for my story, although Rev. William Richardson was a real minister who did missionary work among the Cherokees in the 1750s before taking Waxhaw Presbyterian Church. In the 1760s, he helped establish one of two Presbyterian congregations in the

Long Canes area. Since the earliest ministers were itinerant, I made Rev. Lawrence itinerant and based the idea of his predecessor loosely on Richardson. In 1772, Rev. John Harris was appointed by the Orange Presbytery to supply both vaccines and a pulpit in the Long Canes area. He remained until 1779.

Many characters in *A Cherished Betrothal* who appear in mention or cameo format really existed, and snapshots of their stories are depicted as accurately as possible while still allowing me to complete this fictional story sometime before my memoirs are released. These include Captain George Whitefield, John Stuart, Alexander Cameron, Rev. William Richardson, Captain Moses Kirkland, Captain John Caldwell, Major James Mayson, Major Andrew Williamson, William Drayton, Captain James McCall, Colonel Thomas Fletchall, Captain Andrew Pickens, Patrick and Robert Cunningham, and Thomas Brown.

I did not embellish the tale of Thomas Brown. And he did return at the head of his East Florida Rangers to wreak havoc in the Georgia and Carolina backcountry. That unit disbanded after British troops conquered Georgia in December 1778. Brown raised the King's Rangers and went on to defend Savannah and Augusta until Patriot troops recaptured the colony.

As you can imagine, any time a novelist seeks to include real people, especially *many* real people, things get trickier...as well as when historical records do not always coincide.

One example of this is that some works state that the Loyalists who intercepted the powder and guns being sent to Ninety Six from Fort Charlotte insisted the powder be returned to the fort. Other firsthand records omit this and even indicate that when Colonel Fletchall and party arrived at the town, they demanded *the powder* be surrendered. Hmm. I chose to have *some* of the powder returned.

Speaking of Ninety Six, special thanks to the staff at the

national park who took the time to hash out with me what historical records meant when referring to "the fort at Ninety Six" *between* the time of trader Robert Gouedy's early fort and Williamson's temporary fort. Sources seemed to indicate that when Major Mayson first arrived in Ninety Six, and Drayton followed, they merely fortified the jail and courthouse rather than erecting a fort as we traditionally think of one.

Another big blank I had to fill in regarded the command of Fort Charlotte. The site of the fort now lies beneath the waters of Lake Strom Thurmond, and records are spotty. While it was clear that John Caldwell was initially assigned there with a company of men, he showed up in the action at Williamson's Fort in November of 1775, the Snow Campaign which cleared the backcountry of Loyalists in December, and then ended up fighting on the coast in 1776. So who was in command at Fort Charlotte during the winter of 1775-76? I eventually decided that pursuit of that answer could lead me down a rabbit hole from which I might never emerge, so I made our hero the temporary commander. I hope you will forgive my editorial decisions where history left a question mark. When I make one of those, I note it in my afterword.

Some resources I found especially helpful in researching for this novel included *Militiamen, Rangers, and Redcoats* by James M. Johnson and *Ninety Six: The Struggle for the South Carolina Back Country* by Robert D. Bass.

Allow me to note also my awareness that in many ways, this has not been an easy story—to read or to write! Like many readers, I enjoy lighthearted, feel-good romance, and you will find plenty of those I have penned available through retailers. But I never want it to be said that I shied away from deeper, harder themes when I felt called to write a particular tale. For it is in those stories that we most clearly see God's redemptive and healing power, such as Alex and Elspeth needed. We may not face massacres and brutal wars today, though many in various parts of the world do. Whatever our current circumstances, let us not waver in the face of adversity but rather draw inspiration to act with the courage, honor, and integrity of many of our ancestors. And let us practice grace, forgiveness, and forbearance where they did not.

Many thanks to Misty Beller and her amazing staff at Wild Heart Books for bringing this story and series to my readers. And to my beta readers, Emily Potter and Gretchen Elm.

I hope the frontier action and romance of *A Cherished Betrothal* made your heart pound. I hope you were so thoroughly transported to another time that you began to startle people by saying "'tis" and "aye." If so, your reviews let publishers know my stories are worth continuing to publish. I notice and treasure each one. Please visit me at https://www.deniseweimerbooks.com, and I'd also love to connect on social media.

Monthly e-mail list: http://eepurl.com/dFfSfn

https://www.facebook.com/denise.weimer1

https://twitter.com/denise_weimer

https://www.bookbub.com/profile/denise-weimer

Don't miss the next book in The Scouts of the Georgia Frontier Series!

A Conflicted Betrothal
Releasing June of 2024

SAVANNAH, GEORGIA
SEPTEMBER 2, 1765

"How are ye feelin' this evening, sir?"

The question, posed by the owner of the popular Savannah tavern, spiraled panic through Ansel Anderson. The man leaning on the bottom half of the Dutch door wasn't even speaking to him. But his manner, his tone, and the way the patron in front of Ansel eased forward to answer told him he should have been more prepared.

Clearly, a password was required for entry tonight.

Ansel had been right. The seedling Sons of Liberty group sprouting up in Savannah—calling themselves the Liberty Boys —were congregating here. Most likely, access to the ordinary had been restricted this evening because they would discuss what had happened today in Georgia's Commons House of Assembly. And he'd miss hearing it firsthand unless God granted him a small miracle right now.

What had the patron muttered? A single word, but one with several syllables. Whatever it had been, the owner, James Machenry, backed up with an indulging smile, swinging the bottom half of his tavern's door wide.

Ansel wreathed his countenance with an answering smile —hopefully, one that conveyed ease as well as warmth—and started up the steps to trail the man into the dark interior. But the door swung shut.

The big Scot's benevolence had disappeared. He eyed

Ansel's dusty light-wool suit and riding boots. "Traveled far today, have ye, me friend?"

"A piece. My family has a farm in St. George's Parish."

A true statement. Ansel held the man's gaze. If he told the shrewd tavern keeper where he'd actually ridden in from—Fort Argyle, nineteen miles west of the city on the Great Ogeechee River—he could save himself the trouble of wracking his brain for a password. Instead, he'd get a boot in the backside. And squander any chance of returning.

Maybe it hadn't been such a brilliant idea to get right to work sniffing out the revolutionaries before checking in with the man who had secured his promotion...and his secret assignment. But he could hardly bow out now.

Machenry raised a bushy brow. "What brings ye to Savannah?"

"A visit to a friend of my father's." He twisted his mouth to one side, leaning forward as if rendering a confidence. "In truth, my father hopes I might find a bride. His friend's daughter." Again, all facts.

A bark of a laugh answered his confession. "Then ye're in need of some spirituous courage, son. How are ye feeling about yer new bride, if I may ask? Is she bonnie?"

Ansel's throat worked. That was the entry question, though couched a bit differently. His mind darted here and there. He bought himself a moment. "I'm told both of the man's daughters are fetching, though I've seen neither in twenty years. I was too young to remember them and therefore find myself unable to judge if my father is attempting to pull the wool over my eyes."

"But if he speaks the truth, ye must surely be..." The tavern keeper widened his eyes.

A flash of a memory had him fighting to keep his own eyes from going wide—a snippet from Judge Scott's letter, which

Father had read to him. *They call themselves the Amicable Society.* Could it be?

"Ye can give it to me in confidence, son." Machenry beckoned him closer.

Ansel obliged. "Amicable." He spoke the word with confidence and stepped back, holding his breath and searching his potential host's face for thunderclouds.

Instead, the man nodded. "I wish ye the best of luck. Come in and fortify yerself before ye go a' courtin'."

"Thank you." *And thank You, God.*

A few steps through the foyer, past the stairs that likely led to the family's rooms and the walk-up counter where a barkeep served drinks to two middle-aged gentlemen, and he entered the taproom. Agitated conversation and the scent of roast with a bitter thread of alcohol swirled in the space. From what he could tell through the cloud of sweet pipe smoke and the ripe press of bodies, only one seat remained, and that at a table for two. Like most of the clientele this evening, the man in the other chair was young. Probably in his early twenties, though his crumpled linen coat suggested his purse might be lighter than that of those sporting silk waistcoats and clocked stockings.

Ansel edged his way toward the spot by the window, removed his cocked hat, and addressed the stranger. "Pardon me. Mind if I share your table?"

Golden brows winged upward. "No, indeed." The man rose and indicated the chair opposite. "Please, join me."

"Thank you. Ansel Anderson." He put out his hand to shake his new acquaintance's.

"Jack Weaver." Resuming his seat, Jack picked up his knife and spoon. His pewter trencher held a generous slice of pork roast, potatoes, and buttered peas and bread.

Ansel's stomach growled, his lunch of an apple and cheese

partaken on horseback long gone. "That looks appealing. How do you find it?"

"The food here is good, unlike at some taverns. You're new, aren't you?"

Even in a town the size of Savannah, he should expect to be pegged as a stranger. And viewed with some suspicion. Ansel scooted his chair closer to the table. "Just arrived to visit friends and conduct a bit of business." Hopefully, his companion wouldn't ask what that business was. He'd just as soon no one here knew he'd been brought in to join the Savannah guard of some twenty Georgia Rangers at the beck and call of the royal governor, James Wright. And despite his unexpected assignment, he'd no small aversion to deception.

Thankfully, a waitress arrived. She wore an apron over her shift and petticoat, her brownish-blond hair trailing from beneath her mob cap. He ordered a plate of roast and a cider.

When she hurried away, Jack looked up from chasing his peas with his spoon. "This is the most popular ordinary in Savannah. But you must already know that." His brown eyes fixed on Ansel.

Ah. He meant the password. "Yes, I've heard this is the gathering place for those of a certain persuasion. Though judging from the tenor of conversation, things did not go well today at the Commons House."

Not that he was privy to the inner workings of Georgia's Lower House of Assembly. Besides whatever news trickled over to Argyle, Ansel knew only what Judge Scott's letter had relayed —that the Commons House had endeavored to elect delegates to the Stamp Act Congress proposed by James Otis of the Massachusetts Assembly, which would be held in New York in October. The congress would seek to resist one of the latest in a series of unpopular laws Great Britain had enacted. The Stamp Act, passed by Parliament in March, required imprinted paper to be used for—or a small blue stamped paper to be affixed to

—any legal, commercial, or official papers, as well as calendars, almanacs, newspapers, and even playing cards. The act would not go into effect until the first of November, giving ample time for the stamped paper to arrive from England and stamp agents to be appointed.

Jack snorted. "I'd say not."

When the waitress delivered Ansel's cider, he leaned back and took a sip, attempting a casual air as he surveyed the room.

His companion chewed and swallowed his last bite of bread. "Of course, many here tonight are representatives. Except for supporting their efforts to secure fair representation for our colony, I don't really move in their circles. I'm just a farmer's son from St. Paul Parish."

Ansel grinned. "Same as I, but from St. George's."

Jack nodded. "Well, here in Christ Church Parish, this is the best place to keep abreast of what's going on...long before the *Georgia Gazette* prints the news."

As was the case for most taverns.

Indeed, a voice rose from near the fireplace—unlit tonight, as the evening retained the balmy coastal heat of summer. The voice belonged to a man of about forty with dark hair and a slightly crooked nose, who addressed two younger men—gentleman, all, judging by the tailoring of their coats and the shine of their buckles and buttons. "I share your frustration, of course. But tell me what else we could have done, Clay. Wylly did his part. He set the meeting for us to elect delegates, but without Wright calling us into session..."

"Why do we need him to call us into session?" One of the younger men glowered over his pewter tankard, though his earnest oval face, small mouth, and soft dark eyes negated any true appearance of ferocity.

"Be careful." The first speaker lifted his finger. "'Tis not wise to bite the hand that feeds you."

"My uncle's hand feeds us." The young man glanced at his other companion.

When his dinner arrived, Ansel thanked the barmaid but strained not to miss the rest of the conversation across the room.

"And your uncle's bounty flows from the benevolence of the royal governor. As does the license you and young Habersham enjoy as partners in your import business." The older man swigged his drink. "Let us rest easy. We will receive a full report from the recorder we send to the Stamp Act Congress. The missive we prepared will assure them of our support despite our governor's objections—and our determination to enact any legislation they pass."

Knifing a slice of pork to his mouth, Ansel chanced a glance at the man across the table. Did he share the speaker's confidence in a diplomatic approach, or was he more of a firebrand?

"You know who they are?" Jack tilted his head toward the men by the fireplace, seeming to channel Ansel's curiosity toward the others rather than himself.

Ansel shook his head. "Obviously, men of importance in the liberty movement."

"The one our age is Joseph Clay. As Lieutenant Jones said, he heads an import business with his cousin, James Habersham Jr."

Everyone in Georgia knew who the Habershams were. James Sr. not only oversaw the mercantile firm but a fifteen-thousand-acre rice plantation. It was the other name that made Ansel almost choke on his pork. "Jones?"

"Noble Wimberly Jones, physician and first lieutenant of the Second Troop of Georgia Rangers."

Ansel bolted down a generous swallow of cider.

Jack watched too closely as he wiped his mouth.

Judge Scott had said that Governor Wright did not know whom he could trust among his rangers and militia, but Ansel had not expected to find an officer of the very troop he'd be reporting to in the morning among the Liberty Boys at Machenry's Tavern.

"Would you like me to introduce you?"

"Er..." Heart thudding, Ansel glanced across the room.

Past the knot of men at the mantel, a pocket door slid open. A young woman peeked out, the hood of her dark cloak accenting the paleness of her oval face. "I'd probably better... find lodgings..." Her gaze seemed to latch onto him, and she gave a frantic little flutter of her hand.

"Is she waving at you?" Incredulity laced Jack's tone.

"Surely not. I have no idea who she is." Though never had a distraction proved timelier. Or lovelier. Even from this distance, the pink in the woman's cheeks and lips was visible, as was the snap of her dark eyes. She must be gesturing to someone past him. Ansel swiveled for his final swallow of cider, releasing a soft sigh of relief.

Playing along with Jack had been one thing. If he met First Lieutenant Jones tonight, Ansel would find himself locked into the role of a Liberty Boy when he needed to build relations and gather intelligence among the rangers without prejudice from either side. How careless he'd been.

"Well, I don't, either," Jack told him, "but I'd say she is definitely summoning you." His throaty tone hinted he wouldn't mind being the subject of the lady's attention.

Ansel peeked behind Jack again.

Again, the woman lifted her hand, but this time, she made a clear beckoning gesture.

He pointed at his own chest and mouthed, "Me?"

The dark head crowned with a mob cap under the hood nodded. The door slid closed.

Jack swiveled back from the glance he'd taken over his shoulder and chuckled. "Well, she is quite certain of her powers of persuasion, is she not?"

Ansel pulled coins from his pocket and placed them on the table. "This is an upstanding sort of establishment, correct?"

Jack's chuckle turned into a full laugh. "She is no tavern doxy, if that is what you mean. Yonder is the door to the ladies' parlor."

Of course. Except for barmaids and servants, women would not frequent the taproom. If this tavern made a special accommodation for the ladies, it offered more amenities than most.

His companion rubbed his golden-bristled chin. "Although I'm surprised to see any women here tonight."

"Me too. Perhaps she is in some sort of distress."

"And out of a room of men, she picks a perfect stranger to come to her aid?"

It was Ansel's turn to chuckle. "I own, that sounds fanciful. But I'm prepared to do my best to solve the mystery."

Jack arched a brow. "Need any help?"

"Will call if I do." Ansel winked. "Thank you for sharing your table and your insights. I hope to see you around town." Whatever this woman did or did not require, Ansel risked revealing too much if he continued his current conversation. And he needed to make his exit while Lieutenant Jones faced the fireplace.

Ansel threaded his way through the room on the side nearest the bar, then paused at the rolling door to knock quietly.

A feminine voice answered. "Come."

He entered, then slid the portal mostly closed behind him —not all the way, for he found himself alone in a small parlor with the lady, who faced the other way at a table with a mostly empty plate before her. She spoke before he could present himself.

"This is insupportable, Frankie. I can't hear a thing. Could you find me a spot in the corner..." Her voice trailed off as

Ansel appeared before her and she looked up from picking chicken off a bone.

"Miss." Removing his hat, Ansel made a small bow.

Her fingers stilled, her eyes went wide, and her throat worked. "You are not Frankie."

~

Drat her weak eyes. How many times would they get her into trouble?

Temperance berated herself as she took in the man wearing the same color suit as her cousin, with the same shade of straight mahogany-brown hair tied with a silk ribbon beneath the black cocked hat he now held under his arm. There the resemblance ended. Where Frankie's skin bore the reminder of his childhood battle with smallpox, this man's was unmarked, unless one counted the dimples on either side of his mouth. Where her cousin's face was flat and of a weak chin, this man had high cheekbones, a thin nose, and a square, clean-shaven jaw. And instead of Frankie's almost-lashless brown eyes, she gazed into green jewels framed in a thick fringe of brown lashes.

A small chicken bone fell to the floor. She did not even try to go after it, for with her present luck, she'd mistake it for a crack, and her groping quest would further shame herself before this perfect specimen of manhood.

"Ansel Anderson, at your service. Although, am I to understand I was summoned by mistake?"

"No. Yes." Mercy, the clever words that usually vied for attention in her head dried up like the chicken breast. Normally, she did everything in her power to steer away from males of Mr. Anderson's superior appearance and bearing, and here she'd unwittingly commanded him to her side. "I mean, from across the room, I thought you were my cousin. You are... similarly garbed." She waved her hand, avoiding his eyes.

His smile seemed to bestow compassion on her flusterment. "I thought as much. I could not imagine what good fortune would be smiling on me to be acknowledged by a lady such as yourself. And after I only just arrived in town."

He flattered her. What a poor impression she'd surely made on a newcomer to their city. All of this could've been avoided if her vanity had not prevented her from wearing her spectacles. "Please, I should—I mean, may I offer my apologies? And welcome you to Savannah?" After wiping her fingers on her handkerchief, Temperance attempted to rise, but apparently, she'd placed the chair leg on her petticoat when she'd last seated herself, and now, it pulled her back down.

In a flash, Mr. Anderson was behind her, taking hold of the top of her chair so he could assist with her second attempt at standing. "Allow me."

As he moved the chair, Temperance stepped around it and swung her petticoat free, but the motion brought her closer to the stranger. Ah, he smelled of leather and the outdoors. He'd traveled on horseback rather than by conveyance. "Thank you. I am very sorry to have troubled you, sir."

He gazed into her eyes. "No trouble at all. In fact, may I seek out your cousin for you? This might not be the best night for a lady to find herself unaccompanied in this tavern. The...er... passions of the men in the next room are rather high at the moment."

Indignation for her friends burned off Temperance's usual reserve. "I can promise you, only the finest, the most upstanding, of the city's gentlemen frequent Machenry's."

"I am sure that is true, but I cannot help but notice that you are still the only lady."

"Do you intimate my presence creates some sort of scandal...or temptation?"

Mr. Anderson blinked rapidly, taking a small step back. "I meant nothing untoward, miss."

"Good, because I share the 'passions' of the men in the next room. And they are precisely as elevated as any sensible colonist might expect, given recent events. That is why you are here, is it not?" She raised her brows.

"Uh, I understand. Forgive me." Again, a small bow. "I was only concerned for your comfort."

The faint red creeping up from Mr. Anderson's collar instantly cooled her dander. Her mother was right. When her patriotic ideals were challenged, she truly became another person. "Think nothing of it, sir. And rest assured, I am perfectly safe. I am well acquainted with most of the gentlemen here tonight. Only the silly rule about no women in the taproom keeps me in this parlor." She mustered a smile. "Frankie should return any moment. He only went to get some drinks. When I saw you with your back turned..."

The dimples reappeared. "You thought your cousin had abandoned you for another conversation."

"Precisely."

"In that case, I will bid you a good night." With a nod, he replaced his hat on his head and walked toward the door.

For the strangest moment, Temperance's heart ached, and she cast about for something to say that might justify bringing him back.

And then, with one hand on the frame, he turned, and she sucked in a breath.

He tipped his head. "Might I be bold enough to inquire of your name?"

Of course. He'd given his, but in her embarrassment, she had not reciprocated. She opened her mouth to answer just before the door was flung wide behind him and someone else did.

"No, you may not. What are you doing in here with my

cousin, sir?" Frankie pushed past Mr. Anderson, a glass of flip in one hand and a punch in the other. "Temperance, is this man bothering you?"

"No, indeed, Frankie." She hurried forward to place her hand on his arm. "In fact, I bothered *him*. I spied him across the room and thought he was you. See how similarly you are dressed? I beckoned him over, and he obliged. And now, we should let him take his leave in peace." With a gracious smile in Mr. Anderson's direction, she relieved Frankie of the cup of punch.

Surveying her with that proprietary air that made her squirm, Frankie stowed up one corner of his thin lips. "Dear cousin, what am I always telling you about...?"

She waved him to silence. She knew just where this was going and preferred not to visit that topic in front of this Adonis. She found the courage to face him again. "Good night, Mr. Anderson."

"Good night, miss..." He let the sentence hang, but if she judged rightly, whatever he saw in the taproom had more to do with its termination than a bid for her name. He turned back and glanced around the parlor. "Pardon me. I shall spare myself the trouble of elbowing through that crowd again and instead take the back exit."

Temperance moved to let him pass, her breath hitching as his arm brushed hers. But something in his manner had her sipping her punch and conjecturing after the door closed behind him. Somehow, as mannerly and obliging as he had been, he did not fit in here. And for some reason, she regretted that. Because that meant she'd probably never see him again.

ABOUT THE AUTHOR

North Georgia native Denise Weimer has authored over a dozen traditionally published novels and a number of novellas —historical and contemporary romance, romantic suspense, and time slip. As a freelance editor and Acquisitions & Editorial Liaison for Wild Heart Books, she's helped other authors reach their publishing dreams. A wife and mother of two daughters, Denise always pauses for coffee, chocolate, and old houses.

f X

If you love historical romance, check out the other Wild Heart books!

A Winter at the White Queen by Denise Weimer

In the world of the wealthy, things are never quite as they appear.

Ellie Hastings is tired of playing social gatekeeper—and poor-relation companion—to her Gibson Girl of a cousin. But her aunt insists Ellie lift her nose out of her detective novel long enough to help gauge the eligibility of bachelors during the winter social season at Florida's Hotel Belleview. She finds plenty that's mysterious about the suave, aloof Philadelphia inventor, Lewis Thornton. Why does he keep sneaking around the hotel? Does he have a secret sweetheart? And what is his connection to the evasive Mr. Gaspachi, slated to perform at Washington's Birthday Ball?

Ellie's comical sleuthing ought to put Lewis out, but the diffident way her family treats her smashes a hole in his normal reserve. When Florence Hastings's diamond necklace goes missing, Ellie's keen mind threatens to uncover not only Lewis's secrets, but give him back hope for love.

~

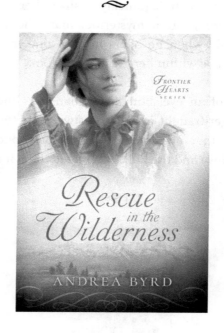

Rescue in the Wilderness by Andrea Byrd

William Cole cannot forget the cruel burden he carries, not with the pock marks that serve as an outward reminder. Riddled with guilt, he assumed the solitary life of a long hunter, traveling into the wilds of Kentucky each year. But his quiet existence is changed in an instant when, sitting in a tavern, he overhears a man offering his daughter—and her virtue—to the winner of the next round of cards. William's integrity and desire for redemption will not allow him to sit idly by while such an injustice occurs.

Lucinda Gillespie has suffered from an inexplicable illness her entire life. Her father, embarrassed by her condition, has subjected her to a lonely existence of abuse and confinement. But faced with the ultimate betrayal on the eve of her eighteenth birthday, Lucinda quickly realizes her trust is better placed in his hands of the mysterious man who appears at her door. Especially when he offers her the one thing she never thought would be within her grasp—freedom.

In the blink of an eye, both lives change as they begin the difficult, danger-fraught journey westward on the Wilderness Trail. But can they overcome their own perceptions of themselves to find love and the life God created them for?

~

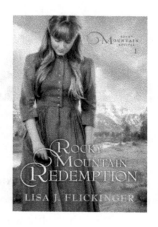

Rocky Mountain Redemption by Lisa J. Flickinger